We hope you
renew it by '

You ca
by ur

Summer
at
Oyster Bay

Also by Jenny Hale:

Christmas Wishes and Mistletoe Kisses
Coming Home for Christmas
A Christmas to Remember
Love Me for Me
Summer by the Sea

Summer at Oyster Bay

JENNY HALE

bookouture

Published by Bookouture

An imprint of StoryFire Ltd.
23 Sussex Road, Ickenham, UB10 8PN. United Kingdom.

www.bookouture.com

ISBN: 978-1-78681-030-4
eBook ISBN: 978-1-78681-029-8

Acknowledgments

I'd like to thank my husband, Justin, who continues to be by my side on this journey.

A giant thank you to Oliver Rhodes for his support and vision.

My editor, Natalie Butlin—I am thrilled to be working with her, and I have truly enjoyed the collaboration we've had on this project.

Chapter One

How ironic that Emily was going to be planning weddings at the prestigious Water's Edge Inn, when she'd just said "no" to her boyfriend's proposal in front of two hundred of her friends and family.

Just three days later, her car full of her things, Emily had driven the hour and a half back to Clearwater from her apartment in the city, locking her door for the last time and slipping the key under the mat, never to return. Her ex-boyfriend, Brad, had conveniently been absent the entire time she'd packed and when she'd left. He hadn't told her where he was, but she guessed that he didn't want to see her. She'd spent ages trying to write him an apology that really expressed how awful she felt, and finally left what still didn't feel like enough explanation on the kitchen counter where they'd always left each other notes and reminders.

She ran her fingers through her long, brown hair, dabbed on some lip-gloss, and got out of her car. Water's Edge Inn wasn't just any inn; it was an enormous expanse of real estate, the biggest in the area. Growing up, she'd seen the inn through the woods of her house, but she'd never set foot on the premises. It engulfed the entire edge of a peninsula, its white clapboard siding fanning out in wings across the estate. It had its own marina and golf course.

The inn staff was in a frenzy. Barely eight o'clock, there was a line of people she'd never seen before expecting room keys; the grounds men were awaiting special orders; a food delivery was outside and, while unloading loaves of bread, the driver was lingering impatiently for signatures; painters were touching up trim and doorways; and a million other smartly dressed bellboys, cleaners, and crew were feverishly buzzing around.

"Welcome to Water's Edge Inn," Libby, Emily's new boss and old friend, said with a grin as she approached the counter. Libby's normally free-falling, golden hair was pinned back into a perfect up-do, her great sense of style showing in her navy pencil skirt, fitted crisscross button-up shirt, and teardrop earrings. She'd hired Emily as an events coordinator right there in the street downtown in Richmond after the catastrophe of a dinner proposal, the solitaire diamond ring still encircling the red roses on the table inside. Libby had been trying for a while to entice Emily to leave her coordinator position at the pub she'd brought to popularity in Richmond. Emily could work at the inn and return to her childhood home to get away from the disaster she'd created.

"There are so many out-of-towners," Emily said, her thoughts coming out almost by accident. "I saw lots of unfamiliar license plates on the way into town."

"It's *full* of out-of-towners. They're everywhere these days…"

It seemed that news of the inn had spread out of the state, which was something new, and it didn't sit well with Emily. She liked her small town and didn't want to see it become commercialized like other nearby beach towns.

"I'm so sorry to bring you on the team right now, but Charles Peterson's coming to stay at the inn, and we're in a bit of a rush to get everything ready for him." Libby made a face. "He's the new owner and we have to impress him."

"Tell me what to do."

"Since we don't have a lot of time, I'd like you to be on call for Mr. Peterson's requests. I'll train you in between, and then once he leaves, we'll go over your position. Did you see his photo in the paper? He's single…"

Emily's shoulders slumped in mental exhaustion. "Libby…"

"Sorry. That was insensitive of me."

She didn't want to talk about Brad or the attractiveness of Charles Peterson. She just wanted to keep her head down, go to work, and come home.

Libby rubbed her lips together as she was thinking, what little red lipstick she'd worn now gone. "He's asked for a few things to be in his suite when he arrives," she said, signing for the food delivery, her eyes on Emily the whole time. "Could I give you the corporate card and have you pick the items up?"

"Absolutely."

"Perfect. When you get back, you can take them to his suite— The Concord Suite. He'll be here in about an hour. Thank you for not running away at the sight of all this," she said, her eyes now a little manic. Libby reached under the desk, unlocked the cabinet and retrieved the corporate credit card and keys to the suite. "Here's his hotel rider. Just do the best you can." She slid the list and the card across the counter.

"Got it," Emily said, looking down at Charles Peterson's requests: three bottles of champagne, a case of sparkling water, moisturizing soap, all-natural sunscreen—sun-proof twenty—and lip balm; set televisions to weather channel, room temperature at sixty-eight degrees.

She slipped her sunglasses on and headed out into the sunshine. Turning toward the wind, Emily watched the sun reflecting off the surface of the water, the salty smell in the air taking her back to all the days she'd spent in this town as a child, the bay offering a childhood full of barefoot, sandy memories. But she didn't have time to think about those things. She got into her car and headed straight for the small string of boutiques near the inn.

The Beach Boutique was just the spot to get the soap, sunscreen, and lip balm. And knowing Francine, the owner, Emily felt pretty good about the quality of the products. She pulled up at the front of the store and got out of her car. With the list in her hand, she walked past the brightly painted crab pots and decorative mailbox flags and into the shop. The ceiling was covered in wind chimes, the walls draped in summer fabrics and patterns—collectible beach bags, sarongs, and swimwear. It was a tiny shop, with all the floor displays extremely close to one another. Emily turned sideways to inch past a spinning display of beach-themed refrigerator magnets and walked over to the beauty section. It was just like it had always been.

"Well, I'll be damned!" Francine said in her southern drawl from over the top of her reading glasses. "I haven't seen you since you ran off to the city! How's your grandmother?"

"Hi, Francine." Emily slipped off her sunglasses to get a better look at her. Francine had aged considerably since Emily had seen her last, but then again, the sun could do that to a person, and she was still heavyset, her love of cooking overpowering her multitude of weight loss plans. "She's fine, thank you," Emily said with a grin. Francine gossiped about everyone, and she never seemed to have a solidly nice thing to say, but Emily liked her. She was always true to herself.

"That's good to hear! Let me know if you need anything."

"Just these, please." Emily pulled the items off the shelf and set them on the counter.

"Going swimming?" Francine asked, pushing her glasses closer to her eyes to view the sunscreen Emily had chosen. "It's a glorious day for swimming! I'll bet the beaches are warm and breezy in all this sunshine."

"I'm working, actually. I got a job at Water's Edge. I'm buying items for the inn." She waved the corporate card.

"Oh! How nice. I didn't realize you were back permanently!" Francine swiped the credit card, set it on the counter, and held the bag of items out toward Emily.

"Yes, ma'am. I'm working with Libby now. I'll be heading over to the market next to get champagne for the new boss," she said, raising her eyebrows in excitement. It was good to have something to take her mind off her breakup.

"Best of luck to ya." With a flourish, Francine ripped off the receipt and slid it across the counter toward Emily, holding it flat with her fingers. Emily pulled a pen from the cup beside the register and signed her name just as the bells on the door jingled. Both ladies turned around.

"Lord have mercy," Francine said under her breath as they both looked at the handsome man who'd entered. He had dark hair cut short, his face was perfectly shaven, his clothes casual but clearly expensive. "May I help you?" Francine called over Emily's head.

"Yes, I'm looking for a unique gift for a woman," the man said, making his way past the beach figurines and hand-painted wine and margarita glasses.

"Well, let me see if I can help you with that." Francine came around the corner of the counter and peered at him over her glasses. She slipped them off and let them dangle from a beaded cord. "How old is this woman?"

"Probably somewhere between thirty and forty."

"That's a range. Know her well, do ya?" she said with a smirk and Emily coughed to keep herself from laughing. She always laughed when she was uncomfortable and Francine was not one to sugarcoat things. Perhaps she should intervene, although she really didn't have time.

"The woman works for me," he said in a very direct way.

"Maybe I can help. I fall into that age range," Emily said, feeling her pulse quicken when his dark blue eyes landed on her. "I'd love to have a few of those margarita glasses. They're nice."

"Mmm," he said, pondering the suggestion. "I don't know if she drinks margaritas."

Emily looked around the store. "Okay. How about, um…" She pointed to the beaded jewelry in a case on the counter. "How about a nice necklace?"

"Jewelry might be a bit personal."

She tried to look at him, but every time she did, the intensity of his gaze and his good looks made her oddly nervous, so she focused on the items in front of her. Francine had disappeared into the store-room, probably calling her gram to tell her that her granddaughter was picking up strange men in the shop.

"What about this?" She held up a box of seashell napkin rings.

"I'm awful at buying gifts." His face gave away the fact that the napkin rings hadn't hit the mark either. "Never mind," he said with a smile that made Emily's hands jittery right there on the spot. "I'll figure something out."

She nodded, slowly turning away from him and heading toward the door. She didn't want to be rude, but she still had to get the rest of the items on the list, and she was losing time.

"I didn't catch your name," he said from behind her.

She turned around. "It's Emily."

He smiled again. "Thank you for your help, Emily," he said.

She smiled and then hurried out to her car.

In an attempt to burn off her nervous energy, Emily put the windows down and cranked up the radio. It had been quite a while since she'd been back in town, and things had certainly changed.

Growing up in the small coastal town, Emily had always known everyone. When they were young, Emily and Libby had spent a lot of time together, having gone to the same white country church on the hill every Sunday that their parents had attended as kids. They'd been able to walk to the string of specialty shops in town after the service without a care in the world—buying sodas and ice cream—because they'd known everyone. Libby was from the nearby town of White Stone, and Emily lived in Clearwater, named after the two rivers that bordered it from the north and the south, with the bay to the east. Both towns were on the sparkling Chesapeake Bay, their streets dotted with grand country houses and hundred-year-old trees. The girls would run through the sprawling green yards, holding their ice cream cones, the sunlight flickering between the leaves of the trees, creating shade on the bricked sidewalks. All the small towns in this area were strung together by a handful of winding roads, making one flow into another and bringing the people of each town together—nearly everybody knew each other.

Emily arrived at the grocery store, threw the car into park, and ran inside.

There was one checkout open. One. Emily grabbed a shopping basket as she passed at least six more unfamiliar people in line.

She stopped along the wall of wines and walked to the end where she knew they always kept the champagne. A pang of sadness swelled in her throat as she remembered buying a bottle with Brad when she'd brought him to meet Gram and Papa for the first time. They'd been celebrating the fact that she was going to move into his apartment in Richmond. Now she'd left that whole life behind her. She'd left her friends, her job, and everything she'd had for the past three years. With a deep breath, she focused on the labels in front of her.

Opting for the top shelf selection, she grabbed a bottle and put it in her basket, then hurried over to get a case of sparkling water. Looking at her watch, she still had about twenty minutes. She rounded the corner. There was a long line still at the register. Things were different here. Life was slower. She had twenty minutes, she told herself. Everything was just fine.

But by the time she'd waited for an elderly lady with a cart full of groceries, who'd wanted to inspect the price of each item as the clerk rang it up and then hand-write a check conceivably slower than anyone could ever write, Emily was starting to worry about getting back on time.

When the clerk finally rang her up, Emily opened her wallet and, to her horror, found she couldn't see the corporate credit card. She rummaged around in her handbag, her heart now pounding.

OhmyGod, ohmyGod, ohmyGod… What have I done with it? Her first day on the job and she'd lost the corporate credit card! Then she remembered, Francine hadn't given it back to her because they'd been distracted by the man who'd come in to the shop. The man who was now looking down at her…

"Lost something?" he asked.

She nodded, unable to breathe.

"Perhaps…" He held the card up between his two fingers. "This?" He handed it to the clerk who was gawking at him as if she were starstruck. The clerk took it slowly and swiped it through the machine.

He glanced down to the items on the checkout counter. When he made eye contact again, she thought she saw compassion flicker across his face. Could he tell how mortified she was? "You have good taste in champagne," he said, a small grin playing on his lips.

"How did you get that card?" she asked, ignoring his comment. Had Francine just given the Water's Edge corporate credit card to a complete stranger who offered to track her down?

"Well, once I convinced your friend, Francine, that I *own* Water's Edge Inn, she let me have it," he said, signing the receipt, his eyes still on her. He took the bag and card from the clerk and thanked her. Then he began walking toward the door.

Emily shuffled up behind him, feeling nauseous. "I'm so sorry," she said. He opened the door and allowed her to exit, the sunshine nearly blinding her. She slipped on her sunglasses. "You came in to Francine's and distracted me."

He turned and faced her, a curious look in his eyes. "Well, if you're going to do the shopping with our card, perhaps you'd better try harder not to get distracted," he said, his expression not quite as harsh as his words. "Why isn't Libby doing the buying anyway? She's the manager that I hired." He began walking again and she followed.

"Libby asked me to go. It's my first day—" Emily stopped talking. She didn't want to get Libby in trouble, and she didn't want to lead the conversation to the mayhem at the inn as they prepared for his visit.

"Are you the new events coordinator?"

"Yes." She felt about two feet tall. "So, you're Charles Peterson? It's nice to meet you." She offered a weak smile.

"Good to meet you," he said, stopping at a startlingly blue BMW. It looked out of place among the other cars in the lot. The headlights blinked as he unlocked the doors from his pocket. He handed her the credit card. "Think you can keep track of this between here and the inn?" he asked jokingly, but it didn't stop the guilt that she felt for leaving it at Francine's. She really had to work on clearing her head. She was a better businesswoman than this.

Emily nodded, at a loss for words. This was not how she'd wanted to greet the boss upon their first meeting. But the good news was that the day could only go up from there. Right?

Chapter Two

Emily hauled her bags past Papa's old Buick, which still sat in the driveway, and up the staircase of the farmhouse at Oyster Bay. Her papa had told her once that the name of the house and surrounding grounds had originated because that particular area of the bay was chock-full of oysters.

Emily was exhausted from work, having spent the rest of the day learning the tasks associated with the job. The commotion in the lobby had finally calmed down by the time she'd returned to the inn, although she'd felt more frazzled than when she'd left. Charles hadn't come back. He'd spent the day touring marinas and wining and dining various community members, she'd heard.

The sun was still high despite the fact that it was after five o'clock. When she planted her feet on the peeling painted boards of the long front porch where she'd played as a child, she noticed the aging wicker furniture sitting against the whitewashed siding, and the streak of sun, coming in at a slant on the faded pots of geraniums. This house appeared so big for just her grandmother now that she was all alone, and from the looks of the porch, it seemed as though it might have become a burden. Even with the deteriorating exterior, being there was like a warm hug to Emily. She loved this house. It was full of so many memories.

"Look at you!" her grandmother said in her silky southern accent as she leaned on her hand-painted cane, after opening the door without even a knock. In her free hand, she was holding a kitchen towel, her hair pinned back as it always was when she was baking. The evening coastal wind was soft, blowing the gray wisps of hair that had escaped from her bun around her grandmother's face. Just seeing her made Emily long for her hugs, her bedtime kisses, and her fireside chats. "I have been missin' you," she said, shaking her head with a grin.

"I missed you too, Gram." Emily embraced her grandmother, surprised by her generally content behavior. She'd expected her to be more melancholy. After all, it had only been six months since Papa died.

"Is that everything?" Gram eyed the bags, her hand still on Emily's shoulder, her other supporting her weight on her cane. She'd had a cane to get around for a few years now, and she always managed to find specialty ones that were like their own works of art. That was how Gram was though. She saw the potential in everything and if she had to have a cane, it was going to be the most gorgeous one she could find.

"The rest is in storage for now like you'd said to do." Not wanting to impose, Emily had asked Gram if she could stay temporarily, but she knew that her grandmother would probably let her stay as long as she liked. Oyster Bay was the kind of place that made a person want to stay forever.

"Well," she said, as if it were a complete sentence, the same way she'd done whenever she had something on her mind. With a consoling smile, she opened the door wider so Emily could enter.

Gram led her down the hallway. "You look so dressed up."

"Really?" Emily didn't feel dressed up, wearing only a nice pair of work trousers and a coordinating top, but then again, maybe she was.

Here in Clearwater people didn't fuss so much about things. They seemed to worry less, work more slowly. It wasn't that they weren't productive; they just enjoyed the task of working a bit more.

As she walked, she noticed the black and white photos of her grandparents on the wall. Emily fixed her eyes on the one of Papa, his trousers rolled up to his knees as he stood in the tide, holding Gram in his arms. Her dark hair was neatly arranged in pin curls, her sundress flowing almost down to the water. They were laughing as if Papa were going to throw her in. The photos had always been there, but she hadn't looked at them much on her visits over the past three years, and suddenly they looked so different. This time, when she looked at them, she realized just how young her grandparents had been at the time the pictures were taken. They looked about her age.

She continued into the kitchen at the back of the house, the smell of shortbread saturating the air.

"You look like a real city girl."

Gram hadn't said anything wrong, but the words stung Emily. She swallowed to keep herself together and walked to the window overlooking the backyard. She'd never wanted to be a city girl and, at heart, she wasn't. She'd tried to chase a life for herself and, for a while, she'd thought she'd caught it. But after spending some time in the life she'd made, Emily realized that she wasn't happy. She'd been happy here.

The view calmed her a little. This old farmhouse sat at the very back of the property. It was all that was left of the original farm, wild grasses and pine trees taking over the land and filling in where the original fields had been. But, as if it were on the edge of the world, there was a clearing at the end of the yard with the whitest sand and the lapping waves of the Chesapeake Bay. She could smell the salt through the open window.

Gram withdrew the pin from the bun at the back of her head, her silver hair falling free just above her shoulders. It rested in soft waves around her face, making her look younger than she was.

"I'm glad you got a job down here," Gram said, her eyebrows raised in interest. "How was your first day?"

"Busy." Emily rubbed her eyes.

"That inn's very luxurious."

"Yes," she said.

Water's Edge Inn had resort-style amenities, yet it was true to the local culture, offering docks for crabbing, tree swings dangling from centuries-old oak trees, and an on-site homemade ice cream shop, although she'd heard it had changed considerably since Charles Peterson took over. She couldn't wait to have enough time to walk the grounds and really see for herself.

Gram used her spatula to scoop two cookies off a tray. She placed them on a small plate and set them on the table. "Rachel's excited to see you," she said, offering her the cookies with a nod of her head.

Emily sat down in the old wooden chair that she'd helped to paint when she was in high school, noticing how the wood was showing through now. "I've missed her," she said. She'd be glad to have time to spend with her sister. She fiddled with the centerpiece—a bouquet of fresh daisies. A petal from one of the flowers came off in her hand. Gram took the flower from the bouquet, snapped off most of the stem, and threaded it through Emily's hair just above her ear. Then she sat down across from her.

"I hope you have time to spend. They haven't given you too many hours at work, have they?"

"It's fine."

"You know, the inn's under new ownership. Rodger's doin' a piece about it for his magazine—he mentioned it to me today when I saw him. But even still, it's all over town—an investor from New York. Have you met him?" she asked, her eyes almost too curious. "Accordin' to local gossip, he only bought it as an investment, and he runs it like some sort of big city business," she said carefully. It seemed as though she were fishing for something. Was she trying to see what Emily thought of Charles Peterson?

"Really?"

"It's probably hearsay… Don't let them work you too hard." Gram nipped a cookie from the plate and took a bite. Then she grabbed her cane and walked to the refrigerator, pulled out a long bundle of carrots, and set them on the table. "Why don't you take these and give Eli a visit? He'll be so glad to see you." She held them out to Emily.

"I can't wait to see Eli," Emily said, suddenly craving the feel of stirrups underneath her feet. She hadn't ridden Eli in years. He had been her horse. Every little girl wanted a horse for Christmas, and, after her parents died, her grandparents had bought her one. She could still remember the big red bow around his neck. "Has his caretaker Shelly taken him to any competitions lately?"

"She entered him in a few ridin' competitions but he's old, you know. He prefers to lounge around and nibble grass. I don't blame him."

"It's been so long since I've seen him."

"I'll bet he misses you."

Emily nodded, unable to speak. She had so many emotions swimming around in her head, but she pushed them away every time they started to surface. She wanted to spend time with her grandmother

and forget the fact that her three-year relationship with Brad was finished. She knew the moment she said "no" to his proposal that she
was giving up more than just him. She was giving up the chance of
a family, at making a life for herself. But when she'd grasped the fact
that she didn't love him, she just couldn't bring herself to say "yes."
So she'd come home the same way she'd left—single, without a plan
in the world.

The last time Emily had been to her hometown was when her
grandfather, whom she called Papa, had passed. She'd come for the
funeral, but with work in Richmond, she hadn't been able to spend
much time. She knew why she'd expected to see her grandmother
still grieving now: Emily had experienced grief like that when she'd
lost her parents, and she, herself, still grieved Papa. Everywhere she
looked here, she thought of Papa, but she knew the sadness would
pass and all the good memories would rise to the top again.

Emily set her cookie down on a napkin that Gram had placed on
the table for her and took the carrots. Then she headed outside.

The farm was full of trees now, the smaller ones having filled out
so much in the last three years. She took a path through the woods
and headed to a large clearing where Papa had built a barn and fenced
off a huge plot of grass for Eli when they'd gotten him. She smiled
to herself as she remembered how Papa had pretended to be put off
because Santa had left Eli and now he had to build the barn and fencing. She could still hear him complaining about how Santa should've
thought of that before leaving him. She missed Papa.

When she got to the clearing, Eli was at the old hay feeder, his
long mane shiny in the sunlight, his tail flicking back and forth. The
field was overgrown, and she worried that the grass was a little too tall
for him. He heard her steps and turned, immediately nickering as he

made his way toward her, and she was glad to see that he seemed okay walking through the brush. She opened the gate and went inside, latching it before meeting him.

"Hey there, boy," she said, offering a carrot and patting his muscular side.

When he'd finished eating it, he nuzzled her, his great snout knocking her off balance a little.

"Haha," she said, offering another carrot. "Miss me?"

He nuzzled her again.

Emily had missed his warm brown eyes, his gentle demeanor, his noble gait. She suddenly felt guilty having left him. Now it was just Gram here, and she probably couldn't go out to see him much.

"I'm back," she said, feeling the emotion welling up again. "I'm here, boy."

He eyed her carrots. With a giggle, she gave him another one.

Emily kicked off her flats and set them by the fence. "Where's your saddle? Is it still on the peg in the barn?" she asked, pacing toward it. Eli followed with a whinny. "It is? Let's get it on ya." She didn't even care that she still had her work trousers on. She wanted to ride her horse.

Eli stopped outside the barn as she went in and dug around to find the saddle. It wasn't on its usual peg. With a tug, she pulled it from under some old, rusty equipment and grabbed a saddle pad and the rest of her gear, stirring up a cloud of dust. Then she walked back out of the barn.

"Will you take me around?" she asked. He stood still, looking at her with those brown eyes of his. He still looked strong and healthy. She tossed the saddle pad over his back, and she could feel the happiness seeping back into her bones. This was where she belonged. This was the place she needed to spend her years. She put the saddle on and fastened it. Then, with one foot in the stirrup, she hopped up, throwing her other leg over him until she was atop his back.

As a girl, she remembered how high up it had seemed whenever she rode Eli. It was an odd sensation being on him now. She tapped his side with the stirrup. "Let's go, boy."

Eli trotted around the field as the sun beat down on them. At first she thought he might be taking it easy on her, but then she remembered that while she'd aged, so had he. As a teenager, she'd gotten caught up in school and friends, and she hadn't ridden him as much as she had as a young girl. Then she went away to college. After that, she was busy working and finding her way in the world. With every quiet stride that Eli made, she felt the tears begin to surface. She'd missed him so much and she was so sorry she hadn't visited him more.

He slowed down and she wrapped her arms around his neck. "I'm glad to see you, boy," she said. "I'm not leaving again. I promise."

Eli made a noise and she could've sworn that he was pleased.

Emily walked out to meet her sister as Rachel's car came to a stop in the driveway. Clara, Rachel's daughter, was sitting in the backseat, wearing pink sparkle sunglasses, her light brown hair pulled into two ponytails with matching bows.

"I swear, you have grown!" Emily said, leaning on the open window while Clara attempted to unbuckle her seatbelt. Emily reached in and helped her.

"I'm four now!" she said proudly.

Emily opened the door for her. "Four! Wow. I can't believe how time flies," she said with a giggle, having seen her only six months ago. She'd been four then too.

Clara hopped down onto the driveway, her matching pink sandals making a smack on the pavement. "See how tall I am?" she asked, tipping up on her toes.

"Yes, you are very tall."

"Come on in and have some cookies, Clara," Gram called from the front door, holding two canes. "Let's give your mama and Aunt Emily a chance to talk." Clara ran up to meet her, taking one of the canes and mimicking her grandmother as she walked inside.

"She likes to be like her gram," Rachel said, then turned toward her sister. "I've missed you so much. You okay?"

That feeling of dread flooded Emily again and she shook her head, unable to verbalize all the emotions she was feeling. It didn't matter though; her big sister could always read her.

"Let's go to the backyard and talk."

They made their way to the sand where their grandfather had hung two swings on one of the old trees. Its enormous trunk was perfectly straight, its branches spreading wide as if it were reaching for the house. Despite all the coastal storms, the tree, and the swings survived, the wooden seats that used to be yellow now as white as driftwood, but the ropes still strong. Emily sat down on one, kicked her shoes off, and put her feet in the sand.

"Gram says there's gossip going around about the new owner of Water's Edge," Emily said, turning toward the bay and letting the breeze blow her hair behind her shoulders. She wanted to hear what her sister thought of Charles Peterson; Emily wondered if she'd made the right decision working there.

"The elusive Charles Peterson," Rachel said with a smile. "Did you get to speak to him when you interviewed?"

"No. Libby hired me." She knew if she mentioned meeting Charles Peterson, her blunder today would eventually come out because she told her sister everything, but at that moment, with the rush of wind across the water and the rustling of the trees, she just wanted to clear her head and try not to have to think so hard.

Rachel pushed herself back and let go, her legs outstretched like she'd done as a girl, the old rope creaking as she swung across the sand. "I heard he's quite easy on the eyes."

Emily smiled and shook her head. "And how would anyone know that? Gossip runs wild in this town."

"Supposedly, he's trying to make structural changes to the inn. I know because Rocky McFadden told us. He's going to meet with him to hear his plan."

"So did Rocky tell you Charles Peterson was attractive?" she said with a grin, teasing her sister.

"No!" Rachel giggled. "His wife did!"

Emily clapped a hand over her mouth to stifle her laugh. "Elizabeth McFadden better not dare be looking elsewhere. Rocky's too handsome himself!"

"Yeah, but I can't get past the fact that he used to eat glue in first grade."

"Haha!" Emily smiled long after the moment had passed. She could always rely on her sister to make her feel better. When they'd lost their parents, Gram and Papa had taken over raising them, and they'd done a wonderful job, but it was Rachel who would crawl into bed with her at night; it was Rachel who sneaked out of class to peek in on her the first day of school each year; it was Rachel who'd put her arm around her when they'd sat on these very swings while Emily grieved the loss of her parents in her quiet way.

"Wanna talk about Brad?" Rachel asked.

"No." Emily bit her lip, trying to keep her face from crumpling at the mere mention of his name. She could still see the fear in his eyes when she'd told him "no," and she could feel the loss of all her life plans.

Rachel plucked a small shell from the sand and tossed it into the water. It made a circular ripple on the surface until the current erased it.

"Do you think you were ever in love with him?" she asked anyway.

Emily turned to look at her sister, blinking her tears away. Rachel had been there for the proposal, and she'd held her after, but they hadn't talked about it until now. "At first. But we just grew apart—at least I thought we had, and then, out of nowhere he proposed. We'd never really talked about it, but I could feel us slipping apart. Maybe he panicked."

Rachel studied her sister, her eyes squinting slightly. "You'll find that perfect person one day. I have faith."

The evening sky was an electric blue without a cloud in sight. "You're a romantic," Emily said. "I don't believe there's a *perfect* person."

"You only say that because you haven't ever felt it, but it's real. I promise. When I met Jeff I felt it…"

To Emily's complete surprise, she saw tears in her sister's eyes as she dropped her head and pretended to be looking for something in the sand at her feet.

"What's wrong?"

Rachel tipped her head back as if the motion would keep the tears from falling, but they fell anyway. "Jeff and I are having a little trouble." She shook her head. "I'm so sorry. I didn't expect to say anything. I know you have enough to deal with…"

The revelation hit Emily like a wrecking ball. Jeff had been one of those people that had seemed like part of the family even before he'd married Rachel. He was like a brother to Emily. She adored him and she couldn't believe anything could come between him and her sister. He had always been so good to Rachel.

"Why? What's wrong?"

"We're at an impasse," she said, her words breaking. "I'm so sorry," she said again. "I didn't want to bombard you with this. I thought I could keep it in."

"I want to know. It's fine. Just tell me. What kind of impasse?" The one thing about the two of them was that no matter what was going on, they could always muster the energy to help the other out. They'd had to learn how to do that when they were little, when they were the only ones of their friends with no parents. They understood each other, and they knew what the other needed.

"He wants more kids—a lot more. And I want to go back to work."

"Why do you want to go back to work so badly?"

"I don't know if Jeff understands this but I feel like I've lost myself a little. I love being Clara's mom, but I want to explore the other sides of me as well, and he's making me feel guilty about that."

"Couldn't you work *and* have more kids?"

"I'm not against having more children—I'd actually like to have more than one—but at this point in my life, I want to focus on Clara and going back to work. He'd have more children right now if I'd let him."

"Have you tried to explain your feelings to him?"

"Many times. He tells me that there are so many working mothers who would want nothing more than I have, but they aren't me."

"I know." Emily understood completely. While Emily played with dolls, Rachel set up lemonade stands, counting the money and deciding how much she would save and how much she would spend. She was always the one they knew would do something fantastic—she was creative, driven, and smart. "I'm sorry." She dug her toes beneath the warm sand until she reached the cooler sand below.

Rachel smiled, but Emily could tell she wasn't happy. They stayed on the swings for a while. They'd done that a lot as kids—sat together in silence as if just their proximity were enough. She missed that.

"Gram's giving Clara cookies before dinner," Emily said with a smirk.

Rachel shook her head. "What are great-grandmothers for, right?"

"Remember when she used to give us dinner backwards and we'd eat dessert first?"

"Yes," Rachel said, chuckling.

The thought of it made Emily laugh, and it felt good to laugh. She kept thinking how great it was to be home.

Chapter Three

"What is that?" Emily asked Libby as she picked up the wooden plaque with a painted blue fish attached to it. She turned it over in her hand.

Libby shot a quick glance over to it. "Mr. Peterson offered it to me as a thank-you for working through the changeover in ownership. He said that he thought my home may have a nautical theme since I live near the water." She leaned in closer, tipping her head to look down the corridor, and whispered, "I feel terrible, but it doesn't match anything in my house. I even tried to consider it for Ava's room, but hers is purple and it just wouldn't go in there. I wonder if I could put it up in Pete's shed? Would that be awful?"

"I actually like it," Emily said. Was that what Charlie had been trying to find in Francine's shop? And to think that he could've gotten hand-painted margarita glasses… Those would've been right up Libby's alley.

"I'll tell you what," Libby whispered. "You can have it. It would make me feel better than hanging it in my husband's shed. It looks expensive. The last thing I need is Mr. Peterson seeing Pete on the water somewhere using it as a bottle opener or something." She made a playfully worried face at her friend.

Libby's awkwardness over the situation gave Emily a little punch of amusement until she looked up and found herself eye to eye with

Mr. Peterson. She sobered immediately, swallowing her laughter, realizing Libby had done the same.

"Good morning," he said, glancing down at the fish before his eyes settled back on her. He was wearing a light, summer gray suit and blue tie, his hair as expertly combed as it had been yesterday, a tiny bit of style in the front.

Emily cleared her throat. "Good morning," she returned. "How did you find everything in your room?"

"It was fine, thank you. I have a few meetings this morning and then I'd like to work out. While I'm in the gym, please send staff to my suite to set up a few tables." He slid a handwritten list of food across the counter, and Emily noticed how neat his handwriting was. "I'm going to show off the place, and I'd like these hors d'oeuvres prepared, along with the drink selections by one forty-five on the dot. I'll be bringing them back at two o'clock. Do you have any questions?"

"No, sir," she said. "I'll begin organizing it immediately."

His lips were set in a straight line, and she couldn't figure out what he was thinking, but she could take a guess: He was probably hoping that she didn't screw anything up like she had yesterday.

"I promise it'll be perfect," she said, looking directly into his eyes. The intensity of his expression made her heart patter with nerves, but she noticed his expression soften just slightly.

"Perfect is good," he said and then he left, with a quick wave as he headed out the door. Emily could feel her shoulders drop the minute he was gone.

"How's Rachel? I miss her," Libby said as she took a sip of her afternoon coffee.

They hadn't seen Charles Peterson for ages and they'd hit a slow patch, so Emily felt comfortable chatting to Libby. "She's doing well…" She didn't want to spill Rachel's secrets, but Libby had known them since they were girls and they'd been very close their whole lives. "What's it like having to go to work and getting two children where they need to go?" she asked. Libby had two kids: Ava, who was seven and a two-year-old named Timothy.

"It's busy, like anything else with two kids, but it's good. Why?"

"Rachel's considering going back to work."

"Oh? That's wonderful."

A patron came in then and requested his room key, which was fine with Emily because she really didn't want to go into too much about her sister. She just wanted to try to understand why Jeff was so insistent that Rachel not work. People did it all the time. But she also knew Jeff very well, and he wasn't an irrational person; he probably just saw his life turning out differently. She hoped he'd come around.

Libby looked at her watch. "Is everything ready to be set up for Mr. Peterson?"

Emily stood up. "Yes. The chef said to me privately, though, that he wasn't thrilled with Mr. Peterson's suggestions for hors d'oeuvres today." She pulled the key to the Concord Suite from the lock box. "He said they didn't represent the local culture at all. I told him it was probably best not to ask questions, although I agreed."

"Good move." Libby got up and handed Emily the armful of white linen tablecloths that they'd stacked on the edge of the desk. "He's intimidating, isn't he? It makes me crazy having him here, and I don't even usually get nervous around people. In fact I never do."

"Yes, he's intimidating," she said to be agreeable. He was, but she was thinking about how he hadn't been terribly hard on her about the credit card. He could've been really upset, but he wasn't. "When you get nervous, just think about Pete opening his beer with that fish. It'll make you laugh." She took the fish from under the counter and slid it down into her bag. "I'll take it home."

"Are you all right to set up on your own?"

"Yep." Emily took the linens, said goodbye to Libby, and walked the long hallway to the steps leading to the second floor. The staircase was grand and arching, with a carpeted runner leading the way. She passed the wall of floor-to-ceiling windows that overlooked the bay and marveled for a moment at how beautiful the day was. Growing up, she'd been so close to it that she'd barely noticed, but having been away, the bay seemed like an old friend, walking beside her, holding her up so she didn't fall. She reached the door to the Concord Suite. A stack of tables had been left by the staff against the wall outside. She turned the lock.

"Hello?" she called, peeking inside. "I'm setting up for the party this afternoon. Anyone here?" she double-checked quite loudly as the space was large and her voice needed to travel. There was only silence, so she opened the door wider and walked in.

The living area was luxurious, with pacific blue wingback chairs positioned at an angle across from an oversized white down-filled sofa with blue throw pillows adorned with embroidered sailboats. The furniture was positioned around a mahogany table that had a blue and white floral vase exploding in yellow blooms of forsythia branches. Emily leaned around them to view a white sailboat as it disappeared behind the rows of perfectly straight, hunter-green umbrellas that dotted the decks outside. She set the linens down and went out to get the tables.

One by one, she brought them in, leaning them carefully against the wall just inside the door. Then she set about moving the furniture.

She dragged the two chairs to either side of the windows, allowing for an unobstructed view but getting them out of the center of the room. As she reached for the table, she swore she heard the click of a doorknob and she stopped in her tracks.

"Anyone here?" she called out.

"Argh!" she heard from the hallway beside her and whipped around to find a toweled and shocked Charles Peterson standing in the bedroom doorway before darting behind a door. It shut and there was silence again.

It took her a minute to register what she'd just seen. His hair was wet, the dark strands glistening in the sunlight. There were beads of water on his bare chest and down the arm that had led to the fist that was holding his towel around his waist. She swallowed, trying to clear the image.

When she'd gotten herself together, she walked over to the closed door. "I did call out when I came in," she said, finding the courage to speak. "Twice."

"How was I supposed to hear you with the water running?"

She heard the bang of a drawer. "You said you'd be at the gym. I was following your instructions."

"The meetings ended earlier than I expected so I went to the gym sooner."

Was she supposed to have read his mind? "How was I to know?"

The door opened and Charles walked out wearing a pair of shorts and a T-shirt that showed off his biceps. She focused on his face.

"I should've told you. I was aware that you would be organizing things, but I didn't know you'd actually be setting them up in the room as well."

"Well, I promised you perfection. I wasn't going to rely on anyone else to do it." As she looked at him, his hair still wet, wearing more casual clothes, bare feet—all of a sudden she realized he didn't look all that dissimilar to the people she hung out with. It made his whole face look different to her now.

She shook the thought from her mind. "I should set the tables up."

He headed back into the bedroom. "What do you think of my hors d'oeuvres selection?" he asked from the other room.

Emily pulled the table legs out until they snapped into position and set the first table upright as she tried to think of a way to spin the fact that she wasn't entirely taken with his choices. While skewered beef sirloin with rosemary, and portabella mushroom bites were lovely appetizers, they didn't reflect the small town, coastal feel of the area at all.

He returned, this time having put on his watch and shoes, and waited expectantly for an answer. Emily fluffed out the tablecloth and draped it over the table.

"You don't agree with what I've chosen?" he said as if he'd read her mind.

"You aren't trying to please me," she said, awkwardly scooting one side of the sofa back against the wall.

Noticing her slight struggle with the sofa, Charles walked over and easily picked up the other side, moving it into place. "What would you have chosen?"

She set up another table without answering. He was putting her on the spot. She should've just said his choices were fine—that was what any good employee would've done, but there was something about his expression that was different from how it had been when he looked at her before. His look wasn't quite as direct; it was more interested.

"You really want my opinion?"

He locked eyes with her, and she couldn't deny how attractive he was. "If I didn't want it, I wouldn't have asked," he said, his tone gentle and unworried.

Reluctantly, she offered her favorites: "How about mini crab cakes with tomato chutney? Or shrimp skewers? For vegetarians… Maybe a white bean soup with coconut milk or something? Look at where you are," she said, peering out at the view. "You want food that will make people feel this." She pointed to the glistening bay outside. "You want crab that was caught this morning, shrimp right out of the sea… There's a certain culture down here, and I'd say appealing to that would be your best bet." He was staring at her, taking her in. "But that's just my opinion."

He looked thoughtful and there was a moment of silence that lasted longer than she felt was comfortable. Finally, he said, "You might be right."

I might?

"See if you have enough time to change what I've ordered. Check with the chef. Then I want you to come see me today at four o'clock." His face was unreadable, expressionless, as he sank further into thought, and she couldn't tell what was on his mind. Then, his phone rang and he turned away from her to answer it. Emily finished setting everything up and left before he'd gotten off his call. As she left, she wondered if she'd overstepped her bounds.

Libby's expression had made Emily worry when she'd told her about what had happened in Charles's suite. She'd spent all day thinking about it—while organizing a new on-site yoga class, reserving space and accommodations for a birthday party, setting up the banquet rooms for business meetings—the whole time, it hadn't escaped her mind. As she sat under one of the umbrellas outside, Emily tried to get her thoughts in order. She'd lost the corporate credit card, she'd walked in on Mr. Peterson half naked, and she'd told him his food choices weren't right. She was going to get fired—that was why Libby had looked at her like that, she was sure.

Emily couldn't lose this job. Mr. Peterson didn't know about the three years she'd spent as an events coordinator at the pub in Richmond, how she'd raised the company's special events food and beverage revenue by forty-three percent, how she'd practically built a management team that ran so well she didn't even worry leaving them. Libby knew it. That was why she'd hired her. But Libby couldn't bail Emily out this time.

It was nearly four o'clock. Feeling low, she stood up, glad the flush on her face was disguised by the warmth from the sun, and walked into the icy cold of inside, heading for the Concord Suite. The hallways that had seemed cheerful and bright now felt as though they were clouded by her worry as she approached. She knocked.

Charles opened the door and allowed her to enter. Emily's mind was swimming. She wanted to explain things, to tell him how trustworthy she was, and how, right now, she wasn't herself. But she stayed quiet.

"Good day?" he asked.

I'm probably about to get sacked, so no. "Yes," she lied.

"Good. Have a seat."

The chairs were still by the windows where she'd put them, so she walked over to the sofa and sat down. She kept taking in deep breaths, trying not to get herself worked up. This wasn't like her, but she had so much going on in her mind that she didn't feel as confident as she normally did. Nervously, she fixed her eyes on the tables she'd set up in the room. The hors d'oeuvres were long gone and she panicked for just a moment, wondering if she'd forgotten to come back and remove the tables, but as she racked her brain, for the missed directive, she realized that he was watching her.

"Are you okay?" he asked, sitting down at the other end of the sofa.

Emily mentally pulled herself together and looked at him. Why was she falling apart now? She was usually so strong—no one ever knew her emotions except her. She'd always been great at her job, poised. Had she hit a breaking point? "Why did you want to see me?" she asked. It was only after he answered that question that she would be able to answer his.

His eyebrows furrowed in thought.

Here it comes, she told herself.

"You are from this area, correct?"

"Yes. How did you know?"

"I guessed by the way you spoke with the woman in the shop the other day and your knowledge of local cuisine." He allowed a small smile. When she didn't respond—not intentionally, more so because she was still trying to ascertain what he wanted—he continued. "I'm planning to make some improvements to Water's Edge."

He cleared his throat. "By improving the inn, offering even more for the visitors, we could publicize nationally, show off its potential... We could build this up to something quite grand."

"So... Forgive me, but why did you want to tell me this?"

"I'm struggling to get the planning commission on board. I'd like you to help me."

"What?"

"I'm hoping you'll be able to advise me on how to best reach the people here. They're pushing back, and I have a gut feeling about you…" This time, he really smiled at her, and she noticed how his whole face changed.

She wondered why the locals were pushing back. What was he planning? His smile seemed so genuine, but was he just trying to convince her to help him?

"I'm meeting with a few people around town soon. It might pull you away from work a few days. I'll talk to Libby. If she needs any help with events, I'll expand her budget to hire someone else for the interim." He stood up and Emily followed his lead. "So, would you be interested in helping me?"

"Of course, Mr. Peterson," she said out of sheer interest. She wanted to know, firsthand, what he had in mind for the inn.

"Thank you. And please, call me Charlie."

"Okay, Charlie," she said, the name feeling overly personal on her lips.

He walked her to the door. "Eight a.m. tomorrow?" he asked.

"Okay. See you then."

Chapter Four

"I'm worried about Gram," Emily said to Rachel while they took an early evening walk. The trees were blocking the last bit of sun as it slipped out of view. "Not that I want her depressed or anything, but she seems almost overly chipper since Papa died. I'm worried she's suppressing her feelings. Has she grieved at all?"

"Well hello, pot! Meet kettle," Rachel teased.

"What's that supposed to mean?"

"You hardly ever express your feelings either." Rachel turned onto the thin path through the woods that they'd used as kids to get to the beach. Her sister was right. Other than with Papa, Emily had been pretty closed off her whole life. She hadn't meant to be, and every once in a while she'd allowed herself to cry in front of Rachel, but most of the time, she didn't open up to people.

The narrow gravel they'd walked down as girls was now overgrown with weeds and grass, but the stones still showed through underneath. Eventually, the dense trees opened up to powdery sand, the bay water slapping the shore in tiny ripples. Emily sat down on the log bench their grandfather had made when they were younger. Emily had helped him cut the wood. Rachel plopped down beside her and kicked off her shoes.

"If you're worried about Gram, why don't you ask her?"

"Maybe I will…" Emily plucked a shell from the sand and tossed it into the water.

Rachel turned back to the bay. Emily followed her line of sight. A speedboat rushed by, agitating the tide, sending it slamming against the shore. The sun was behind the trees now. The sand was cool on Emily's feet as she took off her shoes and set them beside Rachel's.

"Are you ever going to tell me about what happened with Brad?"

"I'd rather not talk about it."

"You never want to talk about anything that bothers you, but it's good to get it off your chest."

"Why?"

"Because you can get another person's perspective."

She didn't need any more perspective on the matter. Emily let the wind calm her. "I just realized that I didn't love him anymore. Is that possible?"

"Of course it's possible."

"I feel like I could cry at any moment. I feel so bad about saying no. But other than that, really that's the end of the story."

A flock of birds flew overhead, their shadows sailing across the water and disappearing over the sand.

"For three years, I'd defined myself by being Brad's girlfriend. Now, I don't really know who I am. And I'm living with Gram again… I feel like I'm right back where I started."

"Then don't live with Gram. Get one of those new condos by the water."

Emily smiled. "Might be nice," she said, but she knew she wouldn't be comfortable there. She wanted space, land, water.

They sat quietly together until the sun had all but disappeared.

"I've got to get back home," Rachel said, standing and stretching her back. "Clara has to have a bath and I need to cook dinner."

"Have you made any headway with Jeff on the working situation?"

"No. He won't even listen to me. I love him so much, but when it comes to that topic, it's like we don't speak the same language."

"I'm sorry."

"I'm so glad you're home. We used to have so much fun—the three of us. Maybe having you back will lighten things up between us. Take the focus off our troubles for a while."

"I hope so."

"Why don't you stop by tonight?"

"Yeah, that would be great. Text me when you want me to come over."

"Okay," Rachel said as Emily looked up at her. In the orange light of the summer evening, Rachel still looked as young as she had when they were in college together. Her cheeks were flushed from the heat, her long eyelashes curling perfectly, away from her big green eyes, and her dark hair fighting the humidity in its elegant way.

Emily stood up and followed her sister down the path, feeling like she was in the right place.

When Emily arrived back at Gram's, a young boy was washing Papa's Buick. The old car still looked brand new. Neither Papa nor Gram hardly ever drove it. The suds ran down the shiny blue surface, puddling in the gravel, making the ground all muddy. The boy waved and she nodded hello. The porch light was on and a single glass of iced tea sat sweating on the weathered wicker table. Emily took a seat, figuring that Gram must be on her way back out. The porch paddle fans were whirring but they didn't do much to cool the humid air that surrounded her tonight. She looked out at the grass. Gram had always kept a perfect lawn but the weeds were taking over.

The bang of the screen door shutting cut through the nightly sounds of crickets and lapping water.

"Oh!" Gram said with a smile. "Back from your walk?" She leaned her cane against the side of the table and sat down.

"Rachel had to give Clara a bath," Emily said as Gram picked up her glass.

"Would you like a drink?" Gram asked.

"No, thanks. I'm okay."

"Are you?" Gram had her hands in her lap, a comforting smile on her lips. "You don't look okay."

"Rachel asked about Brad."

"Oh… Do you miss him?" The old porch light cast a harsh glare on them, revealing the age on Gram's face, but her expression was just as it had always been.

"I made the right decision, but I feel so guilty."

"You can make your life anything you want when it's only you that you have to worry about. The trouble is when you can't live without *him*. But I haven't heard you say that."

"Are you living okay without Papa?"

Gram took in a delicate breath, her thin legs crossed beneath her cotton skirt. "I'm livin'," she said with a smile. "That's all I can do."

"Do you ever get sad?"

"On occasion, but only when I forget."

"Forget what?"

"That life is greatest when we *live* it." She stood up. "It's hotter than blazes out here. Let's go in, cool off, and have a glass of wine." She grabbed her cane and steadied herself. Then she called out to the boy washing Papa's car and told him to knock when he was finished.

On her way inside, the phone buzzed in Emily's pocket. When she pulled it out to view her missed call, it was an unfamiliar number.

She listened to the message as she followed Gram into the kitchen, and her mouth hung open.

"It's Charlie. I'd like to take you to dinner tonight. Can you give me a call?"

"Gram?" Emily said, her heart beating wildly, the phone in her hand. Gram turned around. "Charles Peterson left me a message but my volume was off…"

Gram took a step closer to Emily. "And?"

"He said he wants to take me to dinner." She wondered what it was all about.

"Then go!" she said, thoughts behind her eyes. Emily wondered what they were.

"But we were going to have wine."

"Go, child! Call him back, for goodness' sake! He's probably waitin'."

With nervous fingers, Emily hit the callback button and went into the formal living room for privacy. She sat down on the stiff sofa and crossed her legs underneath her as the phone rang in her ear.

"Hello."

"Hi. This is Emily."

"Yes. I recognized the number. How are you?"

"I'm fine."

The line buzzed with electric silence.

"I'll be taking a few people out to dinner tomorrow. I need to have an exceptional location that shows them I mean business but in an atmosphere that would make them feel comfortable. Where would you suggest?"

"It's a no-brainer. Merroir. It's been featured in national maga-zines, the food is outstanding, and the atmosphere is… well, perfect."

"Feel like a business dinner? I need to go over a few things with you."

"Sure. What time?" Emily leaned over to check her reflection in the mirror. The heat had had its way with her hair and she'd need to at least redo her makeup.

"How about in two hours? Enough time?"

"Yes. That's fine." She only needed about forty minutes.

"I'll pick you up. Where are you?"

She remembered her promise to stop by Rachel's, and she figured she probably should. She had enough time to visit and still go to din-ner. "I'll be at my sister's." She gave him the address.

"Perfect. I'll call for reservations."

"See you soon," she said.

As she turned off her phone, Gram came into focus. She was smiling, her eyes knowing, like she had something she'd wanted to say for ages.

"What?"

She paused. "Glad to see you livin'," she said.

"It's just business, Gram."

"So you say. Go get ready! I heard the whole thing. You'd better hurry; it takes the old hot water heater a lot longer to heat up these days and you need a good shower."

With a grin, Emily headed upstairs.

"Hey, girl!" Jeff said as he opened the door and nearly knocked her over with a hug. Emily had certainly missed him. Jeff was like the older brother she'd never had, her protector. "Glad to have you back!"

"I'm glad to be back! I just wanted to pop by quickly to say hello."

"What are you up to tonight?"

"I'm actually doing a bit of work, but I had a few minutes and I've been here a whole day without coming by! I worried you'd hold it against me," she teased.

"I would've!" He gave her wink and ushered her inside.

"What kind of work are you doing at night, dressed as stylish as you are?"

"Stop flirting," Rachel kidded as she entered the room.

What made Rachel's comment funny was that Jeff was anything but a flirt. He was probably the most genuine person Emily had ever met. Rachel gave Jeff a playful nudge. Watching the two of them as they exchanged happy glances, Emily would've never known there was anything wrong between them. They seemed just as happy as they'd always been.

"You do look nice," Rachel said.

Emily had curled her hair and put on a sundress and wedge sandals, pink lip-gloss, and dangly earrings that Gram had let her borrow. She hoped she hadn't overdone things.

"I only stopped by to say a quick 'hello' because Charles Peterson and I are heading to Merroir. He's picking me up here in a little bit." Before her sister could say anything suggestive, she cut her off. "For a *business* dinner."

"Mmm hmm. I hear ya."

"I'm serious!"

"Hi, Aunt Emily!" Clara said, coming into the living room with a purple bathrobe and matching slippers. Her wet hair looked black, all combed back after her bath. She was holding one of her baby dolls.

"Hi there," Emily said, leaning down to greet her niece. "Who is this?" She pointed to the doll.

"Gloria."

"It's nice to meet you, Gloria," Emily said, grabbing the plastic hand and giving it a little shake. Clara giggled.

"It's time for stories," Rachel said, taking her hand and leading her down the short hallway to her bedroom. "You'll get to see lots of Aunt Emily now that she lives so close." She turned and said over her shoulder, "If you're gone before I get back, text me if anything interesting goes down at dinner."

"Okay."

Rachel and Clara disappeared down the hallway.

"It's so good to have you home," Jeff said, sitting down on the old tweed sofa and motioning for Emily to do the same. "I think it'll be good for Rachel to have family around her again."

"Why is that?"

"She wants to get out more. I know I should take her on dates, we should have dinner parties… She said she wants to go back to work, but she doesn't need to. Maybe if we hung out like we used to, she'd reconsider."

"Have you discussed this with her?"

"Sort of. But we just end up arguing and I don't like to argue with her, nor do I want that tension around Clara. Anyway, it's so good to see you!" It was clear he was changing the subject. He narrowed his eyes. "Even when we get together at Christmas, you never wear earrings like that. You sure this isn't a date?"

"I'm sure."

"If it is, I'm going to make him get out of the car and come in so I can get a read on him. I don't want just anyone dating my little sister."

Jeff had called her his little sister even before he'd married Rachel.
He'd always looked out for Emily.

"It's business. Swear. Apparently the Clearwater planning commission is giving him a fit over doing some sort of changes to the inn.
He wants me to help him with that, and I can't wait to find out why
they won't agree."

"And you're going to Merroir? Fancy."

"He told me to pick a good spot!"

"Well, enjoy yourself," Jeff said, leaning past her to look out the
window. "I think he's here."

She turned toward the window to find the blue BMW pulling to
a stop in the short driveway. Charlie got out and headed up the walk.

Emily said a quick goodbye to Jeff and went out the front door,
shutting it behind her. Charlie stopped in front of her when she'd
made it down the porch's small staircase.

"Hello," he said, a small grin emerging and reaching his eyes.

"Hi."

"Ready to talk about county planning?" he asked as they turned
toward his car.

"Yep." She didn't know a thing about the planning commission.

Charlie opened her door and she got in. As he walked around
the back of the car, she took in the tan leather interior, the quiet
hum of the motor, and the stark difference in temperature to the
heat outside. He got in, adjusted the mirror, and backed out the
drive to the street.

The ride to Merroir was quiet, and Emily was glad that she had
to focus on giving him directions. She found herself a little nervous.
On the stretch of road, when there wasn't anything to say, she tried
to fill the silence.

"So, where did you finally find a gift for Libby?" she asked, having no clue what else to ask. The fish was still sitting on the passenger seat of her car.

He turned and looked at her briefly before his gaze settled back on the road. "The art gallery in town. I don't think it was her style—I could tell by her face, even though she tried her best to hide it."

Emily inwardly scolded herself for bringing up the topic. There was nowhere to go from that question. "For her, I'd have gone with margarita glasses." she said, being honest but worried that she might offend him.

"I actually loved the colors on the fish itself. Even the eyes were hand-painted." He looked over at her to get her reaction, clearly not affected by her comment, which was a relief.

"I did too," she said, thinking how she was going to take another look when she got home. "It would be gorgeous against a bright island-inspired paint—like yellow or pink.

"I'd thought that very same thing," he said, glancing at her again but this time, interest showing in his face.

"Art is subjective," she said.

"Yes."

"Turn here," she said as they rounded the curve.

They bumped along a rocky road, made a few turns winding them down and behind the trees, through a neighborhood, until they reached the shore of the Rappahannock River. Sitting alongside it, just a few feet from the sand, was a bed of white shells set with tables and chairs, strings of lights illuminating the space around the enormous red umbrellas that protected the patrons from sun on bright days.

"It's outside?" he asked, parking the car and turning off the engine.

"Yep. They do have that small screened-in area, but the outdoor tables are so much better."

Charlie got out and walked around the car, meeting Emily. They entered together under the Merroir sign that was suspended with a single pole on either side, creating an entrance for the outside dining area.

A hostess greeted them and took them to a table that sat beneath an oak tree, more white lights encircling its substantial trunk all the way up to the branches. Charlie pulled out Emily's chair as a yellow Labrador trotted past them and settled himself under a nearby table.

"This is quite unique," Charlie said, the breeze lifting the edges of the napkins that had been placed beside their menus.

Emily looked around, viewing the place through new eyes. Despite the fact that the majority of seating was outside, men wore buttoned shirts, pressed trousers; women were in sundresses and sunglasses—the atmosphere was casual yet sophisticated, a lot like the food. Along the edge of the restaurant was Locklies Marina, its docks lined with sailboats, the water gently lapping underneath them, causing them to rock.

The waitress came over to get their drink orders. Emily ordered first. She got a Sandy Crab Ale, a local ale known for its quirky brewer—she'd been friends with the owner of the brewery since they were kids.

"I'll have the same," Charlie said.

The waitress lit a candle on their table before leaving, the flame working overtime to keep its light against the wind coming off the riverbank.

"I've never seen anything quite like this," he said. "It's very different to what I'm used to in New York. I'm glad I decided to ask for your help."

Emily had only been to New York as a tourist, and she couldn't imagine what living there would be like. While it was an amazing place to visit, it didn't fit her personality—she'd go crazy without the open space. Even when she'd lived in Richmond, she'd missed it. She just didn't realize how much. "Do you live in an apartment?"

"Yes. It's close to everything I need. I could walk to work."

"Do you?"

"Actually, no. I usually hire a car or get a cab."

"Why?"

"It gives me a few more minutes to get my work done. The pace is very different there than it is here."

"I'm sure it is. Libby talks about it sometimes. She lived in New York for a while, you know?"

"I do know. That's why I hired her. She was a perfect balance of both worlds. I have to admit that I've struggled with the pace here. I'm used to the hustle of business but down here everyone seems to be on their own time." He leaned over the small airy fence used to separate the dining area from the grass. "Look at them," he said, nodding toward a couple and their dog, walking along the edge of the water. "They were eating a few minutes ago. They've paid the check. I'd have gotten in my car and left but they're still here."

Emily let out a little laugh. "They're just enjoying themselves." She looked back at him, but he was still watching the couple. "In what way can I help you with the planning commission?" she asked.

"I think they see me as threat to the town. They're worried that by improving the inn, the already growing tourism will increase beyond what they can manage. They think I don't understand what small-town life is all about. That was the vibe I got."

"And do you understand what small-town life is like?" Truthfully, she could see their point of view. Clearwater couldn't handle but so much, and if the inn got too big, the roads would get overcrowded, the beaches full of strangers. She didn't want that at all. In fact, she totally agreed with the planning commission.

"That's where you come in. I want you to show me what's important to the people. I want to develop the inn in a way that will benefit the town, but I don't think the planning commission trusts me."

"What do you mean when you say 'a way that will benefit the town'?"

"I will bring a ton of revenue in, which will move along already proposed improvements that the commission has in the works. Improvements that are stagnant at the moment until the town has enough funds. The expansion will be just enough to bring in the amount of income they're looking for. I don't want to overwhelm the city. I just need you to help me understand what life is like here so I can better answer their questions."

She knew exactly what was important to the people and she'd be more than happy to help him build something that would enable Clearwater to thrive, but it sounded like not everyone in town was on his side. Could she trust him? "Okay," she said, nodding slowly.

Excitement flickered across Charlie's face. "Excellent."

The waitress brought their beers over and set them on beer mats. Emily thanked her and took a sip.

"Libby was very quick to sing your praises when I mentioned to her that I was adding to your duties. She told me about your success with the pub in Richmond. I'm impressed. I have high hopes that you'll bring a lot to this endeavor."

"Thank you. I hope to." The couple walking on the beach laughed at something, and Emily's attention was drawn to them once again. They seemed so comfortable here, so happy. What was it that made this area so easy to love? Libby had gone away, but she'd come back and now couldn't imagine ever leaving. She'd given up a very lucrative career in New York just to move back and have a family with her husband, Pete. This area could draw people in and, once they tasted the culture, they often wanted to stay. She worried about what that might do to Clearwater, if Charlie's plans for the inn took off. "Can I ask you something?"

"Of course."

"What improvements do you plan on making to the inn?"

He took a drink of his beer, before responding. "I'd like to make it bigger. I acquired it as an investment property. Water's Edge has huge potential. Tourism in the area is growing. There's not a lot in the way of high-end accommodations to support this growth. I'm going to provide that. But I'm still finalizing things with the architects. We've got a few ideas on the table at the moment."

She wondered how he could possibly make the inn bigger—it was already so vast. Would expanding it more really improve things as much as he thought?

Charlie sat back in his chair, one elbow leaning on the fence railing beside him. He looked comfortable. He took another sip of his beer and peered down at the insignia on the glass. "Is this a local ale?"

"Yes. It's one of my favorites. I like Merroir because they have something as casual as this on the drink menu, but they also serve world-famous wines."

"Tell me what you like to eat," he said, looking down at his menu.

"Well, it's a tasting room. Meals are unfussy; it makes it very easy to entertain for a group. You can order a few things and everyone can try them. It's all made on the grill outside." She leaned on the table and touched his menu to point out her favorites. "I like the roasted red pepper soup, the sea scallops, or the crabcake.

Charlie leaned in to read a description and she got a whiff of his spicy scent. "It all sounds delicious." He looked up at her and smiled, creases forming at the edges of his blue eyes, unexpectedly making her feel warmth in her cheeks. Was she blushing? "Thank you for bringing me here. I think it might be just the atmosphere I need when I try *again* to convince the commission. I'm just thankful they're agreeing to meet me informally."

"Wait a minute." It had slipped her mind until that moment. "There's a man named Rocky McFadden on that committee."

"Yes. Do you know him?"

"He used to build boats with my grandfather. My gram still lets him put his crab pots in the water out back of her house when he has his big Fourth of July parties. I've known him all my life."

"Well, then you're the perfect person to help me understand him."

Chapter Five

"Park here," Emily said as they pulled into the parking lot of the marina. It was much bigger than Locklies and quite a distance away from Merroir. After they'd eaten, Emily decided there was something she wanted Charlie to see. He parallel parked and cut off the engine.

"I've actually been here already," he said. "I wanted to check it out before my photo shoot tomorrow for a local magazine. Apparently, they want to do it here."

"Swanky," she said with a grin.

He shrugged her comment off.

She'd never known anyone who found doing a magazine shoot commonplace, but by looking at Charlie's face, it didn't seem to be out of the ordinary to him.

As they walked along the edge of the property leading to the long piers that housed lines of beautiful boats, he said, "I'm aware that the community is known for fishing. What else can you tell me about the area?" It was clear by his face that he thought he knew what she was going to show him. Yes, Clearwater was known for fishing, and yes, he'd already seen the marina.

"I don't plan to tell you," she said, excitement rising as she thought about where she wanted to take him. "I plan to *show* you." She stopped walking along the enormous dock and peered down at the modest but still elegant speedboat in front of them. "This is our family boat. Rachel takes care of it, and we call it hers, but we all have keys." She stepped across the gap between the dock and the boat and hopped in. Clearly surprised, Charlie did the same.

"Take a seat," she said with a grin. As Charlie sat down, Emily started the boat. She kicked off her shoes to get comfortable and nodded for Charlie to do the same. Hesitantly, he complied. With the motor pattering in low gear, she maneuvered the boat out of the marina toward open water. At first, it took her a moment to get used to steering again—it had been a while, but once she settled in, it came back to her easily, and she could feel her shoulders relax.

Emily relished this time of year, when daylight wouldn't completely disappear until well into the night. With the sun making it's gradual descent, hanging low in the sky, and the water spraying out on either side of the boat as they hit the open bay, she headed for a small island. The island was so narrow, Emily could walk from one side to the other. She'd gone with Rachel as a girl—Papa would take them. They'd sit there in the sand all afternoon, watching the sailboats dock out in the water. She remembered the masses of white sails, and how they looked like angel wings.

Charlie was sitting quite straight in the seat beside her, the wind whipping his hair wildly. It made her smile. The flapping of his shirt in the wind, his bare feet, and the fact that he kept looking over at her was playing with her mind. He was so handsome that she almost forgot they were supposed to be doing business.

"When do you have your meeting with Rocky?" she called loudly above the noise of the boat's motor.

Charlie turned his wrist to view the time on his Rolex. "Five o'clock tomorrow," he said. "I'd like you to come with me." He looked over at her again.

"Okay," she said, a mixture of emotions swimming through her. She wasn't quite sure what to do now. She hadn't had a chance to speak to Rocky yet and hear his side to find out why they were putting on the breaks. But then she relaxed a bit. She'd only told Charlie she'd help him understand Rocky; she hadn't said she'd take Charlie's side. And it would be nice to go to dinner with Rocky. She hadn't seen him or his wife Elizabeth in so long.

Emily slowed the boat down as they approached land. The little island had no trees, the center a slight hill, the sea grasses growing at an upward climb. A beach with the softest sand she could remember ever feeling encircled the whole island. Emily allowed the boat to slide up near the beach, just enough that she could hop off the side. The water splashed up on her dress when she jumped down.

"Hang on," she said, standing ankle deep in the water. "I'll pull the boat up on the shore and you can step onto the sand." She worried about his expensive clothes. He looked as though he wasn't sure, like he wanted to take charge, but he didn't know what needed to be done. With the water's help, Emily pulled the boat by its side handles and dragged it up until it stopped in the sand.

"You should've let me do that for you," he said, hopping down.

"Why?"

"I don't know. It just seems right that *I* help *you* off the boat."

She smiled, flattered by his manners. "Well, I was taught how to get the boat on the shore as a child. I'm used to it. Wanna take a walk?"

Charlie stepped up beside her and she led him toward the grass, where a footpath emerged.

"This is beautiful," he said, looking around between steps, noticeably watching to protect his bare feet from obstacles on the path.

They reached the other side of the island, and just as she'd expected, the view was outstanding. The sun sparkled off the water, and everywhere she looked were sailboats, their white sails fighting against the wind. It was so spectacular that her breath caught. In that moment, for no reason at all, the past three years in Richmond ran through her mind—coming home to Brad, how they'd been looking for a new couch together, the plant in the kitchen that he always forgot that probably needed watering, the spot on the coffee table where he left his coffee cup every day, and the moment when she realized her heart just wasn't in it. Looking back on it all as she stood here, it was as though she had been drowning and she could only now catch her breath.

"Are you okay?" Charlie asked, and she noticed her breathing and her pounding heart.

"Yes," she said with a smile. "I was just thinking…" She sat down on the dune and looked up at him because he seemed to be deliberating on what to do. After a moment, he followed her lead, putting his knees up, his bare feet masculine against the gentle sand.

"What were you thinking about?"

"I had a close call." Her answer just sort of came out in a rush as if she'd wanted to tell it to him, yet she never told strangers this kind of thing, especially not someone she worked for. All her friends had called after that awful meal, but she'd only barely managed to talk to Rachel.

"What kind of close call?" He didn't seem overly bothered by the personal conversation, although he didn't look totally relaxed either.

"I almost…" Should she say it? "I almost married the wrong person."

A look of shock sprung to his face, but he quickly regained composure. Why had she just told him that? What was she doing? Was it the comforting feeling of being back on the island?

He studied her face for a moment before speaking. "Almost?" he asked, visibly curious.

She'd already told him too much. This wasn't like her at all. He was her boss—her boss's boss! But he was watching her, waiting for her answer. "I realized that I didn't love the man I'd spent three years with. He proposed and I had to tell him, 'No'."

"I'm sorry." He looked uncomfortable. Emily inwardly scolded herself for telling him anything at all. What in the world was going on with her?

All of a sudden, he said, "I understand," and looked out at the water.

"You do?"

"Yes. I was with the wrong person as well. But I married her. I knew it wasn't right, but I kept thinking that maybe we could make it work. I should've known better."

"Well, at least we learned from it."

They fell into an awkward silence for a moment, and Emily wondered if he felt as odd as she did having shared a glimpse of his personal life.

"Things certainly are different here," he said, looking down at his hands as he buried his fingers in the sand. "I have to confess that I don't know how to reach someone like Rocky McFadden. I've dealt with communities who didn't want me to build before, but usually it all came down to money, and in the end, I was granted building permits. But what do I fall back on if money isn't persuasive enough?"

"You're creative—I can already tell. You'll figure something out." Emily was struggling. Even though the conversation had returned to business, she was starting to feel the line blur. She shouldn't be telling these things to him, nor should she be hearing his story. She stood up and brushed off her bottom. "I wanted to show you how we relax around here, so I brought you to this island." She looked out again at the bay, now dotted with a few more sailboats. "I should probably get you back so you can prepare for the meeting."

He stood up beside her and followed her to the boat.

Gram was asleep by the time Emily returned from the marina. She went to bed thinking about Charlie, her mind spinning with thoughts of how to help him convince the planning commission to make changes to the inn, but worrying that she might see Rocky's side as well. She didn't want to get caught in the middle of anything. The excitement of the night and the constant thinking about tomorrow's meeting made her sleep lightly, and her shoulders ached the next morning.

As she walked downstairs, rubbing her neck with one hand, she could hear Gram whistling in the kitchen.

"Mornin', sunshine!" she said with a spatula in one hand and her cane in the other. I've got scrambled eggs, bacon, and fried tomatoes for breakfast! The biscuits are still in the oven to keep warm. Grab me the butter, would you, dear?"

Emily retrieved the butter from the fridge and handed it to Gram, so thankful to be home with her again.

"How was dinner?"

"Good."

Gram turned around. "You all right?" Gram's face was overly concerned, worried even.

"I'm fine," she said in the most convincing way she could. She noticed relief flood Gram's face. What was she so worried about? It had only been a bad night's sleep. "I'll come back for breakfast if that's okay. I need fresh air and sunshine to wake me up."

"Of course."

Emily walked to the back door and let herself out. The sun's warmth was already strong enough to cut through the cool bay breeze as she walked barefoot along the path to Eli's pasture. When she got there, she let herself in through the gate and walked to the barn. Eli was inside, resting.

"Hi, boy," she said and he shifted, his great body rustling the straw underneath him. "You relaxing in this heat?" She sat down next to him, leaning against his large side. He snorted and nickered, turning his head so that it was next to her.

She reached up and rubbed his face.

Eli snorted again.

"I just wanted to come say hi." He pulled his face from her hand and laid his head in the straw beside her.

"Well, boy. I'll let you get your rest," she said standing up and patting his belly.

Then she walked down to the beach.

As she looked out at the gorgeous morning in front of her, the way the sunlight shimmied off the water, the feel of the powdery sand underneath her feet, the complete serenity of it, she knew that it was this place that made her whole, and here she could feel the last three years fading away like the sun faded the blue of Papa's boat—until one day, those years would be just a distant memory.

When her parents died, Papa and Gram provided the stability she needed to survive such a tragedy, and this house brought that stability back for her. Everywhere she looked here, she saw their love, and all those wonderful reminders of her life there. Then she thought about Charlie. Maybe she'd agree to those big plans of his, maybe she wouldn't. But either way, helping him to understand the area wouldn't be a bad thing and Oyster Bay would be the perfect place to show Charlie what really mattered down here.

She ran inside and got her phone: *Hi, Charlie. I was thinking about how to explain life here in Clearwater, and I had an idea. I'd like to show you around the house where I grew up. It's my favorite place in all the world, and it might give you the background you need to really be on your game when we meet with Rocky.*

He texted back: *That sounds great. Text me the address and time.*

She texted the address of the farmhouse but explained its proximity to the inn. Then, she told him to come as soon as he could. She couldn't wait to show him around.

Chapter Six

"Here's what I can tell you about Rocky," Emily said, offering Charlie a seat on the porch after he'd arrived. He sat down, his eyes on her, but they looked wary, and had since he'd gotten there. She wondered why. Had he hit another roadblock with the improvements? "He loves this area. He's not going to do anything that might ruin it. So, keeping things on the modest, smaller side might be beneficial. I'm going to take you on a tour of this land and give you a little history of the way we live to arm you with the knowledge that you might need when answering his questions."

"He's a businessman. Wouldn't he understand that big improvements mean big business? I can make his town a lot of money. Why wouldn't he want that?" He was responding to her, but he still seemed very uncomfortable, rubbing the back of his neck as if he had a sudden twinge.

"There's a balance between making money and preserving what we love about Clearwater. There's a different mentality here. Let me show you."

She stood up. Cautiously, he followed her lead. She could tell that he didn't think any of this mattered, but he was wrong.

Emily entered the house and shut the front door, stopping in the modest entryway. "Gram's gone to town, so it's just us here." There

was surprise… or something in his eyes. What was it? Then he made
eye contact. Perhaps sharing some memories with him would put
him at ease. "My grandfather built this house for my gram. He liked
the property because of the wildlife. We have wild turkeys, foxes, and
deer that call this home as much as we do. It started as an old cotton
farm, but Papa let it all go. We've also got a horse out back. It's my
horse…"

He looked more rigid than he had the first day they'd met, and she
couldn't figure out why, but she didn't want to put him on the spot
and ask. If he wanted to tell her, he would.

"Let me pour you a glass of juice," she suggested.

They walked down the hallway into the kitchen and she offered
him a seat, the old chair scraping the floor as she pulled it out to urge
him to sit. He needed to relax, and she was going to show him how.

"It smells good in here," he said.

"It's my gram's buttermilk biscuit rolls. Would you like one?" She
preheated the oven and poured them each a small glass of locally
made grape juice.

The windows were still open, letting in the morning breeze. When
she set the glass down in front of him, Charlie took a sip. "This is
really good."

"It's from the fruit and cheese shop down the road."

He stood up and retrieved the bottle. "Do we serve this for breakfast at Water's Edge?" he asked, peering down at the label, his brows
creased in concentration.

"Not that I know of."

"Call them. Find out how much they can supply. I want to get
this into our restaurant. I can argue with the commission that we'd
provide more revenue to local businesses… If I could get the local

companies' backing… In fact, later I'll make a list of businesses to support. I already have a contract with local builders. It's the biggest account they've ever landed. Let's get as many voices heard as we can."

"What's the name of the builders? I probably know them."

"T & N Construction."

"Yeah! That's Tommy and Nate! They're good friends from high school. They've been building since we were young, and they are fantastic. If anyone needs anything done, they're the people to call in town." Emily couldn't help but smile at this news. "I'm so glad to hear they got the job! Tommy's wife is expecting their first child. I know because I got an invite to the baby shower. I couldn't go," she said, her voice dropping suddenly. "I was working." She'd been too far away to drive, and she hadn't come home for it. Now she felt bad, like she should've tried harder.

In an effort to keep the thought away, she slipped the biscuits into the oven to warm. When they'd gotten just warm enough to melt the butter, she pulled them out. "Cheese?" she asked.

"However you serve them."

"I just put butter." Emily opened the roll and slathered each side with a generous amount of butter. She set the small plate down in front of Charlie, who picked up a biscuit and took a bite.

"Do they have anything like that up north?" she asked.

He shook his head, finishing his bite. "You know, I wonder if we should have local southern fare at the restaurant as well. I hired a chef who grew up here, but I haven't asked him to cook regional recipes. Wonder if we should. It might make the inn more of a coastal Virginia *experience*."

"The chef was on board with the appetizer change we'd made. He'd probably welcome the challenge to create local cuisine."

"You are a lifesaver. You've got me thinking," he said. "Show me more."

She was glad he was loosening up a bit. "I will show you more, but right now, you need to slow down, enjoy your biscuit, and have your juice. You'd said yourself, we move more slowly here. I'd like you to get a feel for that. Let's talk."

"About what?"

"Anything but business. Did you grow up in New York?"

She noticed his mental struggle to leave the topic at hand, but he recovered quite well. "Yes. I've lived in New York and Boston," he said. Did he ever just sit and talk about nothing in particular?

"What took you to Boston?"

"I attended Harvard."

Harvard? She wasn't sure how to relate to that. She'd gone to a state school, taken out student loans, and lived on meager wages that she'd made working at a donut shop. "Did you have fun there?"

"Fun?" He said the word as if it didn't feel right in his mouth. "I didn't have any time for fun."

"I'm sorry," Emily said, noticing the curiosity that showed on his face when she said it. "I had a lot of fun at my college. My sister, Rachel, her husband—then boyfriend—Jeff and I were all there. We used to have these game nights on Fridays. They were so much fun! We still have them, or at least we did until a few years ago when I moved to Richmond. What do you do for fun?"

"I remodel things, although I haven't had a whole lot of time to do it." He'd leaned back in his chair, his body turned toward her, his face so relaxed now. Emily was delighted that what she was doing was working. And she loved that the conversation was beginning to feel more natural between them. She wanted to know more about him, even though she knew that wasn't the goal.

"What kinds of things?"

"Furniture, rooms in my house—I once stripped a room down to the studs just to build it back up exactly the way I wanted it." He smiled, excitement in those blue eyes of his.

"That's amazing. How did it turn out?"

"It turned out great."

"I have something to show you," she said, more animated than she should be. She couldn't help it; she'd found common ground. "Come with me." She stood up, slipped her old boots on, and opened the back door off the kitchen. "Wait right here," she said once they were outside. Then, as quickly as she could, she ran the long path to the barn.

"What is that?" Charlie shouted as she rounded the corner in the old tractor. Its green paint was faded and the tire treads were muddy, the engine vibrating so loudly, she almost hadn't heard his question, but the cab was roomy, and its giant tires could easily maneuver over the rough landscape.

"It's my papa's old John Deere tractor. Hop in!" she called through the open window, unlatching the door.

She could see the deliberation and wariness surface again, but he grabbed a hold of the large handles and hoisted himself up, scooting in beside her. "You can drive this thing?" he asked as he shut his door.

"I've driven this longer than I've been driving cars. I started on my Papa's lap." She put it in gear and bumped along the clearing toward a wide path leading through the woods. "When I was little, my grandfather would put the farm wagon on the back and fill it with straw. He'd give my friends and me hayrides. It was so much fun!"

"And why are we in this tractor now?"

"Because it's too far to walk, and I want to show you something."

They arrived at another clearing, and she turned off the tractor. When the silence had returned, Emily could hear that friendly sound of the water calling to her, begging her to show Charlie. She opened her door and hopped down onto the wild grass.

"You might want to take your shoes off," she said, slipping her boots off with one hand and steadying herself against the tractor with the other.

Charlie, who was wearing dress-casual loafers with his shorts, took them off and set them up inside the tractor. Then he walked around to her side.

"Follow me," she said, her hair blowing into her face. She tucked it behind her ear. With Charlie behind her, she walked over a small hill covered in sea grass and rocks, until her feet met the fine sand of the bay. She swallowed, emotion welling up inside her, as she saw the long dock that her grandfather had built.

She took him over to Papa's old wooden boat, the paint nearly gone, the grains showing through it.

Charlie walked around it, his head tilted to the side, his face giving away his interest.

"I've thought about restoring it," she said.

He looked up.

She'd considered restoring the boat even living in Richmond. She wanted to read up on the best way to strip the paint and apply more without ruining it, but there was something holding her back. A part of her wanted to leave it right there, undisturbed where it had always been.

"It was my grandfather's. I called him Papa. We used to go fishing in it. He built it, along with the pier." She walked up beside him, in disbelief of what she was about to share. She'd never shared it before, and she wasn't sure why she wanted to now. Perhaps it was their mutual interest in restoring old things and bringing them back to life, or maybe it was the way he was looking at her now, as if he knew her better than he did.

"When I was young, my parents died in a car crash, and I was devastated. I was only seven—too young to know how to live without them. Papa never had long talks with me or spent a lot of time grieving, but he brought me here, away from our house and everyone, and he let me cry. I cried the whole time he built that pier. After he built it, he brought me here again and began to build the boat. He could've easily built it closer to his shed with all his tools, but he didn't. He chose to build it here where I could cry. I came with him every day until—and I still remember it—one day, I didn't cry anymore. He asked me to hand him the hammer. I spent the rest of the summer building that boat with him."

She ran her hand along the edge of it, the proximity of it making her old emotions bubble to the surface.

"I feel like that boat represents the love I have for my parents and also for him."

She nodded toward the pier and Charlie followed.

As they'd left their shoes and the tractor, Emily noticed that tension returning in Charlie's walk. Even though he'd had moments when he'd relaxed a bit, that underlying rigidity was always lurking there today.

"Are you all right?" she asked finally, unable to keep her curiosity at bay. She hopped onto the pier, the water swishing underneath it. Charlie stepped up to meet her. He hesitated a moment, his eyes restless, thoughts showing on his face.

"What is it?"

"Originally, I was thinking that we could discuss how to change Rocky's mind. If I could get him on my side, I think the planning commission would follow his lead. I was glad to find that you knew him so well, but now I'm afraid that we've hit a slight bump…"

"What is that?"

"The improvements I'm proposing involve an expansion of the inn. This land that we're standing on now is part of my suggested plan for expansion."

Emily had to cover her mouth with her hand to keep herself from laughing at him. She knew Gram wouldn't sell it. Gram would never get rid of Oyster Bay. When Emily had regained composure, she said, "It's not for sale." There was no way in the world that he'd ever get his hands on Papa's land.

Her tone caused him to sharpen his focus on her. He leaned in closer, those blue eyes locking on to hers. "Everything's for sale at the right price."

She stared at him. What a horrible thing to say. He couldn't possibly believe that, and if he did, he was about to get a shock. If he thought convincing Rocky was difficult, Gram, Rachel, and Emily would be a whole new ballgame. They wouldn't let him get within a hundred feet of Oyster Bay.

It had been only a tiny farmhouse when they'd bought it, but Papa knocked down walls, and, nail by nail, he built the house Gram had always wanted. The cement sidewalk outside had Emily's and Rachel's handprints imprinted in it with their names underneath, the hardwood floors in the hallway inside had the scratches that she and her sister had put there the morning Papa had bought them roller skates. It had rained, and he let them go inside, moving all the furniture just so they could skate. It was the weekend after their parents' funeral, and it had been the first time since then that they'd laughed. Outside, under the maple tree was a large rock that still had remnants of red paint. That paint had spelled "Farley," marking the final resting spot for the family dog that had slept at the end of her bed until his last days.

"I didn't want to say anything about my plans for this land, but I felt terrible holding it in." His face was serious, driven, as if he really believed he was going to buy Oyster Bay for the inn.

He thought he could just walk in and get whatever he wanted. And, by the look on his face, he might just put up a fight to get it. He wasn't joking. He wasn't even considering. It was as if he'd already cleared the land and laid his foundations. Emily felt sick at the thought. "Well," she said, nearly breathless, "I'm sure you have enough understanding of local life now to get you through your meeting with Rocky." She needed to talk to Rocky. She wanted to know everything that was going to happen at the meeting tonight. She felt like running all the way back to the house, but she had to stay calm. She had to be at that dinner. Struggling not to glare at him, she mustered all her energy to sound light about the situation. "May I still come to dinner?" she asked, trying to keep herself under control, her protectiveness for Papa's memory and his things welling up.

"Of course."

"Thank you."

Charlie had hardly left the driveway before Emily had looked up and dialed Rocky's work number. Her knee bounced relentlessly as she sat in the chair in the living room, the phone ringing in her ear, panic rising in her chest. She noticed her shallow breathing as she waited for him to pick up, so she drew in a deep breath.

"Hello. Rocky McFadden."

"Hi," she said. "It's Emily Tate." She picked with a loose thread on the chair, but then realized how it was unraveling the seam, so she stopped and tucked the string down into the crease where it had come loose.

"Hey, Emily. How are you?"

She stood up and began pacing the room. "Not good."

"Did you hear about your grandmother's land?"

"We can't let him have it. Don't let him do it."

"Don't worry," he said gently. "I won't. I've been putting on the brakes every time we meet. I knew you wouldn't want the inn to swallow it up."

Emily let out the air that she was holding in her lungs. She felt the slack in her shoulders as the tension left them, and she plopped back down in her chair. "Thank you," she said.

"To be honest, I'm not really sure that his plans will benefit Clearwater anyway. We like to keep things small, you know."

"Yes," she said, nodding as if he were in the room. "I tried to tell him that."

"When did you speak to him?"

"I work at the inn now, and he's told me a little of what he plans, but I've only just learned about Oyster Bay."

"Sorry about your break up. I had heard…"

"It's fine."

"Well, you don't have anything to worry about with Mr. Peterson. I'm meeting with him tonight and I'll dig in my heels."

"I'll be there too. He's invited me. He wanted me to help change your mind, but I think he knows now that won't happen."

"Great! I look forward to dinner. And we'll just keep it between us—no expansion."

She peered down at the old tapestry rug that covered the hardwoods and all the memories of playing on that rug as a girl, all the fun she'd had, flooded her mind. "You know what," she said. "I'm going to change his mind. I'm going to make him see how great it is here, and then he won't even want to expand."

"If anyone can, it's you. Let me know if you need my help at all."

"Thanks, Rocky. You've done plenty. Just stick to your guns and don't let him talk you into anything tonight."

"Will do."

She and Rocky said their goodbyes and Emily got off the phone feeling so much better. Rocky was right; if anyone could change Charlie's mind, it was her. She was great at selling a place, at changing minds, at highlighting the great things about a location and making people want to be there. That was how she'd made the pub in Richmond so successful, and it was why Libby had hired her as events coordinator. She had to sell the concept of small-town, peaceful happiness to Charlie. Her mind was already spinning with ideas.

Chapter Seven

"While I applaud your ideas to help the area's small businesses," Rocky said as he set an empty oyster shell down on his plate, his eyes darting to Emily and then back to Charlie, "I just don't see the need to rezone the land. The inn is substantial as it is. The farm butts up against a large residential area on the other side. Rezoning would drastically change their view *and* their home values."

Emily could see frustration lingering under Charlie's features. She wondered if he wasn't used to someone telling him no. The members of the planning commission had all left by now, and it was just the three of them—Rocky, Emily, and Charlie. Charlie had delivered an impressive last pitch about increased tourism, county budgets, and lower taxes, but, true to his word, Rocky wasn't budging. She kept noticing his loaded glances, but she didn't even allow a hint of happiness. She'd kept it all business.

It was funny hearing Rocky speak to Charlie. Ever since he was little, he and Emily had played together and been in school together, so seeing this side of him was interesting. But she was impressed by how well he stood his ground.

Rocky rose from the table, set his napkin down, and held out a hand to Charlie. "Thank your for the nice dinner. I'm sorry. We just don't think it'll fit with the planning commission's long-range plans."

Emily could see Charlie's jaw clenching as he shook Rocky's hand. After Rocky left, Charlie sat back down in his chair and ordered a beer. "Want one?" he asked Emily. His voice was short, but she could tell his frustration wasn't directed at her. He was irritated with himself for not changing Rocky's mind, and by the determined look on his face she doubted he'd be giving up.

When she said "Yes," he flagged the waitress. Maybe if they stayed for another drink she could find out his next move.

"I'm sorry," she said, although she didn't really know why she was sorry. She was quite relieved, finally feeling like she could breathe again. Things were going perfectly for her. She felt like a giant weight had been lifted. Gram's house wasn't going to be leveled for now. All Emily's memories would be intact, like a museum of her childhood for her to see any time she wanted. But she knew that, while tonight, she'd won a tiny battle, this might not be the end of it, and she needed to change his mind completely about developing the area so he'd stop trying.

Charlie rubbed his eyes and then looked at her. "To make money on the inn, I have to upgrade the location."

Emily, who'd taken the last sip of beer in her glass as she waited for another, looked up at him.

"And if I can't build onto it, then not only will I not make any money on the sale of the inn but I'll have to let down all the people involved in the expansion."

She thought of T & N Construction. Tommy and Nate were probably banking on that money. "There's enough room to expand on a smaller scale on the existing property. Couldn't you do that?"

He didn't answer her, and she knew it was because that wasn't what he wanted to do. By the look on his face now, she could tell he'd fully expected to convince Rocky tonight and he was scrambling for his next move. The waitress set down their beers and Charlie nodded in thanks, his attention still elsewhere. "I had no idea the planning commission would be this difficult to convince."

"So now what?"

"I keep trying."

She took a sip of beer as the waitress gathered the empty plates. "You hardly ate anything tonight," she pointed out.

"Business dinners are like that," he said with a half-smile. "I'll eat later."

He looked tired, and while Emily was thrilled with the outcome tonight, she felt bad that a great outcome for her had to make someone else unhappy. "Why don't you come back to the house and I'll cook for you." She was crossing that line again. The truth was, the house aside, she liked Charlie. She was going to make him see why keeping Oyster Bay was the right thing to do. With a little persuading, she could change his mind. She knew she could make him love it just like she did.

"I wouldn't want to impose."

"I want to convince you that you don't need my gram's land. It's a business dinner." She smiled at him. He still seemed unsure. "Hospitality is what this place is all about. And you want to understand this town, right? How can you understand it if you don't experience it?"

"Fine," he said. "But you won't convince me."

"Oh!" Gram said, clamping her eyes on Charlie as he and Emily walked through the door.

"Hi, Gram," Emily said. "This is Charlie Peterson."

"Hello, Charles." She smiled in greeting and then turned back to Emily.

"I hope you don't mind, but I called and asked if Rachel, Jeff, and Clara could come over. Have you eaten yet?"

"No I haven't, actually," Gram said, her excitement a little forced. Were they imposing? Emily wondered. "I feel like I've got a house full of teenagers again—all the comin' and goin'," she added. "It's still early. Want me to make us some dinner?"

"We can all help. Are the crab pots full?"

"Probably. You and Charles can go check."

"Please call me Charlie," he said to Gram as she continued to stare at him.

Emily nodded toward the back door as she kicked her shoes off and slid them near the doormat with her foot. "Follow me," she said to Charlie. He took his shoes off and set them beside hers on the way out.

"Do you ever wear shoes?" he asked.

She didn't answer but the question made her laugh.

The sun was low in the sky, casting an orange light on the water as they walked through the grass together, leading down to the tractor that was still parked by the beach near the house. When they reached it, she climbed up in the passenger side.

"I thought you could drive this time," she said.

He stood there for a moment, and then, to her surprise, he climbed up into the driver's seat and assessed his surroundings.

"My papa rebuilt the engine to this tractor so many times that it runs a little differently than most. I don't know if I'd have any idea how to drive another tractor."

Charlie put his hands on the wheel.

"Turn the gas switch. It's over there." She leaned across his lap to point to show him.

He flipped it.

"Now push the ignition and hit the starter button." The motor chugged and then hummed. "Crank that switch up to 'run'." When he did the motor got louder.

Emily watched his concentration, the way the skin wrinkled between his eyes, his slight frown, and his intense focus on what was in front of him. She remembered that feeling when she'd sat on Papa's lap learning the same thing. "Now," she said over the noise. "Pull that lever to release the clutch."

He tried, but it wouldn't budge.

She put her hand over his and wriggled the lever loose like Papa had done for her, but it was odd to feel the masculine hand inside her fist. Just as she processed the feeling, she noticed that his eyes were on her hand, so she removed it and put it in her lap. Best she get her head in the right place now.

"Put it in drive now, punch the clutch and hit the gas."

The old tractor chugged a little and then they were off. Emily watched the way Charlie's hands moved on the steering wheel as he maneuvered the tractor over the rough landscape, the ease with which his foot pumped the clutch. "You're a natural," she said, catching his eye as he glanced over. "Watch the tree!"

Charlie quickly turned back and steered them onto the path again, paralleling the coast as they headed toward the stretch of beach with Papa's pier. "Don't distract me," he said, keeping his eyes forward this time.

She laughed, unable to stop herself.

When they arrived at Papa's pier and the old boat, Charlie said, "Stay put," and hopped down onto the sand. He walked around and opened her door, offering her a hand.

"Well, thank you," she said, grabbing the old bucket from behind the seat, taking his hand for support, and jumping down beside him. "Let's check those crab pots. Ready?"

He grinned at her, but there were thoughts behind his eyes. Trying not to read into them, she led him onto the pier and they walked to the edge, where Emily sat down and hung her feet over the side. She set the bucket next to her. Tied to the post at the corner of the pier was a thin rope. She grabbed onto it and began to pull, the slack from the rope, making wet circles on the dock as she retrieved it from the water. Finally, the crab pot emerged—a wire mesh cage full of Chesapeake blue crabs. Carefully, she stood up, unhinged the trap door, and dumped them into the bucket.

"They're gorgeous," Charlie said, leaning over them as they squirmed around.

Emily turned to respond and stopped when she saw how close he was to her. He looked into her eyes as if he were searching for something. Neither of them spoke for a moment. Then she pulled back. He smiled at her, his face full of questions. Perhaps having him back to the house wasn't such a good idea. She turned and walked toward the tractor.

"We should get these crabs back," she said. "My sister's on her way over with her husband and daughter. We'll need to help them set up the steamer." Then she peeked back over her shoulder at him.

Charlie nodded.

"Do you mind driving back?" she asked.

"Not at all." Charlie picked up the bucket of crabs while Emily tipped the crab pot on its end to dry out on the dock for later. Then, together, they got back into the tractor and headed toward the house.

When they arrived, Jeff was standing at the outside fire pit, starting the fire, and Rachel was setting up chairs in a half-circle. Emily wouldn't have noticed otherwise, but knowing Rachel's struggle about working and how they weren't getting along, she could sense a little something between Jeff and her sister. There wasn't any real, clear sign of it, but Emily could tell by watching their body language. Rachel was working at a clip, not looking up or talking like she always did and Jeff was focused, careful, taking his time at the fire pit. Clara had one of the long skewers with an enormous marshmallow on the end of it. She went over and stood next to her daddy.

"You're going to ruin your dinner, young lady," Emily said with a grin as she walked toward them with Charlie.

"I won't!" Clara said, turning her head and wobbling her marshmallow near the flame as she toyed with her yellow hair bow with the other hand. Jeff grabbed the center of the stick to steady it and keep her safe from the heat. "I'm only having two. Mommy said it's my appetizer."

Emily laughed.

"Hey there!" she said as they neared Jeff. "This is Charlie." Rachel was waiting by the table rather than joining her husband. Emily motioned for her to come down to them. "Charlie, this is my sister, Rachel, and her husband, Jeff." They all shook hands, Rachel's eyes moving back and forth between Charlie and Emily. "And this is Clara."

"Hello," Clara said to Charlie. Her bow had slid down her hair, the wisps that had escaped tickling her face. She scratched her nose and cheek. "I like your blue shirt."

"Thank you," he said, the corners of his mouth twitching in amusement. "I like your yellow dress, but I think it would be too small for me."

Clara giggled.

He's definitely got one of us on his side, Emily thought.

She set the bucket of crabs down next to Jeff. "Ready to steam these?"

When they were younger, it had been Jeff and Papa who'd always steamed the crabs, but now it was just Jeff. She realized right then that she'd taken those wonderful nights they'd had together as a family for granted. She'd spent all that time away from Rachel and Jeff while she was in Richmond just assuming that they'd always be there. What if things didn't work out between them? She may not get to see him anymore apart from the odd birthday party.

"Absolutely! I've got the steamer set up on the patio."

"I'd boiled some potatoes for our dinner, but when you asked me to come over, I just brought them with us," Rachel said. "I figured maybe we could make potato salad. And I brought baked beans. Gram's putting them on the stove now. I'll go in and help her."

Rachel seemed almost eager to help Gram. It was absolutely clear now that she was trying to distance herself from Jeff.

"Wait," Emily said to Rachel. "Should we have some wine?" Emily turned to get Charlie's answer and, to her surprise, he was grinning at Clara. She was showing off, dancing in circles to cool her marshmallow.

He looked over at Emily, his eyes warm. "I'd love some, thank you. But, please, let me get it." He stood up and, before she could protest, he'd left them and gone into the kitchen.

"Tell me quickly," Rachel whispered. "What's he doing here?"

"I asked him to dinner."

"He looked very comfortable driving Papa's tractor. What's that all about?"

"I taught him. He hadn't eaten tonight and I asked him to come back after our meeting. He said okay."

"Wonder why," she asked, her tone suggestive.

"I don't know. Maybe he was hungry and he figured he could get a good meal. We met with Rocky tonight at Merroir—I have tons to tell you. Charlie was so busy talking that he didn't eat."

"He could've just ordered something to go. Maybe he wanted more time with you."

"Don't read into it, Rach. I'm sure he's just being friendly… Enough about me. How are things with Jeff?" she whispered, her gaze darting over to him to be sure he hadn't heard. He was busy with Clara.

"No different." Rachel shook her head. "There's nothing to do really but either weather the storm or let it ruin us. Actually, at this point, I have no idea which is more likely."

Jeff had taken Clara out in the yard. He was swinging her in circles, her laughter sailing through the air. Every time he put her down, Emily could see Clara's silhouette as she raised her arms and jumped around for more. He was a natural at being a dad. He had such an even temperament—he never seemed to get upset. That was what made the current situation so perplexing for Emily. "You and Jeff have always been perfect for each other. You'll work through it."

"This is big, Emily. This isn't a disagreement about where to put the laundry or something. This is about what we both see for our futures. He wants things right now that I just don't. We are drifting apart with every conversation about this. How can I make him wait for more kids? How can he make me want to give up the rest of my working life? I just don't see how we'll get past it."

"Have you told Gram?"

"I didn't have to. She could tell. But I haven't admitted to anything. I'm just not ready to talk about it. I want to see if I can convince him first, although it's not working…

"Where is our wine?" she asked with a laugh, changing the subject. Emily let her, but she wasn't feeling any better about the situation with Jeff and her sister.

"Gram has probably held Charlie hostage with some old story of hers. We'd better save him." Emily and Rachel walked up to the door.

They entered the kitchen and Gram was at the stove, stirring the beans in a deep silver pot with one hand while she leaned delicately on her cane with the other. She was staring at Charlie, her face serious.

Charlie's face didn't look much lighter. Both of them nearly jumped when Emily and Rachel came in. Empty glasses were sitting on the counter; Charlie hadn't even poured any wine.

"Everyone doing okay?" Emily asked.

Both nodded.

"I needed help with my beans," Gram said. "I couldn't… get the can open."

There seemed to be tension in the room—she could feel it. Emily grabbed two glasses, filled them, and handed one to Charlie, wondering if she was making more of the scene she'd just witnessed than what it was. It certainly looked like more than opening a can of beans. Without any discussion about it, she and Charlie headed outside. Jeff had added wood to the fire, its flames licking the light blue sky as they rose into the air.

"Rachel's bringing yours," she said to Jeff. He nodded, his gaze flickering to the kitchen window before settling back on the fire.

"Gram didn't corner you with a long story, did she?" she asked Charlie as they sat down at the patio table. She knew there had been something going on between Charlie and Gram when she'd come into the kitchen for sure. She wasn't crazy; she could tell. Had Gram heard about Charlie wanting the land? Or maybe he'd told her. Had he upset her?

"No. I was just helping her in the kitchen."

Jeff sat down in one of the chairs facing the fire and motioned for them to take a seat beside him. "That fire pit your papa built is really great," Jeff said. "I'd like one in my backyard."

"Yeah, I can remember we used to sit out here for hours, him telling us stories." Emily said with a smile. "He was an amazing storyteller. Even reading bedtime stories, he would pull me into that world and I remember working so hard to keep my eyes open because if I missed the ending, I was afraid the story would slip away from me. If I did fall asleep, I'd make him tell the whole thing again the next night. I wanted to hear it from beginning to end. He was so great at it."

Charlie had his eyes on her, but there was something more behind his pleasant expression. Then he said, "I had nannies that read to me."

"Were they good storytellers?" she asked.

"Some. But my parents had specific books they asked them to read to ensure I was getting the best experience to better my education." He took a sip of wine. "I used to keep a flashlight under my bed, and after they'd gone, I would read the books I wanted."

"Did you go under your covers?" Clara, who'd been setting her dolls in a line on one of the chairs, asked, crawling into Charlie's lap. The surprise on his face made Emily curious. She liked the way he looked when he wasn't in charge, when he didn't have some sort of agenda. It changed his entire demeanor, as if someone had hacked away at that hard, businesslike exterior to reveal who he really was inside, and she couldn't take her eyes off him. Clara was waiting for his answer, her little head turned to the side as she toyed with a button on his shirt. "Sometimes I go under my covers and pretend it's my castle and I'm the princess," Clara said.

"You do?" he asked.

Emily noticed how gentle Charlie's voice was, his warm gaze… She tore her eyes away from him, focusing on Clara.

"Yes," Clara said, pushing her hair out of her face. Her yellow bow was gone. "And sometimes I pretend it's a cave. Did you ever do that?"

"No, but it sounds fun."

"What did you play?" She wriggled off his lap and stood in front of him.

Charlie was quiet just long enough to cause Emily to reluctantly direct her attention back toward him. He looked as though he were searching for an answer. "I don't remember."

Emily's childhood was so vivid, so full of memories that she was floored by his answer, and from the look on his face, he was serious. He really didn't remember playing. Did he grow up without ever having fun?

The back door opened and Gram hobbled through, steadying herself with her cane as she made the few steps down. Emily rushed across the patio to grab the bowl of potato salad from her. She held it with two hands to keep from dropping it and wondered how Gram had expected to get it all the way down to the table. "You should've called through the window, Gram. I'd have gotten this for you. Is there anything else in there that you need me to get?"

"All kinds of things," Gram said. "Rachel's bringing some of it out."

As Emily headed inside, she thought about Rachel. It was unusual for her to stay tucked away in the house, and tonight, she'd taken every opportunity to do that. With the heat all around her, the sky getting dim, and the crackling of the fire at her back, Emily remembered all the times they'd had dinners like this one growing up, her, Papa, Gram, Rachel, and Jeff. And ever since college, Jeff had been there just like now, but things had felt different then. They'd had long evenings on the beach, too many beers with lime, their feet sandy and their faces warm from the sun. They'd talked all night, one voice beginning where another ended.

Papa was always the last one sitting on the beach when they went up to the house to have dinner. He had an old chair that he'd sat in. It was wicker, the weave weathered from the salt and sand. He carried it from the house to the beach and back, and he always sat in that chair. Once he was settled on the beach, it took him forever to come in. He'd say, "You kids go on up. I'm gonna sit here a little longer."

Without a thought, they'd left him on the beach as they giggled under the spell of sun and alcohol. They gave each other piggyback rides and danced in the yard to the music still coming from the small radio they'd used all day. It didn't occur to Emily to pay attention to it all because the next night they'd probably be doing the same thing. But now, as she walked into the kitchen, the invisible wall up between Rachel and Jeff, and Papa gone, she wished she'd have spent a little more time taking in the small things to tuck away in her memory. There was a very real possibility that they wouldn't have any more nights like those. And now Charlie wanted to yank her future memories right out from under her. She wondered if she could ever make him understand how great Oyster Bay was because, from what he'd said so far, he hadn't ever had an emotional attachment like that in his life. He probably couldn't even imagine it. So, how could he ever understand her point of view?

Rachel was at the door, her arms full of things. They divvied up the bowls and the plates and napkins, and they walked out together.

She noticed the slight rigidity in Rachel's face as she handed Jeff the glass of wine that she'd been carrying in the crook of her arm, wedged against her chest. He smiled at her, but it wasn't the kind of smile Emily had seen so long ago when he'd looked at Rachel as if she were the only person in the room. Emily could remember being jealous of that look, wishing someone would look at her that way.

Once everything was on the table, Gram lifted the napkins off the bowls, and they all served themselves a plate. Clara sat down on her knees between Jeff and Charlie.

"Gram," Emily said. "Where's Papa's chair—the one he always took to the beach?"

"It's probably in the barn." Gram was sitting, cracking her crabs in her expert way, the fire flickering in her eyes. "You should take Charlie to see Eli after dinner," Gram said as everyone ate.

Emily gave Gram a sideways glance, trying to tell her with her eyes to slow down. Yes, Emily had invited Charlie to dinner, and she did want to try to make him see how great they had it here, but her grandmother had some kind of motive—she could tell by the look in Gram's eyes. Was she trying to get them alone, set them up?

"Maybe," she said, with another look of warning.

"Eli is your horse?" Charlie said. He scooped up a spoonful of baked beans.

"Yes," Emily said. "Have you ever ridden a horse before?"

"No, I haven't."

"I don't know if the first time he rides a horse should be in the dark," Rachel said with a laugh, and Emily knew exactly why she'd said it. Charlie turned toward Rachel, her laughter clearly causing interest.

"Rachel and I went riding in the dark once," Emily said. She looked over at Rachel to continue the story, but her face had sobered and her head was turned toward Jeff, so Emily continued. "We'd been out too late for Papa's liking the night before, and he took our car keys. He said anywhere we needed to go, we'd have to walk.

"Rachel wanted to see Jeff, and he lived too far to go on foot, so we decided to ride Eli through the woods. We got lost! It took us all night to figure out how to get home. We'd wound our way all the way up the Northern Neck, it seemed. We had to keep stopping for Eli to rest and nibble grass. By the time we reached home, we were deliriously sleepy."

"I remember that," Jeff said. "You two called me to let me know you'd be coming. I fell asleep outside waiting for you. I woke up on the porch swing the next morning with the worst pain in my neck and I teased Rachel for years that she was a 'pain in the neck'."

Jeff and Rachel looked at each other, lost in their own world of thoughts.

"The things we do for love," Gram said, keeping the conversation going. "You girls never told me you did that."

"We didn't want to get in trouble," Emily told her.

"You would've," Gram laughed. "I'll bet you two had a lot of time to talk that night. And I'll bet you're closer now because of nights like that one." She leaned back in her chair, looking younger in the light of the fire. "You know, I told your papa that I wanted a house full of kids…"

Emily shot a protective look over to her sister. Did Gram sense what Rachel and Jeff were thinking?

"I wanted at least four—two boys and two girls. Papa had said the two we had were just enough. Anything more and we'd be outnumbered," she said with a grin. "So we only had your dad and your uncle Joey. That was it. And life was good. Then, I was blessed with you girls.

"I'd like more kids," Jeff said, his expression challenging as if he'd thrown down the gauntlet.

"Well." Gram took in a deep breath and let it out. "Jeff, dear, there's a reason God made that a two-person mission. You know, I've learned that God has his own answers to our lives. And you can't beat yourself up tryin' to figure them out. You just have to make the decisions that will best suit your family at the time."

Jeff sat quietly, thoughtful. "I'm going to the beach. Anyone else?" He stood up and grabbed his wine.

"Your food will get cold," Gram warned.

"It's fine, Gram. I'll get something later." He went down to the beach, Clara following behind him. In the shadows of night, Emily could see Clara reach for her daddy's hand, and he held it all the way to the water.

When she looked back at Rachel, she could swear there were tears in her sister's eyes. Rachel took a large sip of her wine.

"You're outnumbered now, Charlie," Gram said, clearly trying to keep the conversation light. Charlie smiled. Anyone outside the situation wouldn't be aware of the family turmoil going on. "It's just you and us girls."

"I don't mind," he said. "You all are very welcoming. You've treated me like an old friend, and I appreciate that."

"It's easier to be friends than it is to be strangers, I think," Gram said.

Charlie held the stem of his wine glass but didn't take it off the table. He looked utterly interested in Gram's statement. "Why is that?"

"Because when we drill down to who we really are, and we stop trying to be our very best and we're honest with each other, we enjoy ourselves more."

Charlie sat quietly for a moment, as if he were contemplating Gram's explanation. "You're totally right," he said. "This might sound like an unusual admission, but in my entire life, I haven't been around anyone as open as you all are. And now it all makes sense. Since I was a boy, I've been taught to be the best version of me all the time, and I just assumed that it was the right way to live. But I've really enjoyed being with you all. And you are right. It is your honesty and candor that have made it so enjoyable. So, thank you. For tonight and for that perspective."

"You are the age of my grandkids. Please, call me Gram rather than Margaret."

A huff of laugher escaped Charlie's lips but it was out of happiness, Emily could tell. And as he looked over at her, his gaze softened to the warmest look and, despite herself, her heart did a little leap.

Chapter Eight

Gram set her napkin on the newspaper that covered the table. They'd cracked all the crabs. Their drinks needed topping off, so Emily grabbed the newest bottle of wine that Rachel had retrieved when she'd put the pie in the oven to heat for dessert.

"Thank you for a lovely meal," Gram said, leaning back in her chair.

The coastal breeze was still warm despite the dark sky above. Emily had always had meals out on the patio whenever the weather would allow it.

"You all relax and enjoy yourselves. I'll clear the table and bring out the pie."

"Are you sure you don't want help, Gram?" Emily said, while Rachel attempted to stand as well to help.

"No, no. It's been a long time since I've had all you kids home. I'll do it." She shooed them away playfully.

Jeff came out of the house—after they'd returned from the beach, he'd put Clara to sleep. Ever since she was born, she spent her time between her own house and Gram's. Often, when they got together, Rachel and Jeff would put Clara down at Gram's and then pick her up the next morning after Gram had made her a big breakfast. Sometimes, if they were too tired to drive, they'd stay the night as well. With such a big house, there was plenty of room.

Gram began bringing out plates of warm pie and ice cream—it was melting quite quickly. Charlie stood to help her set the plates down on the table. She handed a plate to Charlie and motioned for him to sit.

"Thank you," Charlie said with a smile before Gram moved around to the other side of the table. Then he looked at Emily as he sat back down, his cheeks rosy from the wine. "I hope I haven't monopolized all your free hours," he said.

"It's been fun," Gram interjected.

He smiled.

"Do you have to get back soon or anything, or can you stay a little longer?" Gram asked.

"I don't have anything planned the rest of the night."

"Why don't we have game night?" Rachel suggested. "Gram, do you still have our games?"

"I do!"

Emily remembered how entertaining those nights could be, and she hoped, perhaps, she could show Charlie just how different his childhood had been to hers. She stood up. "The night's about to get really fun! Stay right here." She started toward the door, Gram following behind.

"Weren't you going to see Eli first?" Gram suggested, not so subtly.

"I suppose we can," Emily said, turning toward Charlie and realizing his eyes were already on her. "Will you join us for the game?" she asked Gram.

"No, dear, but thank you. I'm very tired. I'm going to head to bed."

"You sure?"

Gram nodded.

Emily went inside. She checked in the basket by the coat rack in the hallway. Sure enough, the games were still there. She pulled the Crazy Trivia game out and took it back out to the table.

"Oh no," Rachel laughed. "Not that one!"

"Of course this one! We'll be back in just a bit."

"Take your time," Rachel said, looking at Jeff.

Perhaps taking Charlie to see Eli would give Rachel and Jeff some time to talk about whatever had been bothering them tonight, Emily hoped.

Emily pulled the old tractor up to the fence and turned off the engine. Charlie hopped out, ran around to her side, and opened the door for her. She liked it when he did that, although she didn't want to admit it to herself. She wondered if she was just extra sentimental, and she wasn't sure if it was the wine or the fact that Papa's chair might be in the barn. The heavy lid of the electrical box on the light post creaked as she lifted it. She hit the switch, illuminating the entire field with white light—Papa had wired it himself.

Eli, who'd been in the corner, eating, noticed them and began walking over to the fence as Emily let Charlie inside. He hesitated at the gate.

"He won't hurt you," she said.

Eli stopped in front of them, and Emily put her hands on the side of his face. "Hi there, boy," she said. His big brown eyes shifted toward her and he nickered. "I know it's late," she said as if she were talking to a person, "but I was wondering if you'd let us have a ride. This is Charlie."

Eli's great tail swooshed in the air behind them as he shifted on his feet.

"You can pet him," Emily said to Charlie.

Charlie reached out his hand and rubbed the horse's side. "He seems gentle," he said.

"He is. He's old now, but he'll still let me ride him." She looked back at Eli. "Okay, boy. We're going to root around in your barn for a minute and then I'll get the saddle."

She took Charlie by the arm and led him to the barn. When they entered, the musty smell of straw and old wood filled the air. Emily looked up at the rafters, thinking of Papa's hard work and how it had stood even the strongest of storms. She took a minute to look around. The lofts were filled with old riding gear and below were her broken jumps from the days when Emily had practiced for competitions with Eli. Then she stopped. Turned upside down at the back of the barn was Papa's chair. She walked over to it and pulled it out from under some empty boxes, dust flying into the air and making her cough.

She set it upright. It looked a little smaller than it had. Maybe it was because Papa's big personality had made it seem bigger. She sat down in it and put her hands on the worn armrests where Papa's hands had been.

"Is that your grandfather's old chair you mentioned at dinner?"

"Yes." She ran her fingers along the wicker, back and forth. "Even if I could turn back time and make everything new and young again—Eli, this barn, Oyster Bay—I wouldn't change this chair. I sat in Papa's lap until the bugs got too bad on warm summer's nights, right in the sand. I jumped off the seat of it into the bay while he held the back. I remember Papa's strong arms as he carried it over his head across the yard… So many memories." She got up and set it back in the corner, but this time, she made sure it had its own place, moving the boxes to the side.

She grabbed the saddle, the girth, bridle, and the saddle pad and walked over to Charlie, only realizing then that he had an unreadable look on his face.

"What are you thinking about?" she asked.

"Nothing," he said, straightening out his features as he offered to hold the saddle for her. He gently took it from her hands.

"You sure?"

"I just… wasn't ready for all this."

She led him out into the field where Eli was standing. "You weren't ready for what?"

"How much I like you and your family."

She couldn't breathe for a moment. She hung on the softness of those blue eyes, the subtle smile, the slight tilt of his head. She liked having him there as much as he liked being here. Maybe he was beginning to understand. Maybe.

She saddled up Eli, his beautiful back still so brawny, his legs muscular.

Putting her foot in the stirrup, she hoisted herself up and then gave Charlie room to come up. "Put your foot here like I did and swing your other leg over Eli's back so that you're sitting behind me."

Charlie stared at her a moment. Finally, he did as she told him and he was sitting on Eli's back with ease. Emily gave Eli the command and he began walking slowly.

She could feel the closeness of Charlie's body. She sucked in a quiet breath as he put his arms around her waist for support. The only other person she'd ever ridden with was Rachel, and having Charlie behind her felt very different. Taller than her, she could feel his breath against her ear, sending tingles down her arm. The wine from dinner was making her a little lightheaded.

Eli increased his gait to a trot, bouncing her up off the saddle with every step. Charlie held her tightly. All the other times she'd ridden Eli, her sense of safety had come from knowing the skill and trusting her horse, but now—she couldn't help the feeling—she found safety in Charlie's embrace. She steered Eli through the gate, glad to be out in the open.

"Where are we going?" Charlie asked.

"To the beach."

Eli loved walking on the beach. Emily had ridden him there hundreds of times. He'd go so far into the water that his legs were almost completely submerged, the bay lapping up onto her bare feet. It had been a very long time, and she wondered if Shelly ever took him. "Eli, boy. Let's swim!" That was what she'd always told him on the way. He let out a whinny, making her laugh. Eli remembered the way, even picking up speed as he went.

"Isn't your sister going to wonder where we are?" Charlie worried aloud.

"She'll be fine," she said, tipping her head back to make eye contact. She wanted to leave Rachel and Jeff alone a little longer. Gram had surely gone to bed by now and they'd have nothing left to do but talk to each other.

They reached the beach, and Eli went straight for the water, taking off, his tail raised above his back in excitement, despite his age. "Whoa, boy!" Emily yelled, laughing! "Slow, Eli!" She tapped his sides with her foot, regaining control of the horse. "Walk, boy."

He slowed down, wading in until their feet were just above the water.

"I've never seen him this excited," she said to Charlie, laughing again. It felt good to be riding him, and she was glad to give the old horse some enjoyment. Had he been kept in that stable since she'd ridden him last? What if Shelly only took him out for competitions and when he couldn't perform, left him there to spend his days?

With the lights from the barn far behind them now, they were immersed in darkness. The glow of the moon was their light. Eli's noises and the swooshing of the water were the only sounds around them apart from the occasional breeze blowing through the pine trees.

"This is amazing," Charlie said, his arms almost holding her rather than providing support. "Thank you."

When they arrived back at Gram's, Emily was thrilled to see Rachel and Jeff still on the patio, wine in their hands and smiles on their faces. She made eye contact with Rachel, asking in that silent, sisterly way if she was okay. Rachel smiled back at her, setting her mind at ease, and placed red and blue decks of cards on the table. With a grin, Emily sat down, took the cards, and shuffled the two decks as Charlie took a seat beside her.

She had the red deck. "This will be mine and Charlie's." She handed Rachel the blue deck. "This is yours and Jeff's."

Rachel took the cards and then poured some wine into their glasses. The bottle was new, freshly out of the fridge. Had Rachel and Jeff finished the other? That was a good sign.

"I'm not familiar with this game," Charlie said. "How do you play it?"

Emily took a sip from her glass. "I'll show you," she said. "Us first?"

"Sure," Rachel said with a little giggle.

"Okay. It's very easy. You have to draw a card and do what it says. If I guess it correctly, we get a point. That's it," she said to Charlie as she took the sand-timer and prepared to turn it over. "We have until the sand runs out. Ready? Go!"

Charlie took a card and flipped it over. His eyebrows rose as he read it. Quickly, he looked around the table and grabbed his empty plate and a fork. He stood the fork on end in the center of the plate and made whooshing sounds.

Emily watched him, confused.

He took his napkin and held it to the fork.

"Sailboat!"

"Yes!" Charlie said, clearly relieved. "The card said, 'Use items to make your partner say the word 'sailboat'."

"It looked just like a sailboat," she said.

"It did not!" Rachel laughed. "But you got it anyway! Good job, Charlie."

Emily took a card. "We have to keep going until we either miss one or the time runs out on that go. My turn." She flipped over the timer and studied the card. After a moment of thought, she cupped her hands, palm sides up.

Charlie's brows furrowed as he looked at her. "Baby?" he said.

Completely surprised, she said, "Yes!" and laughed.

"That's not how you do a baby! Are you two cheating?" Rachel said in disbelief. "How did he ever guess 'baby' from that? What did the card say?"

Emily, still laughing, read the card, "Using only your hands—not your arms—make your partner say the word 'baby'."

"They're cheating over there," Rachel said anyway. Jeff shook his head and chuckled.

Charlie laughed too and took another card. "Ready?" he asked.

Emily nodded.

He turned the timer over. "Okay," he said as he read the card to himself. He stood up and pushed his chair in. Then, out of nowhere, he started dancing, his arms and legs moving everywhere.

"Haha!" Emily said as he moved around the room. "What is that?" She caught the grin that was just meant for her, and she hid her smile with a gulp of wine. She knew she should slow down on the drinks and have some water, but she was having so much fun tonight that she just wanted to let off some steam.

Then, unable to stop herself, she started laughing again.

Rachel and Jeff were laughing too.

Emily could hardly think of an answer.

"Hurry," he said, still moving around, "the timer's going to run out."

"I have no idea!" She'd doubled over now, her cheeks starting to hurt. "The Charleston?" she said just as the sand ran out.

"Ha!" Charlie said, taking a large stride back over to the table. He grabbed the card and turned it around.

"Oh my gosh!" Emily threw her head back and laughed some more.

"What does it say?" Rachel asked. Emily turned the card toward her sister and Rachel read, "Dance around the room to make your partner say 'The Charleston'." Her mouth hung open. "That's it. This game is rigged. Switch decks with us! You two have memorized that one or something. That didn't even look like the Charleston!" She turned to Charlie and with a giggle said, "No offense."

"I suppose we just think alike," Charlie said, taking a seat and smiling at Emily, his gaze lingering on her a little longer than it should. She wondered if he, too, was feeling the wine.

"That's scary," Rachel joked. "I wouldn't admit that, Charlie."

Emily took another card, turned the timer over, looked Charlie in the eye without wavering, and said simply, "Richard."

He sat there a moment, and then said, "Nixon."

"Yep," she said, her eyes still locked with his. Neither of them moved. Charlie was right. It seemed as if they were completely in tune. There was undeniable chemistry between them and it was all she could do to keep herself from leaning over and kissing him.

Rachel reached across the table, took the red cards, and slid the blue ones in between them while they were still looking at each other.

Emily had offered for Charlie to stay the night in one of the guest rooms. There were plenty of them. But he'd insisted on leaving his car and calling a cab—they'd all had too much wine to drive. Rachel and Jeff stayed, sleeping in the same room as Clara.

Gram had fallen asleep in the chair downstairs with a book in her lap—she'd never even made it up to bed. Before going up, Emily covered her with an afghan and gave her a kiss on the cheek. She'd had more fun tonight than she'd had in a long time, and she couldn't get her mind off Charlie as she unfastened the earrings that Gram had offered to let her borrow for her dinner at Merroir. She went into her grandmother's room to put them away and clicked on a lamp to cut through the darkness. She opened Gram's jewelry chest, trying to swim out of her buzz.

Gram had always let her wear her jewelry. She'd said that someone needed to since she barely ever wore it, so whenever Emily was home, she'd ask to borrow a piece or two. Gram's jewelry was just like Gram: simple but elegant.

Tonight, as Emily lifted the lid to the box, she saw a few new pieces. Gram must have consolidated everything into one box. Her eyes were heavy from the night as she picked up an emerald and diamond ring to admire its beauty. Then, she set it back down gently and pulled out a velvet box at the back that sparked her curiosity.

Emily turned on another nearby lamp and opened the box. Inside was a silver locket. She opened it to see if there were any photos inside, but confusion crawled around inside her when she saw there was only an inscription. On one side, it read, "Margaret, all my love forever," and on the other, "Yours, Winston." While this wasn't anything unusual—people often get things from those who love them—what was unusual was the fact that Winston wasn't her papa's name.

She could feel the heat rise in her cheeks and it wasn't from the wine. Gram had never spoken about anyone named Winston. Who was he? And why was he professing his love to Gram and giving her jewelry? Gram had always said she'd loved Papa her whole life—since she was a girl.

All of a sudden, Emily's head began to throb. She didn't want to think of anyone having feelings for Gram except Papa. She shut the case, and put it back, returned the earrings, and then closed the lid to the jewelry box. After turning off the lamps, Emily stood in the dark for a minute, still processing what she'd seen. Her head heavy, she went to her room and closed the door.

Chapter Nine

When Emily awoke for work, she could smell the rich aroma of fried bacon and eggs, and she could hear the clinking of dishes. She padded down the wooden stairs in her bare feet, the morning giving new light to last night. She was so relieved that Charlie hadn't decided to stay. What had she been thinking, inviting him to sleep there? She shook the thought from her mind and headed into the kitchen. Rachel was showered, her wet hair like a black stripe down her back as she stood in last night's clothes. Jeff was beside her, fixing a plate for breakfast. A basket of steaming rolls sat beside him on the counter. Clara was already at the table. She had the plastic princess cup that Emily had seen in the cabinet.

"Mornin'!" Gram said, puttering around. "Get yourself some breakfast."

"Thank you." Emily greeted the others and tried not to ponder the locket when she looked at Gram. She walked up beside Jeff and made herself a plate.

By the time they all sat down, Clara had already finished and was fidgety, so Rachel suggested she go outside and play. She'd made a house for her dolls last night on the screened porch, and she was eager to get back to it.

"It's rare that I have us all at the same table these days, so I'm goin' to jump right to what I want to say," Gram said as she sat down. She'd made sure everyone had everything first, just like she always had.

Emily and the others gave Gram the quiet she needed to continue. Was Gram going to tell them that she was seeing someone new? Perhaps that was what the locket was all about…

"You have all moved on in your own lives and you have things pullin' you in different directions…" She sat still for a moment, looking each one of them in the eye. Emily could hardly wait for what she had to say.

"As you may know, Charles would like to expand the inn on this land."

He'd told her! That was what they'd been talking about in the kitchen! "I know!" Emily piped up. "Don't worry, Gram. We will do everything in our power to keep that from happening."

Rachel set her fork down and put her hands in her lap, nodding, concern on her face, and Emily could feel that sister solidarity rise up.

"I'm not askin' you to save it," Gram said.

The table was completely silent except for the rush of cold air conditioning through the old vents.

"I've already sold it to him."

What little Emily had eaten settled in her stomach like a cinderblock. "What?" she asked in nearly a whisper. "When?"

"I agreed to sell it just before I found out you were comin' back. I knew you were already dealin' with so much, and I didn't want to bombard you with it. I know you love this house, but it's too much for me to take care of…"

Gram's voice faded as Emily retreated into her thoughts. Last night—the whole time—both Gram and Charlie had known that this land wasn't Gram's anymore. Charlie had allowed her to believe that she could change his mind. He'd said she couldn't, but he'd certainly let her try. Her head started to pound and her hands were shaking. She was angry at both of them for not telling her sooner, but she was also angry with herself. She should've been there more for Gram over the last three years. If she had been, none of this would've happened. Gram wouldn't have felt like she couldn't take care of the house because Emily would've done it for her.

"How could you agree to sell this?" she asked, not waiting for any further explanation. "It's the only memory we have left of Papa." She could feel her eyes burn with the tears that were coming. She looked to Rachel and Jeff for support and it seemed as if they too were in shock, neither of them saying a word.

Gram had scooted back from the table just a bit and turned in Emily's direction. "Papa left this behind because he had to. He couldn't take it with him. Nor can we. Rachel's never shown interest in it, and you were busy making a life in Richmond. And, I can't take care of it."

"I can! And I'm living here now!" A tear escaped and Gram handed Emily a napkin, her face consoling. "Rachel and I can keep it up for you. Where will you live if you aren't here? This is your home— our home! Charlie's gonna bulldoze it!"

Gram reached over and grabbed Emily's hand. "Time can't be stopped, dear. It keeps movin' whether we like it or not. Remember how I said that life is for livin'. If we stay grounded in the past, we aren't livin'. Time flies! Fly with it! If you don't, it'll just make you dizzy."

"What about Eli?" she asked, a sob catching in her throat. "He's an old horse. Where will I keep him? I'm not sure I can afford the rent for a paddock. If I can't who will take him?"

"I've been lookin' for a home for him—"

"This is his home!" She couldn't help herself.

"Emily, dear, you don't even ride him. He's been alone out there for years. Wouldn't you like him to be on a farm somewhere with other horses?"

"What if they don't take to him?" The thought of her promise to Eli that she wouldn't leave him again came to mind, causing her chest to pinch, tears flooding her eyes.

Emily took in a breath to try to ease the ache in her throat. She focused on the two pegs hanging on the wall. They were empty now, but they used to hold their backpacks after school. This house had seen Emily through her grief over her parents' death and brought her through those difficult teenage years. If she lost this house, she felt like she might crumble to pieces.

"But memories are worth keeping too," she said, her voice small.

"You don't need this house to keep your memories for you."

She looked down at her eggs, the yellow blurring in her tears, her head feeling woozy. "How long do we have?"

"A month."

Emily tried to hide her tears by pressing her fingers against her burning eyes. She rubbed them until they hurt and then pushed her hands up her face into her hair, resting her forehead in the palms of her hands. She felt sick.

"And where are you moving?" Rachel asked. She'd been listening quietly, and, as Emily looked up at her, she noticed that Rachel didn't seem half as wrecked about all this as she did.

"Florida."

"What? Where in Florida?"

"Tampa."

Emily couldn't stay silent anymore. "That's crazy, Gram—that would be at least a twelve-hour drive! We'd have to fly to see you! I don't want you that far away from us," she said, the stress of the situation making her eyes ache.

"Have you really thought this through, Gram?" Rachel asked.

"I have. I'd like to move where it's warm year round. I really enjoy the summers here, but the winters are brutal. It's hard on my arthritis. I've found a maintenance-free condo."

There was something very unsettling about Gram living in a maintenance-free condo. It didn't seem like her at all. She'd always been outside gardening, watering the plants, sweeping every surface available outside, clearing the path to the beach. Being away for so long had kept Emily from noticing Gram's decline. She'd always imagined she'd look after Gram when the time came.

That was when it hit Emily: In a month's time, she'd have to not only say goodbye to Papa's memories and all his hard work, but she, too, would have to find somewhere else to live and she wouldn't have Gram with her. She needed Gram. She'd feel lost, knowing she couldn't just come see her any time. And she wanted to be there for Gram if she needed her as well.

Emily took a bite of her eggs, the taste souring in her mouth, her stomach filling with acid. She couldn't eat any more so she got up, scraped her plate and set it in the sink. "I have to get ready for work," she said, before leaving the room.

"We can put a trellis here if you'd like, and perhaps wind roses or some other type of flowers around it. We work with a florist who will be on call for any of your needs should you decide to move forward with us," Emily said with a manufactured smile as she walked beside the bride-to-be, showing her the inn's amenities. It was taking all her energy to not think about the conversation at the breakfast table this morning.

"Could we move these tables and set up white chairs?" she asked nervously.

"Absolutely."

"What if it rains?"

"Let me show you the ballroom we can convert. We have an entire staff on hand who will have it moved in minutes. Your guests would be none the wiser."

"I'm sorry I'm asking so many questions," the woman said. It was true, she'd asked about a hundred and they hadn't even chosen reception colors yet. "It's just that getting married is such a big step. I want everything to be right."

"I understand."

"Are you married?"

"No."

She could see the woman's features slip just slightly and Emily wondered if she was thinking, "How could she know? She's never been married."

"I'm a planner too," Emily said in an attempt to put her mind at ease. "I know what perfection looks like, and we'll meet, if not exceed, your needs on your special day. Nothing will go wrong. If it does, we'll be right there to make it perfect for you, and we'll do our best to make the change even better than the original plan. We've got a very experienced staff; we keep a low number of functions going on at one time. We will be available for your every request. Now," she said with her face as animated as possible, "let's talk flowers!"

As they walked back into the inn, Charlie stepped up beside them. He was wearing a blue suit with a pink tie, and a white highly starched shirt. When he reached out to allow them to enter through the doorway first, Emily noticed his initials embroidered on his cuff. He looked so much more intimidating than he had dancing on her porch last night. When he smiled at her, she had to use all her energy to return a pleasant look, worried the woman with her would see through it and know how upset she was to see him. She swallowed to keep her thoughts from surfacing.

"How are we today?" he said in a businesslike manner.

"Miss Simpson," Emily said to the woman, "this is Charles Peterson, the owner of the inn."

"Oh!" she said, looking up at him. "It's nice to meet you."

"Likewise. I hear you're considering having your wedding with us. I hope Miss Tate is meeting your needs."

"Yes, she is."

"Excellent." He turned to Emily, and she could see a change in his eyes. They were friendly but inquisitive as if he could sense her emotions. "Miss Tate, when you and Miss Simpson have finished—and please take all the time you need—I'd like to have a quick chat. I'll be in the Concord Suite."

"Yes, sir."

He smiled. "Enjoy your planning, Miss Simpson."

"Thank you," the woman said.

"Hi," Charlie said, his face welcoming and happy as he opened the door and allowed Emily to enter, but when she didn't return the sentiment, he studied her guardedly.

"Hello," she said, trying to keep the atmosphere businesslike, but it was more difficult after last night and then this morning—her emotions were all over the place. She walked into the sitting area and sat down in the wingback chair, the sun streaming in around it.

"How are you?" he asked, sitting down in the other chair. He was still dressed up.

"How did you get your car from our house?" she asked, ignoring his question purposely. "I didn't hear you this morning." She knew if he really heard how she was, he might get an earful and she was trying to work. She had three more clients coming in today and she didn't want to be a blubbering mess, nor did she want them to hear the shouting that she would be doing at the inn's owner.

"I had two guys from housekeeping pick it up for me. Libby vouched for them."

"Oh." When she woke up this morning, she'd been hoping he'd pick it up himself but that would've made for an interesting breakfast. He'd better be glad he hadn't been there. She shifted in her chair. "How has your morning gone?" she asked to keep herself together.

"Excellent. I met with the board of supervisors today. I've convinced a few of them to listen to my plans for expansion."

She clamped her jaw shut, her breathing speeding up as he watched her. Was he baiting her?

"I'm wondering…" He sat rigidly in his chair, his stance cautious. "By looking at your face… You've talked to your grandmother about—"

"Yes," she said, standing up. "Why in the world didn't you tell me you already own our land? You've known the entire time! How could you not tell me?" She was yelling, but she didn't care.

He rose from his chair protectively but she pushed herself past him and walked over to the large window. A tear slipped down her cheek.

"It wasn't my place to break that news to you," he said from behind her. "I tried to convince your grandmother to tell you last night! I was pleading with her in the kitchen. I felt awful, but I wanted to allow your grandmother to explain it. What can I do, Emily, to make this whole thing better for you? Is there anything? Do you want me to see if I can have your grandfather's house moved to another lot?"

She stood quietly, trying to organize her thoughts into something that would explain her feelings on the matter. She turned around and tried to keep her voice as even as possible. "The path through the woods leading to the pier—you can't move that. You can't move the spot where my dog is buried. You can't take the tree that holds my childhood swings to a new lot. It's not just the house; it's all of it."

He nodded, looking down at his shiny leather shoes in thought.

For a tiny instant she felt bad for him. It wasn't his fault. Gram had sold him that land before he had any knowledge of how she felt, but the fact of the matter was that he was going to destroy it all, and she couldn't bring herself to feel anything but anger about that. She didn't want to talk about it anymore or she'd end up sobbing right there in front of him.

"I can't talk now," she said, turning away.

She walked to the door, and she felt the brush of Charlie's hand as he tried gently to stop her, but he let her go.

"Charlie's comin' over," Gram said as Emily walked into the sitting room after work. Gram was reading a book.

It had been a busy and emotional day and Emily was tired. She squeezed her shoulder in an attempt to relieve the pinch that had lingered all day.

"Why?" she asked, trying not to spit the word at her. Gram didn't seem to care one bit about anything sentimental and it was driving her crazy. She looked at the faded floorboards, trying to keep her anger in check. She didn't want to shout at Gram.

"He's offered to restore that old boat by the pier."

Emily's head snapped up. "What?" she said a little too loudly. Papa's boat hadn't moved since he'd put it there on the beach. He'd built it for *her*, to help ease her pain, and they'd been the only two who'd ever touched it. Even Rachel hadn't been in it. *She* wanted to be the one who decided when and if it should be restored. She tried to keep herself together, noticing how it seemed that she was the only one who wanted to completely freak out about all this.

"I thought it might be nice," Gram said.

"Doesn't it have any sentimental value to you in its current state?"

"I've told you," she said calmly, marking her place in the book with her finger. "All this," she waved her hands in the air, "they're just things to me. They aren't Papa. But I know we're all different."

Emily was crushed again by Gram's nonchalance.

"Charlie will be over in just a few minutes. I told him he could use whatever's in Papa's shed."

Papa's tools? Without even a response to that, Emily slipped on her boots and ran out back to Papa's shed, ready to stand guard. There was no way Charlie was getting in there. The evening sun cast long shadows across the path as she walked through the salty breeze, her head throbbing with every step. The water was still today, making the bay look like an enormous sheet of rippled glass, but it wasn't helping her to calm down tonight. She pulled the rusty latch on the shed door and unhinged it. It creaked out its age as she opened it up and anchored it to keep it from shutting on her. She pulled the chain for the interior light and looked around the space.

The sight of every item was a reminder of Papa. It made her miss him more. There was a hammer still lying on the counter next to a few loose nails. She wondered what he'd been working on. He always put things away. His plans for a birdhouse were still sitting on the stool, a pencil resting in the fold of the paper. Had it been that? Had he been planning to surprise Gram? Emily fought her tears as she looked down at it. Papa was the last person to set it there. She didn't want to turn around, feeling like any minute, he'd walk in, put his hand on her shoulder, ready to tell her about his latest project. She missed him so much it caused an ache in her chest and an intense guilt that she'd left him for those three years—three years she'd never get back.

"Hi," she heard from behind her. She turned around to find Charlie. He was dressed down tonight, a slight stubble showing on his face. "Your grandmother said I could come around back. I hope that's all right." He took a step toward her, his face showing slight concern. "I wanted to see you. …To make sure you were okay."

"I'm fine," she lied. The laughter from last night still lingered between them like a dream. Laughing with him last night was the first time she'd felt alive in a while; she felt robbed.

"Do you think we could get the boat on the tractor somehow?" he asked, his hands in his pockets, his eyes studying her. "We could probably row it over. Structurally, it seemed fine."

That sadness that was teetering on the edge of anger was tipping uncontrollably. Charlie was going to disturb that boat, shift it from its spot and change it. It wasn't his place to do that. If anyone chose to move the boat, it should be her. She couldn't speak, she was so upset. Finally, when she had enough breath, she said, "I don't want it if you restore it."

Charlie looked down at her and silence hung between them for a moment. "Please let me do this," he said softly. "I feel terrible about how much this is hurting you."

"You don't get to do this. You don't get to try to be the nice guy while you're breaking my heart."

He nodded and looked down then opened his mouth to speak, but before he could, she cut him off.

"You think a boat can make up for taking my home?"

"I know how much that boat means to you."

Her skin prickled with that statement. He only knew because she'd opened up to him, because she'd felt more at ease with him than she had with anyone, ever.

"Please let me do this," he said again. The concern on his face wasn't put on, she could tell.

Was it his fault Gram had sold him the farm? Did she really want to close the door on Charlie? She felt like screaming. He waited as she mentally scrambled for answers, knowing there weren't any easy ones.

"We'll have to walk all the way over there if we're both coming back by boat. I don't want to leave the tractor by the pier," she clipped.

"Thank you," he said as he stared into her eyes. He stood quietly, and she wondered if he was giving her the space to determine their next move. In this moment, he wasn't taking charge; he was allowing her to do that.

She nodded in acknowledgement. Emily took in a deep breath and let the evening air fill her lungs. It remained quiet between them, the sound of a jet ski off in the distance competing with the rustling of the trees in the woods as the breeze came off the bay.

"It's a nice night." He leaned past her into the shed. "Mind if I have a look to see what I've got to work with?"

Heat shot through her veins as he stepped toward the shed. Whatever calm she'd tried to create slipped right out of her body again. She watched every move, just willing him to dare to disturb one of Papa's things. She'd let him have it. Charlie entered carefully, studying the worktable. He reached out, his fingers grazing the hammer and she caught herself standing straighter, rising up almost on her toes. She was ready to pounce. She bit her lip.

Emily watched him gently picking up tools, looking them over, and setting them back in their spots. He acted as if he thought everything in there was as fragile as her emotions, like he understood. He opened a small clear drawer on a box containing washers, screws, nails, and other odds and ends. With his finger, he pushed a few of them around before shutting the drawer. Then, he walked over to the back wall where Papa had stacked old paint cans. "Any of these still good you think?" he asked.

"I'm not sure. They're most likely from when Papa did the house." She grabbed two wooden oars that were propped in the corner and stood outside the door to get out of the stuffy heat in the shed before she fainted.

Charlie pulled the chain to turn the light off and stepped out beside Emily.

"What color would you like the boat to be?" he asked as they started walking across the yard toward the path that led through the woods. He took the oars from her, his height making them easier to carry.

She was really doing this. She was going to let him restore Papa's boat because doing that meant something to Charlie. And, in turn, that meant something to her. He understood he had hurt her, and he cared enough to try to make it right. But she still had to work to keep herself together. "When Papa made it, originally, it was light blue." She noticed his leather flip-flops and thought about his feet as they walked along the brush in the woods. The path hadn't been raked or tended to in quite a while. She'd put on her cowboy boots—what she always wore whenever she had to go into the woods. They were faded, worn in just the right spots to make them comfortable. Things didn't always have to be new and shiny to be perfect.

"Would you like it to be light blue? Or do you want to make it your own?"

"I want it just like he did it," she said, her jaw tight with emotion.

"Okay." He'd propped the oars up behind his neck and across his shoulders, holding them in place at either end.

She stepped on a twig; it made a snap as it cracked under her foot.

"I was prepared to spend my free time on the beach. I didn't know I'd be hiking through the woods," Charlie said, clearly trying to fill the heavy silence with conversation. They stepped around a huge tractor tread in the dirt. "I don't even own a pair of boots," he said, peering over at hers with interest.

"Once you get a good pair, you'll never need another," she said.

He nodded. "I'll keep that in mind." He smiled, reminding her of his face during the card game. She pushed the thought away.

After they'd walked so long that their silence had become easy, they arrived at the stretch of beach with Papa's pier and the old boat that sat in the sea grass on the edge of the sand. Emily had thought about restoring the boat at times, but now, that it was actually happening, she wasn't sure she wanted to disturb it. But, she reminded herself, if she moved it, her reward might be greater than if she didn't, so she walked over to one side and tried to lift it, her arms feeling like jelly.

Charlie set the oars in the boat and picked up the other side.

The boat was small and surprisingly light with Charlie on the other end, lighter than Emily remembered when she and Papa would push it up on the sand together.

"If you guide it toward the water, I'll lift it enough to move it," he said.

Together, they maneuvered the boat until it bobbed in the tiny waves. Emily watched it for a moment. It was like jumping off a cliff—there was no going back now. She slipped her boots off and set them on the wooden seat that Papa had built inside the boat, like she'd done when she and Papa had gone out fishing. The thought of him on his side of the boat, smiling from under his mustache, waving at her as she approached, was like a punch to the gut. She splashed down into the water until it was around her calves. Then she climbed in. Charlie had put his flip-flops in the boat as well, and he got in across from her, sitting in Papa's seat on the opposite side.

He began rowing. The little boat glided through the water fast and even, faster than she'd ever gone before. It was as if she were sliding on a sheet of ice.

Surprised, Emily said, "You're good at this."

"I was on the rowing team at Harvard."

"Oh!" She watched the ease in which his arms moved, the circular motions of his shoulders.

"I'll have us back to the house in no time," he said with a grin.

Suddenly, she didn't want to be back at the house. She wanted to stay out there on the water, away from all her thoughts and memories.

She didn't want to have to face it all again. Right now she was surrounded by the ripples in the bay, the beating sun, and the wind as
Charlie rowed.

"Take your time," she said.

Chapter Ten

Emily was slightly out of breath from carrying the boat all the way across the yard. Charlie had taken most of the weight, but it was still quite cumbersome to lift it for so long. She sat on the edge of it to catch her breath as Charlie rooted around in the shed.

"Let's set it on these sawhorses I found," he said, dragging two wooden frames from the shed and setting them apart from each other. She stood up to assist him with lifting the boat up onto them. "We'll clean the wood today and then let it dry overnight. Do you have something to use to clean it?"

She retrieved a bucket, two sponges, and some soap while Charlie stretched the garden hose from the house, across the patio. He turned on the water and Emily used the force of the water pressure to make suds in the bucket.

"Did you go out on this boat a lot?" Charlie asked as he dipped a sponge into the bucket and began to scrub the side of it.

"When I was younger," she said. "Before my teenage years. Then I was too busy being girly." She watched how his hand moved along the surface of the boat as he scrubbed, the movement of the muscles in his forearms and hands. She turned her attention toward the wood in front of her, scrubbing the abrasive build-up that had left a ring around the bottom of the boat. "We used to go fishing." She reached down into the bucket and filled her sponge with soapy water. "Papa used to put his fishing-tackle box right here," she said as she squeezed the sponge over the seat, the sudsy water running down to the floor of the boat.

Charlie stopped scrubbing to look.

"We caught a ton of croaker using bloodworms. I always made Papa bait my hook." She made a face and Charlie smiled. She didn't want him to smile. She looked away.

Charlie reached for the hose to spray off the boat. She grabbed her boots and his flip-flops and set them aside, standing out of the way of the spray.

The relentless sun and the work she'd done carrying the boat had made her thirsty. As the boat sat, dripping, she asked, "Would you like something to drink? I'm going to get something."

"That would be nice. Thank you."

"Lemonade okay? I'll make us each a glass and we can take them down to the beach." She still wasn't happy with him for taking Oyster Bay, but she also didn't want to veer from the plan. The more she talked to him, the more she thought she'd be able to make him fall in love with the farm. She'd been sure it was working last night and she didn't have to give up hope just yet.

"Sure."

"Okay. I'll be right back."

Charlie began hosing off the sponges as she headed inside. Gram was at the kitchen table, sorting through a box of books, odds and ends, and old photos.

"Hello," she said, the kitchen table wobbling slightly from the uneven floor that had settled with the house over the years. Emily liked the wobble. She felt it was part of the house's character. "It looks like you and Charlie are enjoying yourselves. You two look awfully friendly."

Emily pulled two glasses from the cabinet and filled them with ice.

"Well, we aren't *that* friendly."

"I'm glad you have someone to spend your evenin's with anyway," Gram said, setting a photo on one of the piles she'd made.

Emily offered Gram lemonade but she declined. "What are you doing?"

"I'm sortin' these so we'll each have a pile."

She poured the lemonade from Gram's crystal pitcher and set it back in the fridge. Picking up the two glasses, she peered down at the stacks.

"This one's yours," Gram said.

Emily set the glasses on the table and flipped through her stack of photos. The image flew past her and she stopped, turning photos until she saw it again: Papa holding a fish, the blue boat in the background. She ran her finger over the image of him, emotion welling up, and then looked away, straightening the stack. She wished she could hold onto her Gram; she wished she could keep everything from changing. With a steadying breath, she said, "Charlie and I will be on the beach," while opening the door and picking up both glasses and her photos. She kissed Gram on the cheek and headed outside.

"You all right?" Charlie asked, once she got outside, as he took his glass of lemonade from her outstretched hand.

"I'm fine," she lied. Did it show on her face?

"What are those?" he asked, pointing to the photos in her hand.

"Memories." She grabbed the small radio from inside the shed.

As they walked across the yard leading to the shore, Charlie said, "It's so beautiful here." He was trying to smooth out her mood, she could tell. She looked up at the sky that was still lit by the late evening sun as it made its descent. It was indeed a beautiful night.

When they reached the shore, Emily clicked on the old radio and set it in the sand. She walked over to the swings and sat down on one, the seat wobbling as she made herself comfortable. Charlie lowered himself down on the swing beside her.

"Papa hung these swings over the sand because Gram was worried we'd fall and she wanted a soft spot underneath us." Emily flipped through the photos until she found one of Rachel and her on the swings. They had their swimsuits on, their hair wet and stringy from swimming all day. Emily was missing her front teeth. She turned it around to show him, the image making her smile.

Charlie grinned and then his thoughts seemed to turn inward. "As a child, I didn't get the opportunity to play outside very much."

Emily nodded, his comment making her feel sad. "See that tree over there?" Emily turned and pointed to an old oak tree by the house. "I used to climb that tree and hang by my knees on the top branch right there—the one that's jutting straight out. Whenever Gram saw me through the window, she'd march outside and demand for me to get down, telling me it was just too dangerous. She was right," she said, catching a drip of condensation on the side of her glass with her finger. "I could've fallen on my head."

"Kids don't always realize how fragile life is," Charlie said.

"True, but I should have… On a Tuesday, my mom dropped me and Rachel off at school. She kissed my cheek and handed me my lunch in a brown paper sack. She told me not to forget to write my homework down—I always forgot—and that she'd help me with it that night. That was the last time I spoke to my mother. My father's car was hit head-on that day. He'd taken the day off to be with my mom." As the tears surfaced, she sniffled and said, "I'm sorry. I don't know why that came out."

Charlie gave her the sweetest look—so caring that if they didn't have so much between them, she would want to bury her face in his chest and feel his arms around her. "It came out because you're ready to tell it."

The wind had picked up, blowing her long hair into her face. She twisted it and put it behind her shoulder. Now that the conversation had ended, she noticed the song that was on. "He's playing tomorrow night," she said, pointing to the radio. "He's a good friend of Jeff's. We all swear he'll be the next big thing in Nashville."

Charlie raised his eyebrows in interest, his masculine hands looking out of place on the ropes of the swing.

"Would you want to go?" he asked her.

She absolutely wanted to go. She could call Rocky and Elizabeth—get them to go. She could organize a group of her friends. They could meet up there, show Charlie what living in Clearwater was really like.

But maybe she shouldn't. Did she really want to go out with Charlie? She'd spent enough time with him to know how easily her resolve could slip when she was around him. She liked being with him, but should she give into that, when it might just make things more complicated between them?

He grinned at her. "I'd love to take you."

She bit her lip. "I don't know…"

"It might be fun."

She wanted to see her friends and she wanted to spend more time with Charlie. She couldn't deny it. "Okay," she said.

"I'm excited about tomorrow," Charlie said.

She couldn't help it, but she felt excited, too.

It was Emily's day off. She'd awakened to find that Gram had already gone out. She'd left a note that she'd be out most of the day visiting a friend. Emily couldn't help but wonder what friend—was it Winston?

She made herself a cup of coffee and went out to sit on the back porch. Even with the wind, the morning air was warm. The paddle fans were working overtime above her, but they were no match for the heat. She sat down on a wicker chair and folded her feet under her. The bay was clear today.

Emily looked over at Papa's boat through the screen on the porch; it was still sitting on the sawhorses. What would Papa think of Gram selling Oyster Bay? She had days—she could count them—to sit on this porch with her coffee. What would those days bring? Had Gram really prepared herself to be completely moved out? Maybe she hadn't, and her lack of preparation would delay things.

Emily tried not to think about it. She'd made a list of friends to call about the concert tonight, and Rocky had already agreed—she'd called him first. She was going to have lunch with Rachel and Clara. Then, she'd decided that just in case her plan didn't work, she needed to have somewhere to live, so she planned to call about a few new condos over in White Stone.

Charlie told her yesterday that he'd be out all day, meeting with his architect and a few others. He was moving forward with the planning.

Her nervous energy prevented her from being able to sit, so Emily got up and went into the house, leaving the back door open to let in the breeze. She decided to get ready for the day.

☆ ☆ ☆

Clara sat in the sand, wearing her bright yellow one-piece swim-suit with a little ruffle at the back, wriggling her toes as the water rushed in over them. "Did you see my sparkly nails?" she asked when Emily sat down beside her. Emily stretched out her legs the same way.

"I see them now," she said. "They're pretty."

Clara scooted a little closer toward the next tiny wave as it rippled to shore. "I love Gram's beach," she said, looking at Emily through her pink sunglasses.

"What do you like so much about it?"

"I like that the water isn't deep and I can swim in it. And when I get hungry, I can walk up to her house and have muffins."

Emily smiled. "Does Gram always have muffins?"

"Yep. Because she knows I like them."

"Where is Gram?" Rachel asked, walking toward them with a quilt and basket of sun lotions and towels.

"Visiting a friend," Emily said, still wondering if that friend was the mysterious Winston.

She debated telling her sister about the locket she'd found. But Rachel was dealing with enough and Emily certainly wouldn't tell her in front of Clara.

"I was hoping she'd be here," Rachel said. "I want to enjoy this gorgeous day with her."

The way she was looking at Emily, it was clear what her sister had meant. She wanted to spend time with Gram because the days with her at this beach and at this house were numbered, and then, when this little paradise was gone, they'd be left with just their own lives and all that came with them.

"I'm going to swing, Mommy," Clara said, standing up and running down the beach to the tree swings.

"I'm glad you and Jeff are coming to the concert tonight," Emily said.

Rachel nodded, her thoughts clearly elsewhere. Something was there, on her lips, begging to come out.

"What is it?" Emily asked.

"I need your advice."

Emily grabbed a towel and sat down next to her sister in a foldout chair.

"I don't know if it's some sort of midlife crisis… I've been trying to talk myself out of it…"

"What?"

"I'm not happy with my life."

Emily eyes bulged.

"I'm wondering if Jeff and I aren't meant to be together."

What in the world was Rachel talking about? As far as Emily was concerned, they were the *perfect* couple. "I thought you two were getting along. It looked like it the other night."

"We do get along! … As long we don't talk about our issues. I want to go back to work. I want to be passionate about what I do, and I'm feeling very guilty because Jeff thinks that I should feel that passion by being with Clara—and I do—but I want to be a mom *and* figure out who I am at the same time. I can't live feeling guilty anymore. It's getting in the way of our happiness."

Emily tried to see her point of view but it was so difficult because all she wanted was to have a family, a house full of children, and be there every minute for them. She'd never experienced that, so it was hard to understand why Rachel would want to do anything else.

"I've decided that I'm going to try to go back to work. If Jeff doesn't understand that, then I'm sorry. We'll see what happens from there. There's an advertising agency in Irvington. I've thought about applying. It's been years, though, since I've worked. What if I don't have what it takes?"

"Then you'll figure it out. You're great at everything you do."

"I worry about Clara. Will she wonder why I'm not there every day? Will she resent me putting her in preschool five days a week?"

Emily looked over at Clara. "She's by herself a lot. She might enjoy being with other kids."

"Last year, we tried to have another baby…"

"Really? You didn't say anything."

"I know. Only because it took us forever with Clara, remember? And this time, it hasn't happened for us yet either. I was waiting to move forward with my own life until I knew if we were going to have another child."

"You can't keep your life on hold for the what-ifs. That's not healthy either. But I'm not going to talk you into it. It's your decision."

"I know. Jeff worries that working will cause stress, keep me busy, and make it more difficult to have another child."

"Do you want another child?"

"I wasn't sure at first—only because of the pressure of conceiving. But I *do* want more. I think about you and me—where would we have been without each other? But I'd like to just be me for a little while first." She fluttered her hands in the air, her frustration clear. "We won't solve it today." Rachel reached into the basket and pulled out a small cooler bag. "I brought sandwiches," she said. "Let's stop talking about all this heavy stuff and enjoy this day on our beach." She called Clara over and they made room for her on the picnic blanket.

As they began setting out the food, Emily noticed a dog trotting toward them from down the beach. It looked like some sort of Lab mix—it was brown with a bit of white on its chest. As it got closer, she saw it looked dirty and unkempt.

"We'd better pick up the food," Emily warned, nodding toward the dog. When she did, he made eye contact and began bounding toward them.

Rachel scooped up their plates and stood just as the dog came barreling over, landing on the blanket. It shook, sending muddy water all over them. Afterwards, it sat down, panting, and looked up at Emily.

"Hi, doggy," Clara said, walking toward him.

"Careful, Clara," Rachel said. "You don't know that dog."

Clara, clearly enamored, put her little hands on his face. When she did, the dog whipped around, sniffed her wrist, and planted a big wet kiss on her hand, making her giggle.

The dog put his snout in the air and sniffed until he found the trail of scent to the plates in Rachel's hands. He looked at her, his little eyes seeming so sad.

"He looks hungry," Emily said. "Here, give him my sandwich." She took her plate from Rachel and set it down in front of the dog. With barely a breath, he inhaled the contents. Then, he stood up and pressed himself against Emily. "He's so dirty. I wonder where he's been."

Rachel set her plate down on the blanket and the dog ate the plate clean. "He looks thin."

"I love him," Clara said, giving the dog a hug. The dog sniffed her ear and licked her again.

Emily patted her legs to get him to come over to her. She rubbed his cheeks. "He's very sweet. We shouldn't just let him go."

"Maybe we should take his picture and post it around town. Someone might recognize him."

Emily put her hand to her nose and grimaced. "Why don't we give him a bath first? He smells."

"Yay!" Clara said, jumping up and down. "Let's give him a bath! That'll be fun!"

"Okay," Emily said with a laugh. "We'll take him up to the house and wash him with the hose."

"What should we call him?" Clara asked, walking beside him as he followed their lead.

Rachel picked up the blanket and shook the sand from it. "Oh no," she said. "We aren't naming him because we aren't keeping him."

"Let's call him Flash because he came upon us like a flash," Emily said, feeling a little excited to have found this sweet soul.

"Hi, Flash!" Clara said.

"Don't encourage her," Rachel said with a wink.

"I'll tell you what," Emily told Clara, "if nobody claims him, I'll keep him and you can play with him any time you want."

Clara cheered and clapped sending Flash into a jumping frenzy.

Emily left Flash outside with a little more food and ran in to get her shampoo. On her way through the kitchen, she grabbed a bowl from the cupboard.

When she got back outside, she put the bowl on the ground and Rachel turned the garden hose on low to fill it with water. Before she'd even finished, Flash had his nose in it, lapping it up.

"It doesn't look like he's eaten or had any water in a while," Emily said. "Look at him."

When he'd finished, she held out the shampoo bottle and let him have a sniff. "I'm going to put some of this on your back," she said gently, popping open the cap and squirting it on him. Surprisingly, he let her, though his eyes were wary. She kept the hose on low and wet his back as she started to scrub.

Flash allowed Emily to lather his whole body and rinse him. Before she could dry him off, he shook like crazy, soaking her and Clara. Rachel had ducked out of the way just in time. They toweled him off together.

"I think we need to get him dog food," Clara said, her little head turned to the side as she looked at him.

"We should," Emily agreed. "He needs a collar too. Should we get dressed and take him with us down to the pet store?"

"Yes!" Clara cheered.

"Off we go then!"

It took a little coaxing to get Flash into the car but Emily did it. When they got to the pet store, she kept her hand on him to guide him, but he walked right beside her as they entered the store. Clara settled on a dark green collar with a silver bone engraved with "Flash" on the store's engraving machine. They got a matching leash, a giant bag of dog food, a fleece cushion, some dog shampoo, two chew toys, and a rubber ball.

"What if he belongs to someone?" Rachel said, the dog sitting beside Clara's booster seat in the car, his head out the open window as they made their way back to Gram's.

"I hope he doesn't," Emily said. "I already love him."

Chapter Eleven

"What in the world is that?" Gram said, her handbag hanging on the crook of her arm as she leaned on her cane. Emily was in her bedroom, getting ready to go to the concert with Charlie, and Flash was lying next to her, chewing his toy, his tail thumping on the floor.

"I thought you might need someone to keep you company," Emily teased. She remembered how Gram used to pretend to be irritated by their family dog when Emily was a kid but deep down she loved that dog. She'd sobbed when it passed away.

"Tell me you didn't buy me a dog." She stood in her pressed skirt, her button-up shirt, and low boxy heels. Flash stopped chewing and looked up at her. She was shaking her head, her pearl earrings showing through her hair.

The sight of her unease was enough to make Emily laugh out loud and abandon her bantering. "No," she said, still laughing. "This is Flash. As far as we know, he's *my* new dog. That's unless someone claims him. Rachel's going to put posters up. He came down the beach today all dirty."

"Well," Gram said, pursing her lips. Then, she walked out of the room muttering something.

"You look nice, by the way," she called out to her. Flash's ears went up and down.

"Thank you," she called back with a playfully irritated tone.

Emily laughed again. Flash had put her in a good mood. She didn't even worry about where Gram had been or who she'd seen.

Once Emily was ready, she and Flash walked downstairs to the kitchen where Gram was pinning her hair up. "Y'all want to eat somethin' before you go tonight? I'm cookin' regardless," she said, washing her hands at the sink.

There was a knock on the door then, sending Flash into a frenzy of tail wagging and barking. He bounded toward the sound, his nails causing him to slip on the hardwoods. He slid to the front where he got a firm hold on himself and barked like crazy.

Emily opened the door to find Charlie smiling at her.

Flash bucked around their legs. He threw his snout up under Charlie's hand, nudging him for attention.

"Hi," she said. "This is Flash. I think he's my new dog."

"I'm gone one day and you find yourself a dog?" Charlie said as he bent down and patted the dog's head.

"He sort of found Clara." She let Charlie inside, Flash still hopping around with excitement behind him as he entered. "Are you hungry? Gram wants to cook us something."

"If it isn't any trouble."

"It isn't!" Gram called from the kitchen. "I'm makin' chicken and dumplin's. I've already got it all made up in the fridge. I just have to cook it."

"I've never had chicken and dumplings," Charlie said as they entered the kitchen.

Gram turned around with a look of astonishment on her face. Then she smiled. "Well," she said, reaching into the fridge for the covered dish. Flash threw himself down at her feet and sniffed the air. "You're definitely havin' dinner with us tonight then." She stepped over Flash who was more worried about what was in her hands than the movement of her feet or her cane. "It'll be ready in about twenty minutes." Flash barked, his eyes on Gram. "I suppose you can have some too," she said with mock displeasure. Flash stood up expectantly.

"Do you need any help, Gram?" Emily asked.

"I'm just fine, dear. Why don't y'all go outside and enjoy the fresh air."

"If you're sure," Emily said, giving it one last effort.

"I'm sure."

"Call us when you need us," she said. Charlie held the door open for her and Gram shooed Flash out with them.

Flash ran toward her with the ball from the pet store, which he'd found nearby. He dropped it at her feet. Emily picked it up and threw it across the yard, the dog leaping into the air to fetch it.

She couldn't help but ask the question that had come to mind as soon as she'd seen Charlie. "How did things go with the architect?" She wanted to be on the inside of things, to know what was happening so that she could try to stop it, but every time things moved forward at all, she felt worse, so she hated to even ask, but her curiosity got the better of her.

"Really well," Charlie said with a smile that was beginning to look familiar. His eyes gave away his caution. "It looks like leaving a few acres between the inn and the neighborhood will work out just fine. I'm hoping to make that a selling point when I meet with the commission again."

Emily nodded, satisfaction settling in her chest. She knew Rocky wouldn't budge.

Charlie had moved over to Papa's boat, and it was clear that he didn't want to talk about the architects. Did he worry he'd upset her?

She walked up beside him. Flash came tearing over and dropped his ball. This time, Charlie picked it up and sent it sailing across the grass. He continued to throw the ball so many times that Flash eventually got tired and started rooting around in the woods. Charlie's relaxed demeanor, the way he seemed more comfortable every time he was there, made her confidence grow. She might actually change his mind about what was important down here.

"I was going to come by to paint the boat tomorrow," he said. "You're off, yes?"

"Yes. Today and tomorrow. Tomorrow night I have to go in for a wedding, but that's it."

"Why don't I come over and we'll go to the paint store to pick out some paint? Then I can get the first coat on."

"What time?"

"How about nine o'clock? I'll treat you to breakfast."

"Okay," she said. She didn't want to admit to the flutter she felt when he offered to take her to breakfast. She didn't want to enjoy being with him as much as she did.

Emily called Flash and he came running her way. "Want to get your chicken and dumplings?" she asked as he trailed along beside them like he'd been her dog for years.

When they got inside, the icy cool air conditioning hitting them, Gram said, "I was just about to get you." She'd set the table with the "good plates," as she'd always called them. On each, a portion of chicken and dumplings steamed, the hearty, soupy mixture set off by a tall glass of iced tea and a piece of crusty bread for dipping.

With an extra spoon, Gram dropped a few dumplings into Flash's bowl. He grunted and slurped until they were gone and then settled under the table. Charlie pulled out a chair for Gram and then one for Emily.

"Thank you," she said. Papa used to do that for them, too. As she looked over at Gram, she wondered, by her expression, if she was thinking the same thing.

"This smells amazing," Charlie said, taking a seat and scooting up to the table.

"The recipe's been in our family for years," she said. "It's nothin' special, but it hits the spot when you're hungry."

Charlie spooned some into his mouth. "It's delicious," he said once he'd swallowed.

"What kinds of things do y'all eat up in that fancy city of yours?" Gram asked, draping her napkin in her lap.

Charlie smiled at her. "Oh, I don't know… Nothing like the food you've offered me. I've really enjoyed trying it all." He took a sip of his iced tea and then he said, "Perhaps I can cook you something one night."

Gram clasped her hands together in delight. "That would be lovely! Why don't you and Emily decide what to cook and then we'll get the ingredients you need."

"That would be fine," he said. "But I don't mind getting what I need."

There was a thump under the table and they all looked to find Flash had laid himself out completely, his head resting on Charlie's foot. They all laughed.

"I love having you kids in the house," Gram said. "Never a dull moment."

Emily and Charlie arrived at Tippy's Grille. "Tippy's," she explained, "was named after the original owner, two generations ago. Now it's owned by his grandson." It was a small space, nestled between two other establishments on a strip of land by the water. She could see some of her friends inside through the large window as they walked up.

Charlie put his hand on her back to guide her through the door. She couldn't help but think how much she liked his gesture.

"Hey!" she said as she neared her group of friends. They smiled and threw up their hands, embracing her. Rocky leaned in for a handshake and greeted Charlie before introducing Elizabeth. Emily couldn't stop smiling. It had been too long since she'd been with this crew. They'd all known each other for so many years, though, that her time away had hardly changed a thing. It was as if they'd never left each other.

When everyone had settled into a more normal volume, and drink rounds were ironed out, Emily introduced Charlie to the group. "This is my friend, Kim and her husband Joe," she said, nodding toward them. "And that's Scotty over there with his wife, Ann. And you know Rachel and Jeff." She turned to her sister. "Where's Clara?"

"We got a babysitter!" Rachel said, her excitement clear as she did mini-claps with her hands and bounced slightly. "I haven't been out in ages! I'm so glad to be with everyone."

"I'm glad you're here!" Emily said. She noticed the grin on Jeff's face and she hoped he and her sister could enjoy themselves tonight. Jeff was already drinking a beer, which was a good sign.

"The lead singer grew up with us. His name is Jason Richards," she told Charlie. "He used to play his guitar for us on the beach at Oyster Bay." The memory made her nostalgic. She was so glad she could hear him play tonight.

"Remember that song he wrote about Sally Jenkins?" Rachel said. "It was so good. I still think that could've been a hit."

"Yes, but Sally wouldn't have been happy hearing it on the radio over and over," she said with a chuckle. Then she said to Charlie, "It was a break-up song."

"Ah," he said, nodding, as they started walking toward the front.

"I remember he'd play for us before school at our bus stop and then he'd drag that big guitar all the way to school just so he could play it as soon as the dismissal bell rang."

"I remember that!" Scotty said. "I'm glad we're all together tonight. Emily, It's great to see you."

They all took a seat at a small table on the side of the stage as the place started to fill up. A waitress came over and took their drink orders. Charlie ordered everyone the beers he and Emily had had at Merroir—he'd remembered. "I hope that's all right," he said as the waitress left, leaning toward her, his voice in her ear. "If you want something else, please feel free to get it. I'm buying tonight. I'll get one tab for everyone."

"Thank you. But I don't mind paying for myself," she said. "And I'm sure the others are willing to pay.

"I know. But it's the least I can do for crashing your reunion with all your friends."

"They don't mind, I'm sure."

The band took their places and began to warm up, the notes gritty and southern, Jason's familiar raspy voice pulling Charlie's attention to the stage. Emily was watching the band as well, but she also noticed the interest on Charlie's face as he watched them play. He was enjoying himself. Maybe he was thinking that he didn't want to drown out little places like Tippy's with a giant expansion, maybe he was thinking, like she was, that he could go back to the farm, have a drink on the patio, and talk until the sun rose over the bay.

"Y'all know what we're gonna do first, Clearwater!" Jason said into the microphone, and the crowd went wild.

Charlie sent a silent question over to Emily, his eyebrows furrowing.

Emily couldn't stop the smile that had spread across her face. She held her beer in the air like the rest of the crowd. Then, she leaned over to Charlie as he turned his head to hear her voice over the noise, and she could smell that spicy scent of his. "He has a song called 'Water,' that he always plays first," she said as the guitars got going, the drums kicking in. "He wrote it on Oyster Bay."

"Where's the best place to be?" Jason's voice roared through the speakers, the crowd whooping and cheering.

"IN THE WATER," the crowd chanted as they got to their feet. Emily tugged gently on Charlie's arm, and he stood up beside her.

"What water?" Jason said, the music loud and thumping.

"CLEARWATER!"

Then the drums went wild, the guitars going. The entire crowd toasted their beers and took a drink.

"I'm glad to be home, y'all," Jason said as a waitress climbed on stage and handed him a beer. "Let's have some fun!" He took a sip of his beer and started singing. The crowd erupted into cheers and dancing, laughter and excitement.

Jeff and Rachel had moved to the small dance floor up front. He was spinning her around like he did when they were younger. Rachel was giggling, and, more excitingly, she was looking at Jeff in that way she always had before.

"Would you like to dance?" Charlie said, his proximity startling her. Emily turned toward him in response, their faces so close she could feel his breath. The energy of the moment, the happiness that was bubbling up—before she could think things through, Charlie had her hand and was taking her beer from her. He set it on the table and walked her through the crowd to an empty spot on the dance floor.

The stage lights were flashing through the dim room, the air humid. The music pounded through her chest, the tinny sound of the notes coming off the guitars ringing in her ears.

Charlie spun her around, surprising her. Emily laughed, the movement making her dizzy. He pulled her close and then sent her sailing outward again in some kind of perfectly orchestrated swing dance. His skill was evident.

"Where did you learn to dance like this?" she asked over the music as he guided her, sliding his fingers down one of her arms before taking her hands and leading her backward two steps.

"My mother made me take dance lessons so I wouldn't make a fool of myself at my wedding. Although, I didn't learn the Charleston." He winked at her.

She threw her head back and laughed.

Joe and Kim had joined them. Charlie, so well versed in his dance steps, made Emily look as though they'd practiced together.

"Don't make it tough for the rest of us," Joe teased.

"Hey, I'm just glad you're out here," Kim said to him, taking Joe's hands and swaying awkwardly with him. "Not a dancer, this one," she said, leaning toward Joe. They all laughed.

As Charlie and Emily danced, she was less aware of the noise and the crowd, her eyes on him as he took control, his gentle movements so fluid and perfect that even though she didn't have a clue how to dance like this, he didn't let her fail. There was something so thrilling about dancing with him, feeling his hands moving from her back to her arms and returning to her own hands—it made her wish the night would go on forever.

Eventually, the music slowed, and Jason said into the microphone, "Grab your dates, your friends, the random person next to you! It's time for a slow dance." The band kicked in again. It was a soft, bluesy tune; it balanced Jason's voice perfectly. It was too intimate, and she knew that Charlie would probably lead her off the dance floor, but she couldn't help but hope that he'd stay out there with her.

"Want to keep dancing?" he said in her ear, giving her goose bumps down her arm.

Emily looked up at him. She wanted to say "Yes," but she was afraid to let herself.

"A business dance," he said, a smile lurking below his features.

Charlie wound his fingers around hers, his thumb moving across her knuckles tenderly, and pulled her close. He reached out and took her other hand, moving her toward him. Then he put his arms around her and it felt more like a hug than a dance. It was as if his arms were keeping her together and suddenly, she didn't want to let him go.

Emily slid her arms up around his neck, intertwining her fingers and trying to look away. She didn't trust herself if she looked into his eyes.

They swayed together to the music, the heat, the alcohol, and their closeness making her cheeks feel hot. She stole a glance at him and had to push the breath through her lungs as she saw him looking down at her. Their faces were so close, his eyes direct and warm at the same time. Happiness was swelling in her chest, making her smile at him, but it emerged with shyness. She'd never felt shy before, but she was struggling not to give away her feelings.

"What are we doing?" she said, her eyes darting up to his face only briefly.

"Dancing," he finally said, avoiding the question.

She mustered the strength to look him in the eye again.

"Let's go outside," she said, feeling the need to move away from him, before she lost all resolve and kissed him. With a quick wave to Jason on stage, she let go of Charlie, each of them grabbing their beer from the table, and led him to the door.

Rachel followed after her. "You okay?" she asked quietly.

Emily nodded, telling Rachel in that sisterly way of theirs that she needed to let her go.

"I'll tell the others you had to go if you don't come back in."

Emily nodded and walked outside with Charlie.

The evening temperature wasn't any cooler, but the breeze coming off the bay sent a wave of relief her way. Tippy's long deck, full of tables and twinkle lights, was nearly empty with everyone inside tonight to see the band. She walked to the edge, facing the water. The moon had just started to reveal itself above them.

"This has been a very weird week," Charlie said, walking up beside her and leaning on the railing, his arm brushing hers.

He looked out over the water for a moment, but then turned to her, his body so close that exhaustion was setting in from having to fight the way she felt about him. Right there, in the moonlight, she wanted to wrap her arms around him and not let go.

"I have enjoyed spending time with you, but I worry that we're eventually going to have to face what's before us," he said.

She turned toward him and she was so close that she had to look up. Without warning, without even hesitation, he took her hand, his touch light enough to cause a shiver through her body. "We don't have to face it tonight," she said.

The air carried nothing but the sound of the gentle lapping of the waves and the muffled band inside.

"I want to see you tomorrow," he said, not taking his eyes off her. "I still want to take you to the paint shop and choose a paint for your grandfather's boat."

"Okay," she said, feeling so confused. For the first time in a long time, she felt like she had someone who challenged her, who made her want to be better, and it was the very person who was hurting her. It made her feel like she shouldn't see him anymore, but she knew she didn't want to do that.

Chapter Twelve

Emily stood back and looked at the fish Charlie had bought for Libby as Flash hopped up on her bed and made himself comfortable. She had removed the wreath Gram had placed there and hung it on the wall in her bedroom. The blues were so beautiful that she decided she'd like to paint Papa's boat a similar shade.

Charlie was supposed to come over soon to pick her up so they could look at paint colors. She called down to Gram to ask her to keep an ear out for the door, but when she heard a loud crash, she figured she'd better help with whatever Gram had just dropped. Flash jumped off the bed and followed behind her.

"What happened, Gram?" she called as she came down the stairs but Gram didn't answer. "Gram?" She rounded the corner and headed into the kitchen, her heart pounding harder with every second of silence. "Gram?"

Gram was on the floor, unconscious, broken dishes scattered around her, her cane on the other side of the room. Flash walked up to her protectively and sniffed her face before sitting next to her still body.

"Gram!" Emily yanked her cell phone out of her pocket and dialed 911 as she listened for breathing. To her relief, she heard Gram's breaths, but they were shallow. "I need an ambulance! My grand-mother is unconscious and I think she's had a heart attack or some-thing!" She answered the emergency person's questions while stroking Gram's arm.

The paramedics arrived quickly, and were lifting Gram into the ambulance as Charlie pulled up. He jumped out of the car and ran up to Emily, the sunlight flickering across his shirt as it escaped through the shade of the trees. "What's going on?"

"Will you be riding, ma'am?" the paramedic asked.

"Yes," she said, frantic. The wind blew the trees to the side, send-ing a sharp streak of sun into her eyes. She struggled to focus.

"What happened?" Charlie said, grabbing her arm.

"I think Gram's had a heart attack." She climbed into the back of the ambulance.

Charlie jogged up to the back of it, the paramedic holding the door open but looking antsy to get it shut. "Get in the car with me. We'll ride behind."

"No!" She had to go with Gram! Her head was clouded, her shoul-ders tight, her heart slamming around in her chest. She reached out and shut the doors, plunging herself into the sterile, unfriendly en-vironment of the ambulance. With a small jerk, they were off. Emily reached over and grabbed Gram's hand—it was so still.

She couldn't see Charlie anymore out of the small back window. All she could see was Oyster Bay. As the house slid out of view, she felt the full brunt of what she was losing. She loved Gram so much. If she thought she'd fallen apart when Papa died, she wasn't sure what would happen to her if she lost Gram. There would be no more days at the beach with Gram to calm them, no more of Gram's talks or nights around the kitchen table while she listened.

The next few hours were a manic frenzy of admittance paperwork, insurance documentation, calls to family members, and doctors' prognoses. Gram had had a heart attack and, given her age, they wanted to run a few tests, but it looked like she was stable for the time being.

Charlie showed up, but Emily had been so busy with the hospital staff, she hadn't talked to him. And, as real life set in, she couldn't deny the thought that they might finally have to face up to the truth. He sat quietly in one of the chairs. Rachel was there with Jeff and Clara, only adding to the chaos in Emily's head. She offered her sister a worried look every now and again, but the concern on Rachel's face was almost too much to bear. She hadn't seen that look in her sister's eyes since their parents died.

Charlie had gotten Emily and the family bottles of water, sandwiches from the cafeteria, and he'd kept a steady supply of tissues. When she couldn't stop the tears, when they'd almost overwhelmed her, he reached over and put his hand on hers in a comforting way. He kept it there the rest of the time.

After a while, they'd settled into a quiet slouch in the waiting room, exhaustion finally hitting them. Rachel was on the floor with Clara, drawing pictures on a hospital notepad while Jeff finished filling out a few more forms that the hospital required.

"You doing okay?" Charlie finally asked.

Emily nodded and closed her eyes. She was so tired. Then, she sat up with a start. "Flash is running loose," she said.

"I put him inside before I came," Charlie said.

"Someone should probably check on him." In all the commotion, she'd completely forgotten about him. "Would you make sure he's okay?" she asked Charlie.

"Of course."

"Thank you," she said with a wave of relief as she dug in her purse for her keys. She pinched the front door key between her fingers and held it out to him. "His food and water dishes are by the back door, and he should probably go out."

Charlie took the keys. "Will you be okay?" he asked.

She nodded.

"Does anyone need anything while I'm out?" he asked, his eyes darting to Rachel and Jeff.

"We're good," Rachel said. "Thank you though."

"I'll be right back," he said to Emily.

She watched him leave, and as he walked through the door, an elderly gentleman came in. He looked a little lost. He entered the room, scanned everyone in it, and then left. Emily, alone with her thoughts, wondered about the man. He could've been no one in particular—perhaps looking for a family member or trying to find the restroom. But, what if it was Winston? Was he in a panic, not knowing what had happened to Gram? Had she been meant to meet him somewhere, and she hadn't shown up?

Emily had a sudden urge to run after him and ask, but she stayed put. She knew it was crazy to think he might be Winston. Did this Winston love Gram like Papa had? It was hard to imagine.

Clara was starting to get fidgety, so Jeff suggested he take her for a walk. Rachel, clearly glad for the break, got up off the floor, set the notepad onto a nearby chair, and sat down next to Emily.

"Do you know anyone named Winston?" Emily asked.

"No, why?"

"I found something at Gram's—a locket. It was engraved to her but it was from someone named Winston."

"That's odd…"

"Yeah. She's always said that she's known Papa all her life, that he was the only person she ever loved. Do you think she's found someone now that Papa has passed?"

Rachel's eyebrows rose with this suggestion. "Wow. I don't know, but that would be really fast, wouldn't it?"

"I think so."

"She hasn't said anything to me."

"It would make sense though, because she seemed to have dealt with Papa's loss much better than we could've expected."

"It's difficult to tell, though. People grieve in different ways."

"Yeah, but she isn't grieving at all. She dresses up, she goes out, she makes cookies… Sometimes I feel like I'm the only one who still misses him."

"I miss him," Rachel said. "I still cry over not having him. I worry that Clara won't remember him." Rachel twisted in her seat to face Emily. "Would it be so bad if she's found happiness again?"

"Of course not."

"What would he think if he knew that she'd moved on so quickly?"

"He always said her happiness was his number one priority," Rachel said with a smile. "Remember?"

Emily grinned at the thought. "He told us that when we date someone, he should make us his *number one priority*, and if he didn't, kick him to the curb." She laughed, remembering his frankness. "I miss him."

"Me too."

"Miss Tate?" a doctor in a white coat said from the double doors across the room. Emily and Rachel stood up. He walked over to them. "Your grandmother is stable. She had a pretty tough climb to come back to us, but she did it. I'd like to keep her here for at least a week to monitor her. We've started some medication that she'll need to continue once she's home, but she'll also need to rest. No big changes in her day."

"When can we see her?" Emily asked, relieved to be getting good news.

"You can see her now if you'd like, but let her sleep. She's weak and needs to rest."

"Okay."

They walked down the stark hallway, past rooms with beds and beeping monitors, some patients sleeping, some awake and shifting around under their covers. A pair of nurses walked by, their shoes squeaking on the glossy tile floors. Emily wanted to wheel Gram out of there, take her home to her own bed where she could be comfortable and happy. She wanted to put cookies in the oven and open the windows to let the bay breeze in. She'd do anything Gram asked of her, just to have her home again.

When they arrived at Gram's room, they went inside slowly so as not to wake her. Gram looked older in that bed with her face slack and her hair disheveled.

As Emily looked down at her frail grandmother, she thought about how they didn't have that much time left together. She didn't want Gram to be off in Florida somewhere, away from her, away from Clearwater and everything they called home. What if this had happened after she'd moved? Who would have found her? She needed to be at her own house with her family.

Gram stirred, bringing her out of her thoughts. Emily watched Gram's face, waiting for that smile of hers, but it didn't come. Her eyes stayed closed. A lone tear escaped from the corner of her eye and slid down her temple to the pillow under her head.

Emily waited with Rachel for twenty minutes or so, but Gram never opened her eyes. Finally, Rachel motioned for them to leave.

When they entered the waiting area, Charlie had returned. Jeff was sitting next to him, and to her surprise, Clara was on Charlie's lap. She really seemed to like him. She asked him to bounce her on his knees and she giggled every time she came down. The most surprising part was how gentle his eyes were when he looked at her, how interested he seemed in making her laugh, despite how careful he was.

"Hello," he said, the curiosity remaining as he looked over Clara's head at Emily. "How's your grandmother?"

"She's sleeping."

Rachel took Clara off Charlie's lap and led her to a small table that had a couple of children's books on it. Charlie stood and met Emily in the center of the room.

"How was Flash?" she asked. "Is the house still standing?"

He smiled. "He wouldn't come when I called him and I wondered if he hadn't learned his name yet. I had to search the house to find him."

"Not a guard dog then," she said, missing Flash already. "Where did you find him?"

"In your room. I knew it was yours because your stuff is all over it," he said, smiling again. "He was asleep on your bed. He raised his head when I came in, but he put it back down. I think he's worried."

"Oh," she said, putting her hand to her chest. "How sweet. I guess I can go home and see him now."

"I'll drive you," Charlie said.

"I'll stay," Rachel told her, holding a children's book, Clara now on her lap. "Jeff can take Clara home, and you can text me if you want to come back."

"Okay. Let me know if she wakes up."

"Of course."

Charlie walked beside Emily to the door and held it open for her. As they were walking, he grinned down at her.

"What?" she asked.

"I noticed something in your room."

She waited for an explanation.

"I saw my fish."

She didn't want him to think less of Libby for giving her the fish or get any ideas that it had some sort of sentimental value to Emily. "Art is subjective," she said to him again, hoping he'd remember their original conversation. "Libby wasn't thrilled with it, but I liked it. She let me have it."

"I'm glad you like it."

They walked to the car and he let her in. When he got in on the other side, she said, "That's actually the blue I'd like to paint Papa's boat."

"It's a good color. Could I stop by and do some work on the boat while you're at the inn?"

"It's nice out there by the bay, isn't it? A good place to work outside." She smiled at him.

"Yes. But maybe not all work… I was thinking, I never got to cook for you. I could make you dinner tonight."

"Charlie…" She wanted to have dinner with him but it might be best if she didn't. "I don't know…"

He watched her, and it was clear that he knew why she was hesitating. But he waited, his offer still hanging between them.

"What you said at the concert, you were right. At some point, we have to face the inevitable. If not, things are just going to get harder for us. You can do the boat, but we should probably just end things there."

Chapter Thirteen

"Hey, Emily," Rocky said through the phone as Emily lay on the sofa downstairs. She'd been there a while before he'd called, just thinking about everything. She'd noticed there was a crack that had started in the corner of the ceiling. She kind of liked it there. It made her feel like the house was showing her how many storms from which it had sheltered her.

She sat up. "Hi. What's up?"

"I wanted to make sure you thanked Charles Peterson for getting all our drinks at the concert. I tried to pay my tab and the bartender said Mr. Peterson had run his card for all of us all night! You don't think he was trying to get us in his favor, do you?"

Emily took in a deep breath and let it out. "I don't know," she said honestly.

"I only ask that because I'm starting to get questions from the planning commission. They're considering, Emily. He's been talking to them, convincing them that expansion is what they need. I'm struggling to keep a foothold here…"

"Well, don't back down, whatever you do."

"I won't. I'll do my very best to convince them otherwise. You know I will. I just wanted to let you know."

After she and Rocky ended the call, Emily got up. As she walked down the hallway to the stairs, she looked down at the roller-skate scratch on the floor for a long time. She was going to miss seeing it every day. She wondered if she should take a photo of it. Maybe she could start a memory book with all the wonderful things from Oyster Bay.

She might do that, but right now, she had something else on her mind. Flash followed Emily upstairs as she made her way to Gram's room. Before Rocky had called, she'd been thinking about Winston. She opened the jewelry box and took out the locket, turning it over in her hand. Who was this guy? Was he the reason that Gram didn't mind letting this house go? If he loved Gram and Gram loved him, didn't he deserve to know that she was in the hospital? Emily dug through the jewelry box looking for anything else that might give her a clue, but it was just that one locket. It glared at her from the box, challenging her to find out more.

She returned the locket and left the room, looking for Gram's boxes of photos. Perhaps there was a photo of Winston. Every picture had the names of the people in it and the year it was taken, in Gram's slanted, cursive script, on the back. Then it was filed behind the letter of the first name she wrote. It didn't take but a minute and Emily had located her boxes. They were labeled by year and stacked neatly in the closet.

In no time at all, Emily had gone through over ten years of boxes, and she was losing hope, thinking she should give up, but something made her pull out the next box. She retrieved the 1956 box and flipped through the Ws. Her mouth dried out as she found a photo that said, "Winston McBride and Paul Tate, 1956." She took a close look at the men. Winston was on the left; she knew that because her Papa, Paul Tate, was on the right.

The unknown man was wearing a button-up shirt with a tie, a sweater vest overtop, and he had his arm around Papa. The man was handsome. He had thick hair—dark brown or black; with no color in the photo it was hard to tell—and strong cheekbones. Was this the Winston who had given Gram the locket? And he'd known Papa?

Emily read the date again—1956. So Winston wasn't someone new in Gram's life. Gram married Papa in 1955, so she and Papa were married when this photo was taken. Did Gram have an affair with this man while she was married to Papa? If this were true, had Papa known? Was that why he was always professing his love to her Gram—so that he could keep her from straying? Heat filled Emily's cheeks at the thought, and suddenly her perfect Gram didn't seem so perfect anymore. She covered her mouth with her hand as if it would stop her thoughts from entering her mind.

Flash whined and nudged her arm. Absentmindedly, she reached down and petted him as she kept her eyes on the man in the photo. Still pondering this new possible reality, she put the box away and shut the closet door. Then she took the photo with her to her room and set it on the dresser. Her bedspread was slightly askew from Flash sleeping on it, but she didn't really process that fact. She lay down and looked at the ceiling.

So Gram might not have been perfect. She was human like anyone else. But what was bothering Emily more than anything was the thought of Papa—whether he'd known or not, and if Gram had betrayed him.

For her own wellbeing, she needed to talk to Gram, to figure out what was going on. But she didn't want to put any undue stress on Gram's heart. Why had Gram been crying in her sleep in the hospital?

Emily's head was swimming, but she had to get ready for work. She had the wedding.

With a deep breath, she got up, dragged Flash's bed near the bathroom door, offered him his bone, and then turned on the shower. As the steam filled the small bathroom—the ventilation never was very good in there—her face disappeared slowly in the increasing fog on the mirror. She rubbed her eyes and tried to focus on getting ready.

Emily slipped the long, silky dress over her head and let it shimmy into place. As she looked at her reflection, she watched her breathing rise with the memory of the last time she wore the navy blue dress—the night that had changed everything. Brad had taken her out to dinner. It was a rustic restaurant with brick walls and exposed beams, a wall of shiny taps behind a glossy bar, and windows from floor to ceiling.

To her surprise, the entire restaurant was full—every table—with people she knew, all smiling and glittery-eyed as she took her seat. Brad nodded to the servers and they began delivering champagne to everyone. She knew what was about to happen, and, like a speeding train, she couldn't make him stop. Brad was talking, making them laugh, his hands shaking. All she could think about was the boulder-sized weight in her stomach and the fear that was probably showing on her face. Brad said something about her being his rose, and he handed her a small bunch. They were perfect in every way—deep red and tied with a matching ribbon—but above the ribbon was a platinum ring with diamonds all the way around the band and an enormous square-cut diamond in the center. She had closed her eyes and shook her head just as she was doing now.

The memory was still so fresh in her mind that she struggled to prepare for work. She fluffed her hair and put on her lip-gloss. "I'll be back," she said, reaching over and patting Flash's head.

As she left the house, she texted Rachel to see if Gram had woken up. Rachel texted back immediately, telling her that she'd opened her eyes briefly, but she was asleep again. Emily let her know that after the wedding, she'd check back in. Then she got in her car and headed toward the inn.

Libby, who'd been standing out front when Emily got there, walked straight over to her, a worried look on her face. "The bride has been bugging me for over an hour. The musicians haven't shown up!"

Emily tried to stay calm. "They have two hours. I'll try to call them and make sure they're ready." She pulled out her cell phone and brought up the number she'd saved earlier for the quartet and hit "call," knowing that they should be here and be setting up. She'd told them three o'clock. As she entered the inn, she got their voicemail. The bride came barreling toward her. Emily smiled as if nothing was wrong and gently held up her finger to let the woman know she'd be right with her. "This is Emily Tate at Water's Edge. We're calling to check that you're on your way. Please call us at this number if you have any difficulties." She hung up and turned toward the woman.

"Hello," she said with a smile, trying to keep calm for the bride. "I've just called the musicians and left a message. Voicemail is good. It means they're on their way."

"And if they aren't?" the bride nearly snapped. "How will I walk down the aisle with no music?" There was utter panic on her face.

"I'll go pick them up myself if I have to. But if—and I stress the word 'if'—they don't show, we have music that can be played on the sound system. It's beautiful and no one will be the wiser. Let's give them a little more time before we worry."

The bride was starting to cry. She was standing there, her hair in a curly up-do, a sparkly tiara, diamond earrings, perfect makeup, with jeans and a button-down shirt.

"It'll be okay," Emily said. "Please don't ruin your eye makeup. Remember that you're here to marry the man of your dreams. He'll be yours no matter what music you have. We'll do our best to make this evening amazing and we will deliver. I promise. Now, please, don't worry at all. Get dressed, and I'll check on the cake, the tables and chairs, the flowers, *and* the men. And I will not stop pestering the musicians."

"Okay," the bride said with a sniffle. "Thank you. I'm so glad you're my wedding coordinator."

"You're welcome," Emily said, and she meant it. Then she went to check on everything else.

Charlie came around the corner on the other side of the inn's grand patio.

"Hi," he said as Emily lined up the chairs to put them away.

Her head was pounding and she was tired. She took a deep breath and turned to greet him.

"How did the wedding go?"

"The musicians were late," she said. He took the chair from her hands and stacked it up for her. "But they made it, and everything else went perfectly."

He picked up the patio phone and dialed. "Hello, Libby. Would you mind sending some extra staff to assist Miss Tate with cleaning up

the wedding? I'm going to steal her away for a meeting. Thank you."
He hung up the phone, grabbed two wine glasses from the small bar
that had been set up for the event, and an open bottle of wine. "Walk
with me," he said.

She stood there, deliberating.

"You've had a long day. It's time for a break."

She still had a half-hour of work left, so technically, she was on the
clock and he was the boss; she followed him.

They walked down to the beach where chairs were set up with
umbrellas and little tables between them for the inn's guests. Charlie
set the glasses down and filled them up. Then, he handed one to her.

Reluctantly, she took it. She really didn't think the alcohol would
be good, given the state of her head, nor did she feel that being in
Charlie's presence would make it any better. "Thank you," she said,
kicking off her shoes so the sand wouldn't get inside them.

"How's your Gram?" he asked, sitting down with his glass and
motioning for her to do the same.

"No change yet. She's been sleeping."

He nodded.

The breeze blew off the water, blowing her hair behind her shoulders as she dug her feet into the sand. It felt odd to be all dressed up,
given her surroundings.

"I did catch the very end of the wedding," he said. "You did a
fantastic job."

"Thanks."

"But the whole time, I could see how much you were hurting.
Your grandmother will be okay, you know?"

Emily took in a deep breath of salty air and let it out. "It's not just
that. It's a lot of things," she said. He knew exactly what things.

"Want to talk about them?"

"Not really." There was nothing she could do sitting on the beach at the inn to change her predicament, so why talk about it?

Charlie looked out at the water and sipped his wine. "Well, I'll talk about mine then."

She looked over at him.

"I feel a mixture of emotions. Emily, I don't want to take that house from you, but I can't just stop this expansion. T & N Construction—your friends—would lose the contract and it's probably the biggest contract they've ever had. City Council wants me to expand because they feel that we could capitalize on increased tourism in the summers and, at the very least, overflow from the Urbanna Oyster Festival every year. But it's more than that. Robert Saunders, who's on the planning commission—he's a friend of my father's. Not everyone on the commission agrees with Robert, but he's the reason I bought the inn, the reason I even knew it existed. Robert called me in because he wants this expansion to keep up with the growing demands of the area, and we owed him a favor. I have to do this for him. I'm not lying when I say a lot of people will benefit from this and the more I scale back my plans, the less effect the expansion will have. Rocky is being stubborn; he's the last person I have to convince. Everyone else is on my side. They all feel that expansion would be well-received by the public. And I plan to convince the public. I'm going to meet with the people who own neighboring properties to convince them expanding is a good idea."

The concern on his face made her headache worse.

"You make me feel so guilty," he said. "I enjoy being around you so much. But I know that, too, will eventually come to an end. I will worry about you once I'm gone."

She couldn't look at him anymore for fear she'd start to cry, so she looked out at the bay.

"Have you looked for a place to live yet?"

Emily shook her head. She felt terrible. She didn't want to make him feel guilty.

"Would you like me to help with that?"

"I'll be fine."

"I know you'll be fine," he said. "You'll make sure of it. But would you like my help anyway?"

"No. I know the area. I can find a place to live," she said. She kept her eyes on the bay.

"Look," he said. "Your grandmother will be okay, and you'll adjust to not having the house. I mean, you were able to live without it for three years…"

"I didn't live *without* it for three years," she said, her frustration bubbling up. "The whole three years, it was there because it belonged to my family. Oyster Bay was waiting for me. I didn't, for a second, live without it. And when I was ready to come home to it, it was here for me."

Emily drank her wine, contemplating whether or not to get up and tell him she needed to leave. But she had more to say to him. "You don't understand me or my family. You don't understand how that house is part of me, how I spent night after night in Richmond, wishing I was there, worrying that I'd made the wrong choice and wondering what my life was supposed to look like. You don't know what it is to have a home—a place you love where you can retreat when times get rough. You don't understand the importance of memories because you don't have any. You don't understand how I start to shake every time I think about how my little family might have had some cracks in it… "

She stopped, clapping her hand over her mouth, tears coming to her eyes. Her concerns had just tumbled out. She didn't want to tell him about Winston. It was family business, and she shouldn't bring him in on it. She clutched her wine glass.

Charlie leaned closer to her, his head tilted to the side, concern for her sheeting over his face. It only made the tears come faster.

"Cracks?" he asked quietly.

She shook her head, unwilling to say more, her lip quivering.

"Emily, you can tell me. I'm here for you."

She wanted to tell him. She loved the way he listened to her. And if she didn't talk about it, she might crumble into pieces. "I'm not sure Gram was faithful to Papa. I found a locket from another man that suggests it. What would that say about her character if she cheated on Papa, if she deceived him in some way?"

"I'm sure it would've hurt him." Charlie sat in the chair, his hands resting on the armrest casually. "But it's probably not what you think." He had nothing to lose, and she had everything to lose in the next few weeks. Even though Gram had pulled through, she'd be leaving, and it was possible Gram would leave with all the answers Emily was looking for. "My ex-wife had an affair," Charlie said suddenly. "I didn't know him. He was a complete stranger. It was shocking. But it made me realize that I didn't love her."

"Oh." She set her empty glass on the table.

Emily felt like she'd been hit in the stomach. If Papa had found out about an affair, he might have realized he didn't really love Gram. But when Emily tried to relate Charlie's story to Gram and Papa, it just didn't add up. Gram and Papa *were* happy. So why would she have had an affair? There was no way their marriage could've been an act. Right? "Did your wife ever tell you why she did it?"

"He was very successful…"

"You're very successful."

"He was flashier, had more money, he owned an empire of hotels."

"And that was her reason?" How awful.

"According to her, the reason for his success was passion and the reason for our demise was a lack of passion. It took me stepping away from the situation to realize why there was no passion—it was because I'd never really loved her. I married her because that was what I thought should be the next step. I respected her, so I tried to give her the life she wanted. It turns out she wasn't the person I thought she was. And it made me actually take a look at my life."

They sat together, side by side, the water stretching out before them as far as they could see. The silence between them belonged to their own thoughts. Finally, he said, "It hurts to find out the person you chose to spend your life with doesn't love you. But, in my opinion, it's better to know than not to know, and that's what makes the story of your Gram and Papa so interesting to me. It seems like, from what you tell me, they had that passion. So why would she look elsewhere? Maybe he was just an admirer."

"Wouldn't it be odd to keep the necklace then? And why would this other man profess his love to her? It rubs me the wrong way."

"Things all work out for a reason."

"Do they? It's easy to say that, but do they really work out to fulfill some grand plan, some reason that lies in the heavens? Or do we just fumble blindly with our own lives and hope to come out on top?"

"I'd like to believe there is a reason. And we just get frustrated when we can't figure out that reason. But eventually, we see. I was a wreck when my wife left me. I'm not used to failing at things. But with time, I was able to see how right she was to leave. Did she handle things in the right way? Maybe not. But the end result was the right one."

Emily thought about all the things in her life going wrong at the moment, and she wanted to believe him, but she just didn't know if she could. "Time will tell," she said.

"You seem tired," he said. "Let me cook you dinner. I said I would. I'd like to stay true to my word."

She wanted to spend time with him, but it just didn't make sense. "I don't think so."

"I'll be there to do the boat anyway. It would be no trouble at all."

His cheeks were pink from too much sun and his hair had lightened slightly since he'd gotten there. Even those blue eyes of his had changed—now, when he looked at her, she saw so much care and interest. She wanted to have his arms around her, but instead, she took a deep breath.

"I'm sorry, Charlie, but I have to say no."

Chapter Fourteen

"Is your Gram doing better?" Libby asked.

Emily had gone to the hospital last night to relieve Rachel of her duties for a bit, but the nurses finally shooed her out around midnight, telling her it was well past visiting hours and she needed to go home.

Libby and Emily had been organizing things and sorting flyers all day for the charity event that was being held in a few minutes and they had hardly even had a moment to talk. She took an orange stack of papers and set them by a peace lily on the corner of the table.

"She's doing okay. I went to see her this morning and she was sleeping, but the doctors said she'd been awake. They told her where we were and what had happened." She placed some more fliers next to a stack of giveaway magnets with a company's logo on it. "I'm going to go see her again after work."

"That's good.

They both stood back to look at the table.

Libby turned to Emily. "I heard that Charles isn't backing down on expanding."

"I know," she said with the sinking feeling that came whenever she thought about it. Emily was touched, though, by Libby's concern. The older of the two of them by a year and a half, as kids, Libby had always watched over Emily as if she were a second big sister. It was clear, by the direct way that her friend was looking at her that Libby had wanted to ask.

"I can't believe he isn't even considering your feelings on the whole thing," Libby said, a stack of leftover fliers in her hands, her head tilted in an apologetic way.

Emily took a deep breath and let it out. "He's already bought it from Gram."

Libby shook her head, clearly at a loss for words.

"What's so unexpected is that I like him, but I don't want to. I want to hate him for taking my family's land. It makes the whole thing harder."

"You've spent more time with him than I have. What's he like?"

Emily ran her hand along a small bubble in the linen tablecloth, finishing off the display. "He's strong-willed when it comes to business, but when he's just hanging out, he's nice, easygoing," she said almost against her will. "He's going to restore Papa's boat for me."

"Really?"

Emily nodded, wondering if she should still let him do it. "I have no idea what I'll do with it if I have to move into a condo, but I suppose I'll find something."

"Put pillows in it and make it a sofa," Libby said with a laugh.

"Ha! Don't tempt me."

Emily had successfully organized the charity event and spent the rest of the afternoon in her office, completing paperwork and booking events before heading to the hospital. She'd booked three more just today, and she was feeling good about her efforts.

As she left work, driving down the narrow road leading toward the farm, the bordering coastal grasses swaying from the speed of the cars, she let the wind blow in through her open window. The sun was bright today, causing her to squint even with her sunglasses. She slowed down as she passed Oyster Bay.

It was nearly hidden, the trees full and dense from spring growth, but she could make out, down the long, winding drive, the edge of the sea and the tip of Papa's boat. She took in a deep breath of fresh air, and hit the gas. She couldn't wait to get Gram home and back to her comfortable surroundings. Even if it was only for a short time.

When she finally got to Gram's hospital room, the door was cracked, so she let herself in. Gram was partially sitting up, her bed at an incline, and her eyes were open.

"Hi, Gram," she said, smiling. It was so good to see her awake.

Gram twisted a little to view her, the IV in her arm keeping her from turning the whole way. "Hello, dear."

"How are you feeling?"

"Apart from my sore hip—we think from the fall when the heart attack happened—I feel fine."

"Did the doctor say that you could come home soon?"

"Friday. As long as my tests remain normal."

"I'm so happy to hear that! I can't wait to get you home."

Once, as a girl, she'd tried to make breakfast in bed for Gram, pouring dry cereal in a bowl and making instant coffee with cold water and coffee grounds. She'd balanced it on a small tray all the way upstairs to surprise her gram. Gram's smile right now, at her comment, looked like it had then.

"Have I missed anything?" Gram asked.

"Not much. Charlie told me he's meeting with our neighbors tomorrow to convince them that expanding Water's Edge is a good idea."

Gram nodded, her mind still working. Was she reconsidering her actions?

"Rocky's giving him a hard time, but I don't know if he can hold Charlie off forever if he already owns the land. Charlie's got the City Council's backing. Do you think it'll really happen?"

"Does it matter?" Gram asked gently. "It's not our land anymore. Not in three weeks anyway."

"Are you still fine with that?"

"Of course. It was a decision that I didn't take lightly the first time."

"Oh." Emily looked down and fiddled with her ring. She'd hoped for a different response. "You know what I noticed?"

"What's that?"

"When you first became stable after your heart attack, you had a tear in your eye. I watched it go down your cheek. Do you remember why?"

Gram's face dropped from its usual pleasant expression to one of contemplation. "I do."

"Would you tell me why you were crying, Gram?"

"When I felt the tinglin' in my arm and the kitchen began to spin, I couldn't help but get excited because I thought it was finally my turn, that God wanted me now, and I'd see Papa again, but then I came to. I could hear y'all talkin', the beep of the machines, and I could feel the bed underneath me. I knew Papa wasn't there, and it felt like I'd lost him all over again."

A lump formed in Emily's throat, closing it up, the air catching on every attempt to get a breath. Gram wanted to be with Papa. Everything would change if Gram left them—*nothing* would be the same. While Rachel and Emily had always had each other, it was Gram and

Papa who'd held them all together, and without Gram, what would happen to them? Emily feared the grief would just swallow her up. But through the tears that surfaced, she felt a wave of relief. This was the Gram she knew and loved, the one who would wrap her arms around Papa and kiss him right in the kitchen for everyone to see, the one who danced in her apron, grabbing Papa's hands, their feet moving effortlessly on the kitchen rug.

"I'm absolutely sure that Papa misses you, but I still need you. I'm so happy you're here with us. I love you so much, Gram."

"I suppose you're right. And Flash needs me," she teased, and Emily laughed through her sniffles. "Somebody's gonna have to train him. Is he eatin' my furniture and gettin' hair on my sofas?"

"No. He's sleeping on my bed. He's been depressed since your heart attack. I think he can sense that something is amiss. He'll be happy for Friday, too."

"Have you found any pet-friendly condos?" Gram asked.

"I… haven't started looking."

Gram sat up a little more in her bed. "Emily, dear. You need to find somewhere to live. The house will be gone in three weeks. I've put out ads to sell the furniture. You'll need to have somewhere to sleep."

"You're selling the furniture? What if I want some of it?"

"Then tell me what you want, and if anyone shows interest, I'll say it's sold already. What would you like to keep?"

"All of it."

Gram gave her a knowing look. "You won't fit the entire house into an apartment. And if you don't find a place, Rachel's house is too small to put any of it in there. She has enough on her plate without addin' you and the dog to the mix."

"I wasn't going to impose on Rachel." She sat on the edge of the bed and fidgeted with the thin hospital blanket.

"Then where are you plannin' to live?"

"I'll find something."

Gram clicked the button on the adjustable arm of the bed, sitting herself up a little more. "This isn't goin' away, dear. You're goin' to have to figure it out."

Emily looked out the double window, obscured mostly by thick gray drapes.

"Oh!" Gram said, remembering something. "Did Charlie ever cook for you?"

"No." Gram was changing the subject. Emily let her.

"Call him or you're goin' to make me upset. You have a life to live."

"I don't know."

"Listen, Emily. I know how you think, but you can get yourself into a lot of trouble by prioritizin' memories over real relationships. Don't be afraid to have them. It's the relationships that will carry you through the hard times and help you grow. Not the memories."

Emily kissed Gram on the cheek. "I love you. I'll be back in the morning."

Gram pursed her lips in disapproval, and Emily knew it was because she hadn't said she'd call Charlie. But she said, "Love you too, dear," and as she did, her face softened just a little.

Chapter Fifteen

Charlie stood at the front door, holding a can of paint in each hand. She couldn't help a grin spreading across her face, but there was a tiny part of her that felt protective of the house, and didn't even want to let him in.

"I got the paint. I've been waiting until things settled down to bring it over. It's the shade of blue like the fish on your wall."

"Let's bring it around back." Emily shut the front door, joining him on the porch, and headed down the steps to the path that led to the shed.

"You're barefoot," Charlie said, following her as she hopped through the grass.

"Yep," she said over her shoulder.

"You might get a splinter or stub your toe."

"I might. But *you* might get paint on your shoes."

They stopped outside Papa's shed, and she noticed how he was smiling at her. She turned away from him toward the boat, inspecting the wood to make sure it was in good shape before they painted it. It had spent many days in the elements out on that little stretch of beach.

Charlie set the cans down and took off his shoes, placing them to the side and walking barefoot into the shed. "We'll need to sand the boat first."

Emily waited outside in the breeze, anxiety pecking at her while he rooted around in the shed, eventually returning with Papa's electric sander.

"Is there somewhere I can plug this in?"

Emily reached just inside the door of the shed, where Papa had the extension cord hanging, and pulled it out for him. Then, she pointed toward the outlet. Charlie plugged the other end into the outlet above his worktable. He tried to turn it on, but nothing happened. He took a step inside to inspect it, Emily standing behind him.

"That one doesn't work," she said. "It hasn't worked for years. You have to plug it in the bottom one."

He wriggled the outlet—it looked loose. Then he pulled the plug from the top socket and put it in the bottom. The sander let out a squeal when he turned it on.

"It looks like the outlet's gone bad."

He turned off his sander and set it on the worktable next to the stack of photos she'd inadvertently left when she'd returned the radio the other night. When he did, it shifted a piece of wood, moving it from where Papa had last set it, and Emily could feel the drumming in her heart. She tried not to watch, instead focusing on the photos. The one of Papa was on top of the stack and she looked away, not knowing what to do.

"Mind if I unscrew the cover to take a look at the wiring—make sure it's safely wired? I might need you to turn the circuit breaker off." He reached for Papa's screwdriver.

"No!" she heard herself shout "No," she said again more calmly. Papa had wired it all himself and he'd always been fine with just the bottom one. There was no need to start dismantling things in his shed.

"It's an easy check," he said, reaching again for the screwdriver. This time, he picked it up. "I promise I won't set the shed on fire." He was looking at her, his brows coming together, showing his confusion.

She grabbed his arm, stopping him. "The bottom one works. Just use that one."

Changing the boat was one thing. It would rot out there by the beach; they'd used it all the time, moving it in and out of the water. But Papa's shed was another thing entirely. It had been his place—no one else's. It had always been just like this and there was no reason to change it.

"It's fine, Emily. I don't mind looking at it."

Carefully, Charlie turned toward the outlet, lining up the screwdriver with the center screw in the plate, and Emily could feel the frustration rising from the pit of her stomach. She felt out of control, like a speeding train with no destination, just waiting for the end of the tracks when she'd free-fall. As his hand began to turn, loosening the screw, she pushed him away with all her might, knocking a piece of wood and the stack of photos off the worktable. She shouldn't have left them there. They fluttered through the air and scattered across the dirty floor.

Charlie stared at her in silence, a shocked look on his face, but she didn't care. She found two pieces of wood that Papa had glued together—they had fallen to the floor when the photos fell and split into two pieces. She tried to fit them back together, willing them to stick, to go back to the way they had always been, but they kept falling apart.

"What was that?" he said incredulously, but she ignored him, trying to get the pieces together, her hands shaking.

When she looked up, she saw Charlie walking away but it didn't matter. She didn't want to see him.

A sob escaped as one piece of wood slipped from her hands and crashed again on the floor. She set the other piece on the worktable, trying to get herself together. With slow, deliberate movements, she leaned down on it for support—like Papa had always given her—and finally cried, her face in her hands. She felt sick with grief.

But then Charlie returned. She looked up at him, his jaw set, his breathing slow and steady as if he were working to keep it even. "I can't get out of the drive. There's a car in my way and a man standing out front."

"Hello," an unfamiliar man said as he stood in the driveway, holding a piece of paper in his hand. "I'm here to take a look at the car that's for sale."

Flash had been there first to greet the stranger. The man bent down and rubbed Flash's head. Emily looked at Charlie, confused, but there were no answers on his face. Surely, this elderly gentleman was at the wrong house.

He held out his hand and showed her a photo that looked as though he'd printed it off the Internet. There, on the paper, was Papa's Buick with Gram's name and details.

"It was on the Clearwater trading website," he said. "Is this it?" he asked, walking over to the car and peering in the windows. In typical Gram-form, it was unlocked. He opened the door and sat himself down in the driver's seat, his hands on the wheel, his eyes roaming the dashboard. "The ad said it only has 50,000 miles on it. Is that still correct?" he asked from inside the car, the door still open, his foot protruding out and planted on the gravel. He looked out of place in it.

"Um… I believe so. I'll get the keys…" She noticed Papa's hat still on the back window, and she felt as though her chest might explode. "May I see the printout you have?" she asked, trying to keep her words even.

He handed it to her.

She left Charlie with the man as she peered down at the paper on her way to get the keys to Papa's car. From the looks of the ad, it seemed that Gram had posted this about a week ago. Her heart sank as she read it.

Once inside, she shut the door behind her. Every time she stood in that entryway, she could feel Papa around her. She looked around for some sign, some guidance, but it was just her. As she collected herself in the silence, the anxiety she'd felt in Papa's shed replayed like a bad dream, and suddenly, she felt terrible for the way she'd acted toward Charlie. She wasn't being rational at all. Charlie was only trying to help. She walked to the table in the hallway where Gram always kept her keys and pulled them from the basket. Then, she opened the ring and slid the single Buick key off.

Charlie was making small talk with the man as Emily walked onto the porch and down the steps, with the paper and the car key. Flash was nearby in the woods, but came running over when he heard her come out. She faced the man, handing the ad back as Flash leaned against her leg. She was glad for that, because her knees felt weak and she needed the support.

"I'm not the owner," she said as she gave him the key. "I'll have to call her if you're interested in the car."

"Okay," the man said. "May I take it for a test drive?" He held out his hand. "My name's Randolph Smart." Emily shook Mr. Smart's hand. "If you'd like me to leave something here to be sure I bring back the car, I'd be happy to do that."

"It's fine. Take it out for a drive and if you like it, I'll call my gram. It's her car."

"Thank you." Mr. Smart put the key into the ignition and started the Buick. Then, he closed the door, fastened his seatbelt and headed down the long drive, Papa's hat, still sitting in the back window, fading away in the distance.

Mr. Smart offered to buy the car on the spot. He had his checkbook with him, and after a quick call to a friend to drive it off the property, the car was gone. Emily put Papa's hat on the hat rack, and a few coins from the car's coin tray onto the hall table. Selling the Buick was a wake-up call.

Charlie, who'd stayed through the sale of the car, had left, and she was alone. She'd apologized profusely to him, telling him she didn't know what had come over her. She'd felt terrible for pushing him, and she made sure that he heard the complete regret she had.

But before she really felt like she'd finished telling him, he'd said, "It's fine, I understand." Never once during her apology or his response, had he looked her in the eye. He wanted to leave, and she could tell, so she didn't say anything else, and then he'd walked to his car and gone.

The house was eerily quiet, and the silence made her anxious, so she clicked on the radio, the station fading in and out but providing enough noise to make her feel better, and she opened the window to let the sound of the bay come inside.

As she walked around the house, she made a list on a small notepad of all the things she wanted Gram to keep for her. There was the old hat rack that Papa had made out of scrap wood and antique crystal doorknobs. She was definitely keeping that, as well as his hat—an old baseball cap. The brim was weathered, the edges fraying, but if she put it to her face, she could still smell Papa. She didn't let herself though. She'd been behaving so irrationally and she needed to keep hold of her emotions.

She wrote down her childhood bed—an old four-poster that Papa had painted white to go with her pink room as a child. It was beautifully intricate, the spindles curly and feminine. Papa had read her bedtime stories in that bed, and she'd hid under it when she heard him coming up the stairs to tuck her in. Emily would pop out and he'd pretend to be startled.

There was the old recliner that Gram would playfully call hers whenever Papa was in it. Emily added it to the list.

She wrote down the floor lamp in the hallway that was always left on after dark when she and Rachel were playing outside, catching lightning bugs, and climbing trees.

She had so many memories, and they were wonderful, but she kept thinking about how she'd acted with Charlie and how Gram had warned her about prioritizing memories over real life.

She called Flash who came leaping up the stairs so quickly that his paws slipped. He had to scramble to get to the top. He came to her, panting and snorting, pushing his head against her leg to say hello.

"Hi, Flash," she said, rubbing his head. Why was she the only one losing it and reacting this way? She sighed and shook her head. She didn't have the answer, but she knew she needed to get out of the house. "Want to go see Eli?" she asked Flash. He wagged his tail.

What started as a walk, turned into a run. When she reached Eli, she opened the gate and jogged to the barn, grabbing her riding gear. She saddled her horse and swung herself up onto him without a moment's breath. "Hey, boy," she said, knocking his sides with her feet, the frustration over her emotions getting the better of her. "Let's go."

She wanted to be close to Eli. She wanted him to know that she loved him. As if he knew, as if he felt the fear of knowing she might leave him again, Eli took off, his old body sailing through the woods, toward the beach, Flash trailing after them. Eli was flying, tearing through the trees, giving it all he had. While the wind pushed against her, Eli's hooves sinking as they sped through the sand, she thought about Charlie. She couldn't get her mind off him. She didn't want Charlie to think this was who she was, because she had so much more to show him.

Eli finally slowed to a walk, his aging body probably spent. She lay down on his back and hugged his neck all the way back to the barn, tears falling faster than she could stop them. "I'm so sorry," she said. "I didn't want to leave you. I wanted to stay. Please forgive me." Eli was silent the rest of the way.

When she got back to the house, Emily went upstairs, ran a brush through her hair, and looked at herself in the mirror. She was finally alone and calming down, but all she wanted to do was talk to Charlie to try to make things right.

She picked up her phone and dialed his number.

"Hello?" he answered.

"Hey. It's me." He didn't say anything, so she continued. "Charlie, I just wanted to say again how sorry I am for the way I acted. I feel awful."

Silence buzzed in her ear. She wanted him to tell her it was okay, that he forgave her. He had to know that she knew she'd acted irrationally and she was sorry.

"Please let me make it up to you. Maybe you can come over and I can cook for you." She needed to see him, to read his expression, to study his eyes—he always spoke with his eyes. "Or maybe you could make that dinner…"

She hung on the emptiness, waiting, hoping he'd say "Yes." Then, the doorbell rang, startling her.

"Hang on just a second." She took in an anxious breath and headed down the stairs to get it.

Emily held the phone as she walked down each step slowly, not wanting the conversation to be interrupted. He had to say something, or she'd go crazy. "Charlie, I don't know who that was in Papa's shed today. I don't push people. That's not who I am." She rested a hand on the doorknob, her focus on making Charlie understand. "I know I messed up and I'm so, so sorry." She waited again, her hopes dashed when she heard a breath on the other end. It seemed expectant, like he was waiting for her to say or do something more. What could she do? Her chest ached with the need to hear his voice.

Finally, Charlie cleared his throat. "Didn't you say there was someone at the door?" Her heart fell.

"No I didn't. But there is." She turned the doorknob and opened the door, only to find Charlie standing with the phone in his hand, grocery bags at his feet.

"Hi," he said with a grin.

Chapter Sixteen

Flash jumped around the kitchen excitedly as Charlie set the bags of groceries on Gram's kitchen counter. He'd bought oysters, garlic, oregano, parsley leaves, red peppers, and all kinds of other delicious ingredients. There was a moment where it seemed like he had something he wanted to say, his face serious, apologetic even. If she hadn't been looking directly at him, she'd have missed the slight nod of his head, as if he'd decided something. He turned to her and allowed a small grin to emerge. She smiled back. It was as if they'd silently agreed not to think about things too much tonight, to simply enjoy themselves.

While Charlie preheated the oven and put the oysters on a baking sheet, Emily filled Flash's bowl with food, but he ignored it, sniffing around near the counter instead.

"I'm just going to go change into something more comfortable," Emily said, and she immediately saw interest in Charlie's eyes. He quickly blinked it away. "I've been riding Eli in these clothes. I'd like to put on a clean pair of shorts and a T-shirt." His face resumed a more regular look, but the speculation of what he thought made her smile despite her attempts to straighten it out. "Be right back."

Flash followed her upstairs.

Emily went into her room, allowing Flash to come in, and then shut the door. She squatted down and rubbed his cheeks. "And what do you think of Charlie cooking for us?" she asked him quietly. Before she could pull back, Flash gave her a big wet kiss, making her laugh. "You like it when he cooks?" she giggled. "I wonder if he can cook like Gram," she whispered and Flash kissed her again. "You think he can? Well, let's get ready then." She stood up and pulled a pair of shorts off the chair in the corner.

Flash flopped down onto his cushion and chewed his bone as Emily slipped her clothes off and threw on a T-shirt and her shorts. Then, she headed downstairs, her little shadow behind her.

When she got to the kitchen, Charlie had found one of Gram's oven mitts and was pulling the oysters out of the oven. "I heated them up a few minutes so they'd pop open. Now, I'm just going to remove the top shell. Do you have a butter knife?"

She opened the drawer and retrieved one.

"Do you mind prying them open for me, please? You can throw away the top and then loosen the oyster on the bottom. I'll mix the other ingredients together." He opened the cabinets until he found a bowl. Then, he put in breadcrumbs and spices and started mixing.

Emily finished opening the shells as Charlie began peeling the outer covering off the garlic. She pulled the garlic press from the drawer and set it beside him. "Do you make this a lot?" she asked.

"I've made it a few times." He picked up the garlic press, loading the garlic. "Thank you," he said, holding it up.

"You seem to know your way around a kitchen."

"I live alone. If I don't cook, I'll starve, and I refuse to hire someone," he said with a grin.

"Why?" She stood next to him and scooped the garlic peel off the counter with her hands, throwing it away.

"I suppose I like to be in control of what I cook. Growing up, I didn't get to choose, but as an adult I can. I like having the ability to cook however I'd like. If I want more butter, I can add more butter," he said as he looked over at her.

"So you like taking charge. Not surprising."

He grinned. "I like this recipe because it's easy. I have to add a little olive oil and some chicken stock." He reached into the bag and pulled out the rest of the ingredients, pouring the stock in last. "Now, I'll just spoon this mixture on top of the oysters and really pack it down. Then, we'll pop them into the oven."

"I'll make us a salad."

"Sounds good."

As Emily moved around the kitchen with Charlie, she thought about the day that unknown man had walked into Francine's, and now look at them. She filled a bowl with lettuce, thinking how she'd never done this with Brad. She'd cooked. He'd eaten. And neither of them had really ever questioned it. But here was this man who treated her so differently, and it was as if just now she realized what she'd been missing. The thought scared her to death, but she was going to push it to the back of her mind tonight.

With a few shredded carrots and a chopped cucumber tossed in the bowl of lettuce, she set it on the table with a glass of iced tea for each of them. Charlie plated the oysters, the stuffing sizzling in each shell. The buttery, herb smell washed over her, making her stomach rumble.

"Wow, that looks delicious."

"I'm glad," he said with a wink. He pulled out her chair.

She poked her fork into one of the oysters, the breadcrumbs golden and crispy on top. "How do you eat it?" she asked, holding the entire thing on her fork.

He chuckled. "You just put it in your mouth. It's not that big."

"It's too big of a bite for me!"

He chewed on a grin. "Would you like a knife?"

As she attempted to stab it with her fork, he let out a little laugh, smiling now, his chest rising and falling with his amusement, and she couldn't help but find him attractive, which made her mind wander. Their little conversation just now made her think of something. She struggled to straighten her face out, heat from embarrassment burning her cheeks, but she could see he'd noticed.

"What?"

"Nothing." She got up, trying to hide her thoughts, and grabbed a knife from the drawer as he followed her with his eyes. She had to get herself together.

"What?" he asked again, with more emphasis, a crooked grin on his face.

"It's just... I realized something. But it's nothing. Really."

He was staring at her, waiting, an adorable look on his face. His eyes were daring her to say what she was thinking out loud, his smile different than it had been before, more personal, as if she were someone he'd known for years.

"Oh, okay. Fine." She took a sip of iced tea to try to cool her burning face. It didn't help. It was a stupid thought but now she'd made such a scene she'd have to tell him or his curiosity would get the better of him. She took a deep breath. "Aren't oysters supposed to be... aphrodisiacs?"

"Ha!" He threw his head back and then looked at her again. "I've heard that, yes. But it hadn't occurred to me."

"Well, I'm glad it hadn't!"

"Why?"

He was still smiling, but his face was baiting her, she could tell. What was going on between them? They'd spent time together, and, while she could feel herself letting her guard down tonight, she didn't know quite what to do. She couldn't believe how she'd turned the conversation. What was she thinking?

He seemed to sense her confusion as he said, "Personally, I think wine is more of an aphrodisiac than oysters any day, and we've made it through that on several occasions just fine. I'm sure, given that we're drinking iced tea, and we have an entire kitchen table between us, that we'll be able to control ourselves," he teased.

She didn't even want to think about that bottle of white wine he'd brought over. It was still in the fridge. She looked down at her food, trying to stifle the grin on her face and the blush in her cheeks, and in both instances, she was unsuccessful. She needed to change the subject.

"You said you eat alone in your apartment." She mustered the courage to look up and found him looking at her affectionately, a slight smile on his lips.

"Yes."

"I rarely eat alone so I can't imagine that. Don't you want to talk to someone?"

He shook his head. "No. I enjoy the silence. My job back in New York is quite demanding. I have about fifty employees—who are probably wondering what has happened to me, by the way."

"You haven't checked in?"

"I do, via email." He stabbed a piece of lettuce with his fork. "This is the longest I've ever been away."

"What about when you did your renovations? Weren't you away then?" She leaned on her forearms casually, more interested in him than the food.

"I did them at night."

"You worked all day and then renovated your house at night? That seems like a lot of work."

"It's amazing how living in a construction site will motivate a person." He chuckled. The modest chandelier above the table sent a yellow glow around the room, casting a light shadow on his face.

"True. When I'm alone, I like to take walks or sit out by the water. I'll bet Central Park is amazing. Do you ever take walks there?"

His face was thoughtful as he shook his head. "Not very often."

"Why?"

"I'm too busy when I'm home."

"Life is about balance, though, isn't it? You seem to be finding that balance here."

Charlie let out a quiet laugh. "This is not what I call balance. This is me barely working. I'm on vacation."

"So when you have only a meeting or two a day, you call that a vacation? What would you do if you had no work at all for two weeks?"

"I'd probably go crazy. Wouldn't you?"

"Not if I were in the right place."

He nodded slowly as if reconsidering. "Yes, you might have something there. I've been here almost every day and I haven't been bored once."

Emily tried to keep the thrill of that revelation behind her features.

When their plates were empty, Charlie said, "I got us a movie. Still hungry? We've got the popcorn and wine."

"First oysters, now wine," she said, feeling comfortable enough with him after their conversation to tease him. His honesty just now had made her feel like she could tell him anything.

"Ha!" he laughed. "I swear," he said, holding his hands up in the air. "I'm innocent. I just thought it would be nice with the movie."

Emily could see the sincerity in his eyes, but she could also see the excitement, and it sent a thrill through her chest. She found herself enjoying having that look of happiness directed at her. "Okay, fine. Pour us some wine, I suppose."

They cleaned up dinner together. Emily popped the popcorn and put it into a giant bowl, while Charlie poured them each some wine. Then, they went into the living room where Gram still had the small television and DVD player.

"I'll just get Flash a treat and grab a blanket," Emily said, setting the large bowl onto the coffee table. She had to hold Flash's collar to keep him from diving into it. Charlie put in the DVD and turned on the TV.

As the screen came to life and Charlie sat down, Emily covered them both with one of Gram's quilts, the bowl of popcorn now between them. Flash was finally settled on the rug with his treat.

"Why are we covering up? It's scorching outside?" Charlie said.

"I always cover up when I watch a movie. That's why I've got the paddle fan on," she said, "Get comfortable." She wriggled herself closer to him, getting into a cozy position, the popcorn tipping precariously.

He caught it and set it upright.

"Can I ask you a question?" she said, hitting pause on the remote. The image froze on the screen, and he looked at her. "Forgive me if this sounds rude because I don't mean it to be. I'm just curious."

His head tilted just slightly to the side as he waited for her question, curiosity all over his face. He looked so handsome and vulnerable right then that she wanted to put her hands on his face and kiss him. She shook the thought from her mind and continued with her question.

"You work a desk job and live in an apartment."

Charlie turned completely so that he was facing her, the popcorn tipping again. He caught it.

"So, how did you get so good at building things?"

A small smile emerged. "It was a talent I stumbled upon," he said. "When I bought my apartment, the one thing I really hated about it was this half-wall separating the kitchen and the living area. It looked so out of place that I wondered if the resident before me had had it built and it hadn't been part of the original plan. It didn't belong there at all. I decided—since I had just ordered new flooring anyway—to knock it down. I got out my hammer and started hitting it. By the end of the night, it was gone. The floor crew put new hardwoods right over it. After that, I started doing small projects whenever I had time— which wasn't much. I realized that I really enjoyed it, so I read about different projects I wanted to do, and I could always just do them."

"So restoring Papa's boat relaxes you."

"Yes. I don't ever just sit. Doing things is my way of relaxing."

She really hadn't ever seen him just sitting still. "Then why did you buy a movie tonight?" They could've easily painted the boat instead.

He smiled at her. "Because I thought you might like it."

"And since when have you decided to be so concerned about what I might like?" she teased.

He stared at her, so many unsaid words on his lips. It was as if he were deliberating, what he wanted to say clearly right there ready to be said, but he didn't know if he should say it. Then, finally, he said, "Since the moment I decided that I wanted to kiss you."

She sat still, her eyes on him, feeling the impact of his words in her chest. "And when was that?" she asked slowly.

"At your grandfather's pier, when we got the crabs. You were barefoot, your hair blowing in the wind, that adorably concerned look that you always have on your face, your perfect lips pressed together except when you talked. Then."

"It wouldn't be very professional of you," she said cautiously, the thought of his lips on hers making her dizzy.

"No."

"The owner of a company doesn't go around kissing his employees…"

"Certainly not," he said, setting the popcorn on the side table beside him and turning back toward her.

Flash got up and positioned himself on the floor next to the table with the bowl, but Emily barely noticed.

"It could make working together quite difficult in the future."

"Yes," he said, leaning toward her, his hands on either side of her, their faces only inches apart, his blue eyes so intense that it almost took her breath away.

She wasn't pulling back. That was because she welcomed his advances. In that moment, she didn't plan ahead, she didn't think about what would happen tomorrow when they faced each other at work, she didn't think about the loss of Oyster Bay. None of it mattered because of one important factor: *she* wanted to kiss *him*.

It made no sense at all, but she reached out and put her hands on his face. Before she could process the feeling of his skin against her fingers, the masculinity of his jaw, the day's growth in his beard, his lips were on hers, moving effortlessly, eagerly, and then softly, making her lightheaded. She moved her fingers around his neck to his hairline, grabbing on lightly for support as he continued to kiss her. Their kiss had so much built-up energy, so much passion, that she didn't know if it would ever end, which was fine with her.

Charlie's hands found her back as he leaned her onto the decorative pillows that sat in the corners of the sofa. His lips moved from hers, to her cheek, and then to her neck, his breath causing the hair on her arms to stand up. He found her lips again and she couldn't get enough of him. She let her hands move along his back, onto his sides, as she gripped his shirt in her fists. For the first time in her life, she understood what Gram meant by *living*. She'd never felt more alive than she did right now, in this moment. And she was happier than she had been in years.

When his kisses lightened, the energy dissipating to a more regular level, he pulled back and looked at her, his grin filling his entire face and causing the little creases at his eyes. "Wow," he said, running his finger along her neck where his lips had been. Neither of them moved. They were both right there in that moment.

"You said you don't like to sit still. You're not moving and you look relaxed now," she teased.

"Well, I don't *always* have to move." He grinned. "And staying still on this sofa is a lot easier since I don't have the stress of wondering how in the world I'm going to get you to kiss me anymore."

She laughed quietly, enjoying the feel of him wrapped around her still. "I think it was the oysters."

He laughed, making her stomach flip. "Want to turn on the movie now?" he asked.

"Okay."

Charlie hit play on the remote and then dropped it down onto the floor beside him, just as his lips found hers again.

Chapter Seventeen

An unfamiliar beeping sound swam through Emily's head, as she lay under the warm blanket, more comfortable than she could remember being in a very long time. She opened her eyes and blinked, trying to register the source of the beeping. To her confusion, she realized that she was looking at the alarm clock from her bedroom, but it was on the end table and she was still on the sofa. Beside it was a piece of paper. She sat up and opened the note. It read: **I woke up before the sun was up. I checked on Flash to let him outside for you. Go out to the boat. I left you a surprise. See you at work. Charlie.**

Emily pushed the blanket off her legs and stood up. She padded across the house and went out the back door in her bare feet. She could hardly wait to see what Charlie had done. As she approached it, the boat was in the same spot as before, but its beautiful new coat of paint made it look as if it had been pulled right out of her memory, only better. The blue was so pretty. She walked around it, admiring his work.

Flash came running up from the sand, his fur all wet from swimming, his tail thumping the sawhorse. "Hey there," she said, patting his side, as she continued to look at the boat. Then she saw something and a smile spread across her face. On the wooden seat inside the boat, Charlie's artistic talent overwhelmed her. He had painted a perfect picture of Papa's fishing-tackle box, open with all his pretty glistening hooks, lures, and spools of line. Papa always sat it in that exact spot when he was fishing. As Emily looked down at the painting, still marveling at it, she couldn't imagine a better surprise. She peered into the shed. The photos that had been left strewn across the floor were in a nice neat stack with the one of Papa back on top. Charlie must have picked them all up for her.

There was another note taped to the sawhorse. She reached over and pulled it off. It said: *Careful, it's probably still wet. I sanded and painted it by hand. Hope you like it. Charlie.*

Charlie had not been at the inn all day, which had been good for Emily, as it meant she could focus mostly on work. She had spent a large part of the day booking events and doing inventory for the inn, the whole time smiling—she couldn't stop smiling.

She checked in at the hospital to see how Gram was doing. Then she called Rachel while she sat outside on the inn's patio, telling her both about last night and the fact that, on her lunch break, she'd secured herself a condo. Getting a place had been easy—only three phone calls and she'd found one. It wasn't permanent—a sublease for the summer—but it was dog-friendly, fully furnished, and near the water, so she accepted. She'd be able to move in next week, as it was currently vacant to allow summer renters.

"Guess what!" Rachel said.

"What?" she asked, feeling her sister's excitement through the phone.

"I got an interview at that marketing company!"

"Oh, that's fantastic!"

"I'm so excited! It's Wednesday at two o'clock. But I have a favor to ask. Is there any way you can watch Clara for a few hours while I do the interview? I know you have to work, but I was wondering if you could arrange your schedule by any chance. I hate to even ask, but Gram can't, and I don't have anyone else."

"I'd be happy to. I'll figure it out."

"Oh!" she said with relief in her voice. "Thank you so much! I owe you big time!"

"No you don't."

"Love you!"

After a quick bit of small talk, Emily got off the phone with Rachel and decided that she'd been away from her desk long enough. It felt good to be working, making plans to see Clara, hearing about Rachel's job interview. It was a nice change of pace. It was as if she were finally in the real world again. She got up and headed back inside with renewed energy.

Emily wanted to see Charlie. She'd managed to go all day, but now she was losing the ability to focus. She picked up her office phone and ran her finger through the index until she found the phone number for the Concord Suite. With excitement pumping through her, she dialed the number and let it ring, hoping he'd be back.

There was a click. "Charles Peterson."

He was there! She smiled, hearing his voice, and cleared her throat. "Yes. This is the events coordinator. I have a few questions and was wondering if I could request your presence in my office, sir."

There was a tiny huff of laughter on the other end. "Certainly, Miss Tate. I'll be down in… thirty seconds."

"That's awfully fast."

"I like to get straight to business."

Before she could say anything more, the line was dead. Still unable to get her smile under control, she hung up the phone and took a deep breath to steady herself. She ran her fingers through her hair, pulling it behind her shoulders and sat up tall in her chair. As she made herself look busy by moving things around on her desk, there was a knock at the door.

"Come in," she said.

Charlie opened the door and then closed it behind him.

"That might have really been thirty seconds," she said, standing up and walking around the desk to greet him. He looked down at her and smiled, sending her stomach into somersaults.

"I said I like to get right to business."

"To what business are you referring? You don't know why I called you down here. I might need new tablecloths. We're short three."

He put his hands on her waist, his expression swallowing her up. "I'd better keep control of that corporate card," he teased. "I'll have them ordered today," he said, his mouth near hers, his breath on her lips.

She pulled out of his grasp, her head whirring with the exhilaration of being near him, but she kept her cool. "I also need an artist. I think it would be good for the displays in the restaurant."

He had a quiet determination about him as he took a step toward her again. She turned to face him and this time, she put her hands around his neck. "Know any good artists?" she asked, looking up at him. "Because I do."

He smiled a crooked grin as he leaned down and pressed his lips to hers. Then he looked at her, his eyes happy. "Did you like it?"

"I loved it."

"I'm glad."

"Where did you get the paint for the tackle box?"

"I'd seen it in your grandfather's shed. There's a wall full of paint cans. When I needed certain colors, I mixed a few together until I had what I wanted, or at least close to it."

"You're very talented. No wonder you have a knack for renovation. You have an artistic eye."

"Thank you." He pulled her against him.

"Now about those tablecloths…" She wriggled out of his embrace.

Charlie chuckled. "Would you like to come up to my suite and assist me with ordering them? I'd like to make sure I get the right ones."

"I have work to do."

"That would be work."

She cut her eyes at him playfully. "Perhaps we can order them later. I wouldn't want to get sidetracked."

"I won't take no for an answer," he teased. "If you need tablecloths, then, by all means, let's buy them."

She finally allowed herself to laugh. "Just hush. What are you doing tonight?"

"Nothing, why?"

"I want to hang out on Gram's beach. I talked to Rachel and she said they can come."

"What time?"

"I need to visit Gram again—I'm bringing her some books to keep her busy. After that, say six thirty?"

"Shall I bring anything?"

She smiled. "Your swimming trunks."

"All right."

They had an easy way of being together, as if they'd always been meant to be, and she remembered Rachel's words to her about finding someone. Her sister was right, because Emily had never felt like this before.

"Hey, how did the meeting go with the residents?" she asked, all of a sudden realizing why she hadn't seen him all day.

"It went well."

"Don't get too excited yet," she said, still smiling at him. "You still have to wait for the planning commission to approve the rezoning. But if they do, I think I'll be okay with it."

He looked into her eyes and reached out, pulling her close again. Then, he leaned in for another kiss.

Chapter Eighteen

"I'm the last one, Emily," Rocky said after she had called him for an update. She took a chance that he'd be in the office after five o'clock, and she'd been right.

Things were eventually going to have to move along—she knew that—and Rocky was in an awful spot.

"I really don't have an argument. It's a good move, expanding the inn. He's proven that he's going to be cognizant of the area with the build. The residents are happy, there are some big tax advantages that could come from this, he already owns the land… It just doesn't make sense to say no."

Emily sat on the sofa, chewing on her thumbnail, her knee bouncing relentlessly. "Rocky, you've done a great job for me and I'm so thankful that you've put up a fight, but if you feel that it would be a better business move to expand the inn, then agree to it." She closed her eyes in disbelief of her own words.

"Honestly, I don't know how much longer I could've held them off. They're starting to see through me—they know I'm doing it for you. If I had even a few people on my side it would be different, but I don't."

"I understand. I'm sorry to have put you in that position."

"Don't worry about it. It's fine. I'd do it all over again if I had to."

"Thank you."

The sunlight was hanging on, its heat-laden rays still powerful enough to require Emily to wear sunscreen as she sat alone on the beach. It would be a few hours yet before the sun dipped low enough to cast shadows on the sand. Emily swiveled in her beach chair and looked toward the house where she saw Clara running full speed across the yard. She had her swimsuit on, her sparkly sunglasses, and a tiny striped beach bag over her shoulder.

"Aunt Emily!" she called, out of breath. "Charlie's here too! He's talking with Mommy and Daddy!"

She continued to sprint, her thin brown braid bouncing with every step. She slowed down near the shore, trotting over the path through the sea grass that led to the sand. Her little chest was pumping up and down as she took in large breaths.

Clara squatted in the sand and dug into her beach bag. She pulled out a bright blue and pink circle float and held it out to Emily. "Will you blow this up?"

"Sure." Emily took it and opened the plastic cap. Then, with a deep breath, she puffed into the float, the surface expanding only slightly. She puffed again. With her cheeks full of air, the float hanging from her lips, Emily spotted Rachel, Jeff, and Charlie coming across the lawn. From that distance it seemed they were talking and laughing, and it looked like they were old friends. It reminded her of when she was in high school and she and Rachel would have Jeff and the guys over to swim. The boys would walk across the yard with their floppy hair and bare feet, their skin tanned from being in the sun all summer. Rachel and Emily would whisper about them, giggling, stopping only when they were within earshot. Charlie had the same sort of look on his face as her high school friends had had, and she couldn't help but get excited about it.

"Hey," she said as they all reached the beach.

Charlie walked over to her, and Rachel and Jeff began unpacking their things on the sand. "Hi," he said. "I don't mind blowing that up. Clara had asked me on the way in." She handed him the float. He put it to his lips and blew it up until the edges were tight with air. Then he secured the cap and handed it to Clara.

"Thank you," Emily said, trying not to notice how good he looked in his T-shirt and swimming trunks. She could see the bottom of his biceps peeking out from below his sleeves.

Clara went running into the water, the spray splashing all the way up to her face. Jeff had already waded out to be with her. He grabbed Clara and lifted her into the air before toppling over as they both fell under the water. Clara came back up giggling. "Do it again, Daddy!" Jeff picked her back up.

"How was Gram?" Rachel asked, setting up their three chairs.

Emily sat down on hers, and Charlie followed in another. "I popped in to see her on the way home. She's fine. I trust the doctors, but I really wish they could send her home before Friday."

"They probably just like to keep her there so they can bill the insurance," Rachel said with a laugh. "Does she seem lonely? I haven't been by today…"

"She was her usual self. I took her some books. I think she was glad for that."

"That's good to hear."

"Are you all ready for your job interview tomorrow?" Emily asked.

"I hope so. I'm a little nervous. I've been out of the game for a while." She leaned forward to address Charlie on the other side of Emily. "I'm interviewing for a marketing job and I've been out of the working world since Clara was born."

"Ah," Charlie said, nodding. "You'll do great."

"Thank you."

"How's Jeff dealing with the news of an interview?" Emily asked, keeping her voice lower, shooting a quick glance at Jeff and Clara still in the water splashing around.

"He hasn't said anything. He didn't offer to take off work or to help with finding childcare either."

"I'm sorry."

Rachel shook her head. "I can't stop my life from moving forward. I'm just going to go for it, let fate have a hand. Maybe I won't get it and Jeff won't have anything to worry about for a while."

"Or maybe you will," Emily said, raising her eyebrows with enthusiasm for her sister.

"Yes," Rachel said. "Maybe I will."

They sat there quietly for a little while, Clara calling out to them to watch as Jeff threw her into the water. Finally, Jeff and Clara came up onto the beach. "The water is so warm," he said. "You all should get in. It feels great."

"Yeah," Clara agreed. "Get in please, Mommy."

Rachel stood up and looked down at Emily. "I suppose we should, since the water's so nice. Do you have your suit on under your clothes?"

"Yep," Emily said, not moving from her chair. She'd never cared how she looked before, but she found herself wanting to look attractive for Charlie. She reached down into the beach bag and fumbled for the bottle of suntan lotion to stall, suddenly a little bashful. She pulled it out and pretended to read the ingredients.

Clara grabbed Emily's arm. "Please come in the water, Aunt Emily. It's fun. You can bring Charlie." She let go and ran toward the water, Rachel following behind and diving in.

Charlie and Emily both stood up. He pulled his shirt over his head, the sight of him causing her to drop the bottle. It fell in the sand with a smack.

"You okay?" he asked, a smile twitching at the corners of his lips.

"Fine, thank you." Emily picked the bottle up and shook it in the air to release any leftover grains before she chucked it back in the bag. Why was she so nervous? He'd had his hands all over her last night. She shimmied off her shorts and folded them, placing them in her chair and then she pulled her shirt over her head. When she did, she saw the way his eyes roamed her body despite his attempts to keep them on her face.

"Ready to swim?" she said.

They waded in together, the bay water just cool enough to be refreshing in the intense summer heat.

"Let's play Marco Polo!" Clara said, swimming inland just a bit until she could touch. She was wearing bright orange floaties on her arms. "Do you know how to play that, Charlie?"

"Is it where someone closes his eyes and calls out 'Marco' while the others say 'Polo' and he tries to tag them?"

"Yes," Clara said. "I play it with Daddy, and he's really good. Do you want to play?"

"Okay," he said.

"Yay!" Clara splashed around. "Close your eyes!"

He looked surprised. "You want me to say 'Marco'?"

"Uh huh!"

Charlie's gaze flicked over to Emily just before he shut his eyes, and she wondered if he was taking stock of her position in the water. He wouldn't dare.... But the lightness in his attitude today made her think he might. She took a big step toward the shore as a wave came in, trying to cover the sound of her movement.

"Marco," Charlie called, immediately turning to where Emily had been. She had to restrain herself from laughing. She moved toward Rachel. Charlie whipped around, zoning in on her movement. "Marco," he said again.

"Polo," she said quietly.

"Polo!" Clara yelled out.

Charlie waded toward Emily. She backed up out of his reach.

"Marco," he said, a smile playing in his features. He knew he was close, she could tell.

"Polo," she said, darting out of the way just as his hand came near her arm.

"Marco." His strides were too large for her to escape and he was so close to her that she couldn't possibly move fast enough. It was clear that he could hear the swoosh of the water and his reaction time was impeccable.

"Polo."

Slowly, he raised his arms out of the water. And then, as quick as a flash, he grabbed her, tickling her sides and making her squeal as he opened his eyes. "Got you," he said with a grin and let her go. "Your turn."

"You think you're slick," Emily said, still recovering, and he laughed. She liked the way he looked at her when she'd made him laugh. "Well, Clara and I will both try to find *you*. How does that sound, Clara?" she said, turning to little Clara. Charlie raised his eyebrows, a flicker of excitement in his eyes.

"Yes, yes!" Clara cheered.

Emily waded over to Clara as Jeff and Rachel, both eyeing her, spread out. "Okay, Clara. Ready?" Clara closed her eyes and Emily did the same. They waited for everyone to get their positions before Clara called out, "Marco!"

"Polo." Charlie's voice was to Emily's right. She started to move in that direction, the water swishing rapidly around her when he moved.

"Marco!" Clara said again, flapping around, trying to hear her mom as Rachel called out to her.

"Polo," Charlie said. This time the voice was behind Emily. She could hear his amusement in the word.

"Marco," she said this time, jolting quickly toward where the sound had come from. There was a loud splash.

"Polo," he said with a laugh. Another splash.

Her stomach was fluttering every time she heard his voice. She knew where he was. Slowly and deliberately, she waded through the water, listening as the ripples made their sound.

"Marco."

"Polo."

With all her might, she tackled him, sending them both under water.

When they came back up, his arms were around her. She opened her eyes and his face was so close, his arms so strong that she wished they were in that water alone because she would've kissed him right there.

He pushed a strand of wet hair out of her face. "You got me," he said with a grin.

She pulled out of his grasp with a giggle, turning toward the others.

"I got Mommy!" Clara yelled.

"Good job, Clara!" she said.

Clara swam over to the sand and got out, turning to Rachel, her limbs dripping wet. "I'm hungry, Mommy. Can we eat?" And just like that, the game was over.

Emily and Charlie stayed in the water while Jeff and Rachel took Clara in for an early dinner, a bath, and finally bedtime. They'd pulled in two lounger floats. Emily was on one, lying on her belly, holding on to Charlie's float by the cup holder to keep them from drifting apart while he lay on his back. They bobbed together as the waves washed ashore from a passing boat.

"I like how close you are with your family," he said out of nowhere, and she couldn't help but feel happy. Perhaps she'd gotten him thinking.

There was a kite in the distance. It was so far up in the sky that it looked like a tiny rainbow speck among the clouds.

"Would you ever want to have a family of your own?" she asked, her eyes on the kite for a moment before she pulled her float up next to his and rested her chin on her hands.

"I'm not sure…" he said. "I don't know if I'd be any good at it."

She lifted her head. That was quite a big thing to admit. "None of us know if we'll any good at it. We have no way of knowing what little souls we'll receive or what will fall in our paths."

"I think all the time about how glad I am that I didn't have kids when I got divorced. I wouldn't be able to raise children alone, and there's just no guarantee that your partner will be there."

"You're right. There are no guarantees. But I'd be willing to take that chance."

"Why?"

She looked at him for long time, trying to get her thoughts straight. "So I can play Marco Polo and know that my child will remember it for the rest of his or her life. I can teach my child to drive Papa's tractor. I can make Gram's sugar cookies and that child will know the recipe that's five generations old. Maybe when I'm Gram's age, I'll be able to have my child visit and bring her own children…"

"You're keeping your grandfather's tractor?"

"Of course. I'm going to drive it to work every day." She was teasing because she didn't want to think about how much of an eyesore it would be at the condo or imagine it decaying out in some junkyard somewhere because no one would want it. She was having a good day, and she wanted to keep it going.

Charlie chuckled at her joke, but she could see the same thoughts in his eyes.

"Are y'all gonna just stay out there and get all pruney or are you going to have some dinner?" Rachel called from the backyard, the kitchen door still open. "I ordered us a pizza. Jeff's going to pick it up."

When Jeff had returned, he and Charlie had the fire going in the fire pit and Emily had pulled the patio table over in front of it to give them a little light and keep the bugs away. Rachel, who'd brought the pizza box out with four beers, was tuning the radio.

"Did Clara go down okay?" Emily asked her sister.

"Yeah. I put her in Gram's bed. I might just stay the night. We can all three fit in that big bed and then I wouldn't have to wake her."

"That'd be fine."

"Do you have to work in the morning?"

"Yes, but I'm taking a half-day to watch Clara while you're at your interview. Haven't run it by the big boss yet," she said, giving Charlie a wink, "but I've cleared it with Libby."

"I suppose I'll let you off," he said with a smile. "Since it's for Clara's sake."

"And mine," Rachel said, handing out beers. "I really want to get this job."

"Who will watch Clara if you get it?" Emily asked.

"Her preschool has extended day, and next year, she'll be in kindergarten. It's actually the perfect time to go back to work, and I'm so ready. I just hope I'm still on my game."

Jeff sat silently at the table. Emily wasn't really sure what to say to him. She wanted to make him feel better about the situation, but ultimately, she wanted to encourage her sister.

"Knowing you, you'll be fine. You've probably been reading up on the latest trends for weeks."

"Months," Jeff piped up, then took a sip of his beer.

Emily could see the distance in his eyes. It wasn't good. It was clear by Jeff's demeanor that he didn't want to ruin the night. He smiled at her before taking another sip of beer.

Rachel passed everyone a paper plate and opened the box of pizza.

"What are you planning to do with Clara tomorrow afternoon?" Charlie asked Emily.

"I thought I'd take her to that little playground in Irvington. Then, maybe have some ice cream. Wanna come with us?" she asked.

"Sure. I might have to meet you there, though, because I'll be with the city planning commission that day. Can you give me directions?"

"Just text me after the meeting." She didn't want to think about the meeting tonight. There was nothing she could do to change it, and eventually, she'd have to face the fact that things were going to be different.

"Okay."

"So, I ran into Francine today," Rachel said, balancing the large wedge of pizza on her fingertips, preparing for a bite.

Emily shook her head, already wondering what her sister would say. Francine was known for gossip, and Emily never knew what would come out of her mouth. She leaned over to Charlie as he took a bite of pizza. "That's the woman in the shop with the margarita glasses. The one who gave you the corporate card back."

"Yes. I remember her well," he said with a chuckle.

"I told her I was coming over tonight to see you," Rachel said. "And I mentioned that Charlie would be here. You should've seen her mouth hanging open."

"Why do you indulge her like that? You could've just told her you were coming over."

"She doesn't mean any harm and it's fun to wind her up. She did say that, given your luck lately, you deserve a handsome man like Charlie." Rachel grinned sweetly at her sister and then winked in Charlie's direction. "And then she remarked how you two must be on *very* friendly terms if you call him Charlie because she's only ever heard people call him Charles."

"How does she know?" Emily said amused.

"Because she said she'd met him personally."

"Lordy. He was only in her shop five minutes. That was it."

"Well, she knows," Rachel teased. "And she said that if you two get married, she'll hand paint all the wine glasses for the wedding."

Emily's eyes got as big as saucers. "Married?"

"Francine said she's just thinking ahead."

Charlie quietly put his beer to his lips and drained what was left in the bottle. "Would anyone like another beer?" he asked. "I'll grab one from the kitchen." He stood up.

"I'll have another," Jeff said.

"Great. Emily, do you mind just coming in with me a sec?" he asked.

Given his face just now, she followed him in. He looked as though he had something he wanted to say to her.

As soon as they were inside, the door closed, he turned toward her. "I'm scheduled to fly out of Richmond on Friday," he said with no introductions at all.

"To go home?"

"Yes."

"That's in three days."

"I know. I have to get back home to take care of some things at work. It's proving difficult to run the business right now without me there on a regular basis. We're about to lose a major property." He turned toward the window, leaning on the sink as he looked out into the yard, but it seemed as though he wasn't processing the view—he was thinking. Then he turned back around.

"I don't just do this sort of thing," he said, frustration showing in his jaw. "I've never done this in my life. You've completely sidetracked me, derailed my plans entirely. I don't want to play a round of golf! I'd rather sit on your grandfather's patio and eat greasy pizza."

Emily smiled.

"You haven't known me long enough," he continued, "to realize that this doesn't happen to me. I don't run around after people. I don't change my plans… Because I've never had a need to."

"Then stay a little longer."

"I can't." He walked closer to her. "Why don't you come to New York for a while?"

She shook her head. "Sorry," she said, feeling deflated. She didn't want to go to New York. She needed to be here for Gram right now, for her family, and for herself. "I need to stay here. I spent three years away from it and I don't want to spend a single minute more somewhere else."

Charlie nodded, his face unreadable.

Chapter Nineteen

As she drove to the playground with Clara humming in the back, Emily thought about Charlie. He had been pleasant but quiet last night after their conversation in the kitchen. No one else seemed to notice, but Emily had, and when he decided to leave, she felt like he'd been waiting for a good time to make his exit. He was so stubborn. He wouldn't compromise at all. He had his job in New York and either Emily went with him or she didn't. He was knocking down her home regardless of how anyone felt about it. And because of that, he'd probably made the right decision by pulling back last night. But it left her feeling like something wonderful was missing.

She hadn't heard from Charlie all morning. He'd been in meetings. She'd texted but she'd received nothing in response. Now, as she made her way to the playground with Clara and Flash, she hoped that he'd still meet her like he'd said he would.

"I've never been to this playground," Clara said from her booster seat in the back of Emily's car. Her hair was in braids again, and she had a pink tank top and purple shorts with pink flowers on them. Flash was sitting beside her, his nose to the window.

"I think you'll like it. It has a lot of big, shady trees."

"It is hot. May I put down the window?"

"If you want to," Emily said, with a grin, peering in her rearview mirror as Clara hit the window button, letting a rush of heat into the car. The warm air reminded Emily of so many days she'd spent driving these roads with her windows down as a girl. Flash moved cautiously to the other side of the car. He sat in the floorboard at Clara's feet with his head tipped up toward the fresh air coming in.

Emily pulled onto a side street just past the main road running through the center of Irvington and parked the car by the little playground. There was a swing set, a curly slide, and a seesaw. As Clara unbuckled her seatbelt, Emily checked her phone. Nothing. She slipped it into her pocket.

"Swing with me, Aunt Emily!" Clara said, running to the swings and hopping on, the bright sun making her squint as she pumped her little legs to get going.

Emily let Flash out of the car and came over to grab a swing next to Clara.

"How high can you go?" Clara said, sailing past her.

Emily pushed off and glided forward, then pushed off again to get herself going. "I don't know," she said with a grin, "Pretty high!"

"I can go higher!"

"Are you sure about that?"

"Look at me!" Clara flew up and then back down, her braids hanging low to the ground behind her as she straightened herself out and stretched her legs as far as they'd go.

"I think you've won," Emily said, affection for her niece bubbling up. She loved spending time with Clara.

They continued to swing, Clara talking about the playground at her preschool and how her mommy had told her that she might get to swing at preschool every day.

"And what do you think about that?" Emily asked.

"I'd love it! It's so much fun! And my friend, Hannah is there. We play in the playhouse together. She pretends to go shopping while I cook the food." She was excited.

Clara pumped her little legs to get going faster. "Is Charlie meeting us?" she asked.

Flash found a shady spot under a tree and lay down in the cool grass, panting and wagging his tail.

"I'm not sure." Emily pulled her phone from her pocket and checked it again. "He's in a meeting. He'll probably text when he gets out."

"I like him."

Emily slowed the swing down until she was just sitting. "What do you like about him?"

"He's nice. And he's good at Marco Polo."

"Yes," she giggled, "he is."

"It's hot." Clara skidded her sandals against the dirt, stopping herself. She pulled on her shirt collar.

"It's very hot," Emily agreed, laughing again. She looked over at Flash. He was still panting. He sniffed something near an exposed root.

"Can we get ice cream now?"

Emily wanted to stall, hoping Charlie would get out of his meeting so as not to let Clara down. "How about a game of Hide and Seek?"

"Okay!" Clara jumped off the swing. "I'll hide first. Count to ten."

Emily covered her eyes, peeking out through her fingers to keep an eye on Clara. "One... Two... Three..."

Clara ran behind the large oak tree that shaded the area as Emily continued to count, Flash following her to the other side, his tail wagging feverishly. When she'd gotten to ten, Emily got off the swing and walked slowly toward the bench along the side of the play area. She looked under it. "Not there," she said loudly so Clara could hear her. She heard a giggle from behind the tree and acted like she hadn't noticed Flash dashing over and barking, giving Clara away.

Emily looked two more places before she heard a ping on her phone and saw Charlie's text: *So sorry I'm late. Tell me where to go.* She felt a wave of relief. He was coming! As she looked down at his text, she couldn't keep the smile off her face.

"Got ya!" Emily said, peeking behind the tree and sending Clara into a fit of giggles. "Charlie just texted. Want me to tell him to meet us at Henry's for ice cream?"

"Yes!"

Emily gave Charlie the location and told him she'd be there in five minutes. "Okay, let's get in the car! It's ice cream time!" The summer heat was unbearable, and she was glad to get Clara out of the sun. She started the engine and cranked up the air conditioning.

Flash hopped in, getting comfortable on the backseat as Emily helped Clara buckle herself up. Then, they were on their way.

Henry's ice cream was a diner-style building. It had walk-up windows, an outside seating area on grass, and picnic tables with giant red umbrellas. It was a perfect place for Flash to relax and have a little water while they ate their treats.

They pulled up and got out. Emily, who had put Flash on a leash to keep him safe from the road, grabbed his water bowl and a thermos from the backseat.

"What flavor of ice cream are you going to get?" Emily asked Clara. With his leash around her wrist, she took Clara's hand, and they walked over to an empty table.

"Mommy and I do a tasting game."

Emily slipped Flash's leash under the table leg and poured water in his bowl. He lapped it up sloppily and loudly, his tail batting back and forth. "Oh? How does it work?"

"Henry gives us little spoons with different flavors. We close our eyes and try to guess what it is! Want to play that?" Clara bounced up and down in anticipation.

"If it's all right with Henry."

"It is! He always lets us."

Emily felt a jolt of excitement as she saw the familiar blue BMW pull up. Charlie got out, wearing clothes that were too formal and hot to be in the sun eating ice cream. He'd come straight from his meeting. He put up his hand, that caring look in his eyes, making her feel like somehow everything would be okay.

"Hey there!" she called out.

"Hello."

Flash stood at attention, his ears perked up.

"We're going to play a tasting game," she said as he got closer. "We have to close our eyes and guess the flavor of ice cream."

"Sounds fun." Charlie smiled down at Clara as she tore away from them, headed toward the counter. He seemed to be his easy, relaxed self again.

They walked up to the window where Clara had already gotten Henry's attention.

Henry smiled as they approached. "Who's first?"

"Charlie!" Clara said.

"So I close my eyes?" he asked Clara.

"Yes!" she said hopping around.

"Okay."

Charlie closed his eyes.

Emily loved the fact that he wasn't self-conscious about joining in and indulging Clara. "Here's the first bite," she said, taking a small spoon from Henry and putting it near his lips. He leaned forward as she offered it to him and he bumped into the spoon. Emily let out a little laugh. She couldn't help but look at him as he tried to figure out the flavor. Dragging her eyes away, she tossed the spoon into a nearby trashcan.

He licked a drip off his bottom lip. She watched his expression while he deliberated.

"He doesn't know it!" Clara said, beaming.

He swallowed. "Yes I do." Charlie opened his eyes.

"What is it?" Emily asked.

"If he gets it right, all three of you can have ice cream on the house," Henry said with a devious grin on his face.

"Is it Caramel… Praline?"

Stunned, Henry leaned out the window and looked at the ads below. "How did you guess that? I didn't have it listed on my sign."

Charlie chuckled, clearly proud of himself. "There's a small coffee shop down the street from my apartment that makes caramel praline custard. It's my favorite treat and I get it occasionally."

"Ha! Well, it looks like you all will get free ice cream." Henry looked down at Clara. "Would you like to keep playing the game or do you want your sundae now?"

"I want a vanilla sundae with chocolate sauce!"

"Want to share one? They're big," Emily said to Charlie.

"Sure. Order whatever you like."

"Two vanilla sundaes with chocolate sauce then," she told Henry.

"Two vanilla sundaes, coming up!"

They walked over to the table where Flash was lying in the shade. He'd had his eyes closed but popped up to a sitting position when he saw them approaching. By the time they reached the table, he was standing, his tail wagging, his eyes expectant.

"Hi, Flash," Charlie said, patting his side. Flash leaned against his leg and Emily worried about the dog hair that might get on his expensive trousers.

"Clara, how was the playground?" Charlie asked, taking a seat at the table.

"It was very hot but I got to swing and play Hide and Seek."

"I'm sorry that I missed it." When he said it, his face was sincere.

"It's okay." Clara was sitting with one leg folded under herself as she waited for her ice cream.

"We'll have to go again sometime."

Emily looked at him. She knew he was just trying to be kind, but she wished he hadn't given Clara an empty promise. In two days he was leaving to go back to New York. He wouldn't be back to go to the playground with Clara. Even though she wanted to say something, she stayed quiet for Clara's benefit.

Henry brought over their sundaes and set them on the table. Each one was served in an enormous hurricane glass, filled to the brim with bright white vanilla ice cream, dark chocolate sauce sliding down the inside of the glass, and topped with a mountain of whipped cream and a maraschino cherry. Emily took one and slid the other one to Clara.

"Don't feel like you have to eat it all, Clara," she said. "That much ice cream will give you a bellyache."

"I won't," she said, her eyes on the ice cream as she pulled her spoon out and licked the end of it. Flash was at her feet, sitting, his tail wagging in the grass and his ears back as he followed her spoon with his eyes.

"I like to mix mine up," Clara said, stirring the concoction and taking bites. Whipped cream and chocolate sauce were oozing over the edge of the glass and puddling under it on the table. "It's yummier this way." Clara was on her knees, her head tilted to the side and her petite arm working hard to mix the thick concoction. She pulled the spoon out and licked a lollipop-sized glob of dripping brown ice cream.

"You're gonna make a mess," Emily laughed. But she didn't try to stop her.

She turned to Charlie, spooning a bite of ice cream for herself. "How did the meeting go?"

"Very well," he said, a hesitancy in his voice. He scooped a spoonful for himself and took a bite.

"Tell me about it." He might as well just be honest. She was a big girl; she could handle it.

"I've got my team together for one last meeting this afternoon regarding rezoning. I had to call in my architect, my engineers, and my lawyer. My lawyer thinks we might be able to get a variance or a conditional use permit for the land. They're talking now with the planning commission. And then tomorrow I hear from Rocky. It all hangs on that."

Emily knew that if it all hung on Rocky then Oyster Bay would be gone. She'd accepted that things had to change, and she'd been trying so hard not to feel sad about losing the house, but the thought of it actually being demolished and crumbling to the ground, just hurt. She couldn't help it.

"I'm all done. My tummy's starting to hurt," Clara said. She'd barely eaten any of her sundae, but it was fine with Emily because, she worried, with the size of it, that Clara would ruin her dinner.

She took a napkin and wiped Clara's mouth, the paper sticking to her lips as she tried to pull it across them. "You're really sticky." She balled up the napkin and set it on the table, gathering their trash.

But then she stopped, unable to hide her laugh. Clara had taken one more bite. She had chocolate down her chin and on the tip of her nose, and, because she'd attempted to lick it clean, she had vanilla on her upper lip. "Let me get a photo." Emily would clean her up but she had to show Rachel. It was priceless. She snapped a photo and then cleaned Clara's mouth with the wet napkin.

A woman walking by saw them and stopped. "Oh, dear! Please! Let me take one of all of you. You can even get your dog in the photo." She nearly jogged over to their table. "You are such a lovely looking family," she said with a smile, and Emily got a pinch in her chest. They were so far from a family. The comment made her realize how unsettled her life was at the moment.

Emily handed the woman her phone and they all posed—even Flash. She smiled—that smile she was so good at making whenever she didn't want to have to explain to someone what she really felt.

"There," the woman said with a satisfied expression. "I hope you all have a wonderful afternoon." She handed the phone back and Emily slipped it into her handbag.

Charlie offered her a bite of ice cream. Emily kept that smile on her face. "You can have it," she said. Then, she busied herself with cleaning up Clara and getting her ready to go home.

☼ ☼ ☼

With trembling hands, Emily pulled the blue BMW up beside her car and put it in park. Charlie had insisted on taking Flash back to the house so that when she took Clara home, she could have a little time with Rachel to find out how the interview went and get the latest on Gram, since it was Rachel's day to visit. Rachel's house was small and close to the road—not a place for a dog like Flash—so she couldn't take him with her.

Emily had refused to allow Flash in Charlie's BMW. She just knew he'd get nose prints all over the windows and dog hair on the interior. She didn't know what she'd do if his claws scratched the leather. So Charlie proposed that she and Clara take his BMW and he'd drive Flash home in her car. He wouldn't take no for an answer. She gave him her keys, hoping that her seats were clean enough not to put any spots on those fancy trousers of his.

When she got up to the front door at Oyster Bay, it was un-locked, so she went in, but Flash and Charlie were nowhere to be found. She walked to the kitchen, where she saw her keys on the table, and looked out the back door. Charlie had set up two beach chairs from Papa's shed in the sand by the water. She grinned re-membering how she'd told him to get a beer from the fridge while he waited for her. She could make out the bottle in his hand, his arm on the armrest of the chair as he sat facing the water. His back was to her—almost a shadow against the sunlight. He was throw-ing Flash's ball into the water and Flash was retrieving it in excited leaps. She walked outside, shutting the door behind her, and made her way down to the shore.

When she approached Charlie, she laughed, clapping her hand over her mouth. He'd unbuttoned the top button of his shirt and rolled up the sleeves, his trousers pulled up almost to the knee. She didn't want to think about the wrinkles that would be in them, and she hoped he had a good dry cleaner back home.

He turned around. "What?"

"You look… comfortable."

"I am, thank you." He smiled and took the ball from Flash's mouth, chucking it into the water. He patted the seat next to him and Emily sat down.

"How can you not love it here?" she asked.

"I do love it."

She felt the hope leap right through her. "Then how in the world could you destroy it?" She turned and looked at him, waiting for his answer.

He had concern in his eyes. "Why do you need this whole house to remind you that your grandfather was a good man? Why do you need this land to tell you that it was okay to grow up here? You know those things without this house."

"I know that," she said, the tightness in her chest returning like it always did whenever her views on Oyster Bay were in question. Flash dropped the ball by her feet. Charlie picked it up and threw it back toward the water. She watched it sail through the air and plop underneath the surface, a splash in the current.

Charlie got out of his chair and kneeled down in front of hers, grabbing her hands.

"You're going to ruin your trousers," she said.

"I don't care."

Emily had always thought that Oyster Bay would remain under Gram's watch and that she'd pass it along to the next generation. She'd assumed she and Rachel would be the next ones to inherit the house. But with her move to Richmond—three years spent away from her home—it had seemed Emily hadn't wanted it. The guilt over that consumed her.

"Come to my apartment in New York," he said carefully. "I know you said you need to stay here, but I want to show you something else, another perspective. You might love it."

"It isn't me," she said, getting her emotions back in check. "I wouldn't be happy there. This is where I belong. Even if I'm not in Papa's house. This is where I'm happy."

"Are you?"

"Yes," she said. "Even if I seem sad. I'm going to miss Oyster Bay terribly. There's so much I want those walls to see." She turned around to view the back of the house, the patio sprawling along the edge of it, meeting the screened porch, and she had to turn back around to keep herself together. "I want those walls to see Papa's great-grandchildren. I want those walls to see parents who made it! Parents who spent sleepless nights with their children, who celebrated little birthdays with party hats and homemade cakes, giving their children what I wasn't able to have. I want a family in that house. I want Papa to look down from Heaven and know that all his hard work building it was so that a big family—his family—could spend lazy days here, enjoying each other and having a blast."

When she focused on Charlie's face, his eyes were restless, showing his thoughts. He wasn't saying a thing. He picked his beer up from the sand where he'd set it and walked out to the water, the bottle swinging between his fingers.

She got up and walked down to him. She didn't want to make him feel bad. "But even if I can't have all that, Clearwater is where I belong."

He didn't look at her. His eyes were on the bay.

Chapter Twenty

"I'm going to have to tell Charles Peterson yes today," Rocky said through the phone as Emily sat outside the hospital. The heat was building in the car—she'd had the engine off for the last few minutes, trying to figure out some last way to offer to Rocky to save Oyster Bay. But there wasn't any.

Emily understood the pressure he was under. He couldn't go against everything he was supposed to do just to make her happy. And he'd warned her, so it wasn't a surprise.

"I can't believe Gram sold it," she said more to herself than to him. She shook her head, the phone pressed against her ear. "I'm sorry to have put you in this situation in the first place." She couldn't tell him that enough.

"I'm sorry too," he said. "I wish I could do more."

She said goodbye and hung up the phone. Then, stepping into the bay breeze, she went to get Gram.

"The movers are starting Friday," Gram said, shifting in her bed, the IV, now removed from her arm, having left a dark bruise. But other than that, she looked well, the color had returned to her face, and she was alert and pleasant. Emily could feel tension she hadn't known was there leaving her shoulders. Gram smiled at her. "Would you mind packing the hall closet where I keep all my photos and the drawers with my jewelry? I'd rather you do that than rely on strangers."

"Of course," Emily said, sitting down at the foot of the hospital bed.

"The movers have a list of what will be going to Florida."

"Yes. Speaking of… How are you going to get around in Florida without your car?"

Gram's eyes dropped down to the tan hospital blanket that was covering her. "I've been thinking a lot about Florida as I've sat here with nothing to busy my mind."

"What have you been thinking?" she asked, trying not to get excited by that comment.

Gram looked up. "I'm having second thoughts about moving."

"You are?" She couldn't help her delight from showing.

"When I agreed to sell Oyster Bay, you were in Richmond with the man I thought you planned to marry. Rachel was busy with Jeff and Clara, building her own family. There was no need for me to stay. But now with Rachel trying to go back to work and you moving home, I worry that I've made the wrong decision."

"Can't you back out of the sale? You *could* stay!"

"Even if I could, that house is too big for just me. I've already put a deposit down on a place in Tampa, and it's nonrefundable. The weather is better in Florida too…"

"You're trying to talk yourself into it."

"I'm trying not to sell myself short. I'd like to get a fresh start on these last few years of mine. But now you're all here, and it scares me. I don't want to miss out on anything."

They fell silent for a few moments before Gram piped up again. "Has anyone called on the furniture?"

"No. Just the car."

"What will I do with it all?"

"Well, if you move, we can put it in my storage unit until it sells. I can also call around to some antique markets in town to see if any of them want to buy anything. But if you don't move to Florida, we could look for a place to live together and move it there."

"For now, let's see how much we can get into storage."

Emily took a deep breath. While she wanted Gram to stay, she also wanted her to be happy, so, ultimately, the choice was Gram's. But she wasn't going to let her off without a discussion. "Well, I should get to work. And I need to check on your discharge time tomorrow. I'll be so excited to have you back home! Then we can talk more about you staying here in Clearwater."

"I cannot wait to sleep in my own bed."

Emily got up and kissed Gram on the cheek. "Do you have enough reading material to get you through today and tonight?"

"Yes, thank you. Now, go, go! Enjoy your day."

"I feel like we need to host more public events at the inn," Emily said to Libby as they sat on either side of Emily's desk. She'd called Libby in to discuss some ideas she'd been having. "I do weddings and special events, but what if we hosted something big—say a regatta or a county fair? Maybe even a wine expo. It might bring in more revenue and get the inn on the map, so to speak."

"I love that idea," Libby said. "A regatta or wine tasting would be my suggestion. It would keep with the upscale nature of the place. I know Charles is really pushing to make it less about small town and more about luxury."

"Maybe I should speak with him about it as well," Emily said, wondering if Charlie still felt that way. Did he still want the same things for the inn that he had when she'd first met him? Or had she changed him? "Is he around today?"

"I think he's got back-to-back meetings, as he flies out tomorrow. I know he has his cell phone though since Rocky's supposed to give the final green light today."

This was it—her last day to save Papa's house. There was nothing to do but wait for the inevitable. But right now, she didn't want to think about it, so she changed the direction of the conversation and went back to work.

Emily hadn't seen Charlie at all, and, given the circumstances, she wasn't surprised, but she did think he owed it to her to tell her one way or the other.

She'd spent the evening alone at the house. She'd brought Papa's old wicker chair up from the barn after seeing Eli, and sat in it most of the afternoon.

She was still out there when the heat had finally become too much, so she went inside and curled up in the recliner in the front living room. Through the window, she saw the BMW pull up, and her heart began thumping in her chest. Charlie got out and started up the walkway as she opened the door. She didn't speak. She only wanted to hear what he had to say.

As she went down the steps to meet him, he walked toward her, his face stoic.

Her chest went cold. This was the moment that could change everything. She braced herself. Had she been able to plant any doubt in his mind at all?

"I got the rezoning approval," he said evenly as he reached her.

Bam. There it was. She was glad he hadn't tried to sugarcoat things with introductions, but she felt like she was going to be sick. She stood there, still hoping for a miracle, willing him to tell her he wasn't going to do this.

"The plans are laid, the crew is organized, and the preparations are in place to finalize the closing and break ground. We're moving forward."

Emily had known this probably would be the outcome, but until it was confirmed, she had been able to hold out hope for a miracle. Now, having heard the deal was sealed, her emotions washed over her like a tidal wave. She didn't move, unable to speak. Seeing him and knowing he'd be gone in a day, coupled with the news that she'd be losing the house, caused a gush of emotion, and her eyes brimmed with tears. Her Papa holding on to the back of her bike seat as she wobbled along the front path, the water fights she and Rachel had had with the garden hose, the smell of the gas oven as Gram baked cookies—all the memories came flooding back, so many that she couldn't process one completely before another surfaced.

"But do you know what surprised me the most?" he asked, stepping close enough that he had to look down at her.

She swam out of her thoughts, scrambling to keep herself together. Her throat was tight and if she tried to open her mouth she'd only cry. She had to be strong. She wiped her tears away but more replaced them as she tried to focus on him. The weight in her chest was almost unbearable. She met his gaze.

"I couldn't enjoy the success of it." He wiped a tear away from her cheek.

Emily took a step back, trying futilely to keep calm.

"What I realized was that I want to be with *you,* Emily. I want to share every day with you. I want you there because when you aren't with me, I miss you terribly. Tell me we can get past this."

Emily let the tears fall now. She couldn't tell him what she felt because if she tried, she'd just yell at him. She thought she'd be okay when she finally lost the farm, but the truth of the matter was that it was entirely within Charlie's power to save Oyster Bay for her. And he wasn't going to. Yes, he had already bought it before he knew her, but here he was, telling her that he wanted to be with her, yet he was going to go through with his plans anyway without even a discussion about how he could fix this.

"Do you hear what I'm saying?"

"Yes," she managed. "And no, we can't get past this. I won't raise my children here because of you. I won't get to carry on our family traditions here because of you. But you don't seem to care at all about that, which shows you don't care at all about me because if you did, you'd understand how much it means to me," she said, her voice rising. "Can I live without it? Absolutely. I could live without my parents too, but that doesn't make it right! So, no. I'm not going to get past this just to make you feel better.

"Emily. You're hearing the news about the house, but, if you take that out of it, you're not hearing me."

Yes, she was. Brad's proposal slammed around in her mind—all those faces looking at her while Brad went on and on about his undying love for her. That feeling of defenselessness overtook her again just as it had when she'd realized that what Brad was saying had absolutely no meaning to her because he'd never demonstrated those feelings outside of that proposal. She was scared.

"Yes, I hear you. But those are just words. You haven't shown me that they're true."

He stood there, his bright blue eyes baring down on her, so much thought and frustration on his face that she didn't know how to read him. "I've spent every free moment I've had with you. What more do you want me to do?"

"You're creative! You haven't even considered a compromise. Why can't you find a way to make us both happy? You know what I think? I think that it's because you're so used to getting your own way that you won't even try." She turned around and walked up the stairs of the old farmhouse.

When she got to the top, she looked back at him, waiting for him to show some sort of grand gesture, something to prove his feelings were real, but he said nothing. She'd hoped he would, because the truth was, she wanted nothing more than to have him beside her too, to tell him about her day, to laugh with him. But when he offered nothing, and it was clear he wasn't going to, she went inside and closed the door.

Charlie ran up the stairs after her but she closed the door in front of him. Emily had nothing more to say, and he couldn't use that persuasive business talk of his to make things any better. He might have convinced the planning commission that this was a good idea, but he'd never convince her. She watched him pace the porch for a few minutes through the window. He dragged his fingers through his hair, his jaw tight, his lips pursed.

Eventually, he got back into his car and drove down the long drive to the main road. As Emily stood—alone—in the empty house, she felt just as empty. She had nowhere to go, nowhere to cry, no one to hold her. She looked up at the ceiling, her eyes focusing on the small iron chandelier Papa had hung. "I'm so sorry, Papa," she said through her tears. She needed him there to fix this—he could always fix everything. As more tears fell, she sat down on the floor with nothing but silence around her.

Later that night, she got a text from Charlie: *I miss you.*

She couldn't answer it. She couldn't bring her fingers to move. There was nothing he could say that would make this all better.

Chapter Twenty-One

Most of Gram's jewelry had been boxed. Even if Gram was staying in Clearwater, it wouldn't be at Oyster Bay. Emily had spent much of the night changing sheets, cleaning, and packing. She'd moved on to the hall closet that had the rest of the photos that Gram had told her she still needed to go through. She'd pulled the boxes out, stacking them against the wall in date order.

At the back of the closet, she found a slightly larger box. Needing a break anyway, Emily sat down and opened it to see what was inside. It was filled with all her old artwork as a child, school reports, certificates she'd received for perfect attendance. She pulled out a rainbow she'd drawn at the age of eight—the colors dramatically scratched in an upside down U-shape, little flowers along the bottom and a sun in the upper corner. She placed it back in the box. She found a paper kite she'd made in art when she was probably ten or so. The edges were bent from being squeezed in there for so many years. She found all her lists for Santa and the letters she'd written from summer camp as a child.

Emily pulled out the stack from camp and set them on her lap. They were secured with a rubber band. As she straightened the rubber band, it snapped and the letters fell loose in her hand. She could see her youthful handwriting, memories and emotions nearly over-whelming her. Those had been her hardest years when she'd held in the most grief. She flicked through them. As she got ready to tie the rubber band back on, one of them caught her eye and she pulled it from the stack. It didn't have her swoopy handwriting. She knew ex-actly whose handwriting it was—Papa's.

She opened the letter and the memory came rushing back. Usu-ally, at camp, they all wrote paragraphs to their family about what they'd been up to and how much fun they were having. But that time, she'd felt so homesick that she couldn't get her hand to write. Papa could always calm her, and with him not there, she was struggling. She wrote simply, "I miss you, Papa. I wish you were here." Her camp leader had mailed it to him just like that.

She could still remember getting the letter from him. She'd brought it home in her gym bag and Gram must have saved it. He'd written back to her on that same paper. Underneath her note, blinking to clear the tears as she looked at it now, his words had new meaning so many years later. She read, "I miss you so much, Emily. You are stronger than you think. It feels like I'm gone, but remember I'm right here. I'm just a thought away, wherever you go. I love you. Papa."

It was like he was talking to her now. With sobs welling up, she stood and put the letter in her pocket. Then, she continued packing the rest of the closet.

Emily was exhausted. She'd slept terribly. Her mind had been full all night, and she'd tossed and turned until the wee hours of the morn-ing. So she made sure to have a double-shot espresso when she arrived at work.

She was apprehensive about seeing Charlie, so she decided to stay out of his way. There was a part of her that just wanted him to wrap his arms around her to make her feel better. But the other side of her wanted to never have to see him again. When she'd asked—blatantly asked—him to show her how he felt about her, he'd walked away.

All day she replayed their time together in her head and it just didn't make sense. How had she not made him see? Why hadn't he understood? She couldn't come up with an answer.

For the rest of the afternoon, she tried to keep her mind on her work, but she couldn't. She thought about how hard it had been to lose her parents, how difficult to say to Brad that she was going to choose a different life, how sad she'd felt when Papa had died. The one constant in all those things was that she'd gotten through them. They'd made her stronger than she thought she was. She had to tap into that inner strength of hers. She'd given saving the house all she had, but in the end, it wasn't meant to be. Now, she had to go on living like Gram wanted her to do so badly. When three o'clock finally came, she said goodbye to Libby and headed out to get Gram. She never did see Charlie. Had he left without even saying goodbye?

The next day was moving day. Gram wasn't allowed to lift anything heavy. She wasn't supposed to go up and down the stairs. She was under strict orders to rest or she'd have to return to the hospital. So when the movers came and started packing things up, Emily had to help them do everything. She had to load the boxes of old family photo albums and Gram's jewelry—Winston's locket—onto the trucks for Gram, she had to assist the movers with wrapping up her mother's teacup collection, and she marked what furniture would be going into storage—which was most of it, it seemed.

By the end of day one, she was exhausted. The movers had started to disassemble rooms, packing the dishes, wrapping furniture, rolling rugs… Gram was sitting in one of the living-room chairs the movers had left for her, reading and seemingly unaffected by everything going on. Emily wanted to shout, "Doesn't any of this bother you?" The thought surprised her so much because, growing up, she'd never wanted to yell at Gram.

She sat down on the floor beside her. "Why aren't you the least bit upset?" she asked as calmly as she could.

"Sorry?" Gram looked up from her book.

"Doesn't this bother you?" She waved her hands in the air. "And I thought you were considering staying. Have you thought about asking Charlie if you could buy Oyster Bay back from him?"

"Emily, things move on, and we have to move with them."

"But you aren't still going to Florida, are you? Tell me you're not." This conversation was wearing thin. Emily knew that. But moving on didn't have to mean that everything needed to fall apart. They might not have Oyster Bay, but they could still be together. Gram had said she worried about leaving them.

She wanted Gram to say, "I was wrong to sell Oyster Bay and I want to stay with my family," but she wasn't saying that. Why had Gram even mentioned the possibility of staying? Didn't she know how important it was to Emily for Gram to stay close to her and Rachel? She was so frustrated.

Gram looked back down at her book. "I don't know whether to go to Florida or not, to be honest."

"Well, have you thought about where you'll stay while you're making up your mind? Is Winston still alive? Maybe you could stay with him." It was a low blow, coming out of nowhere and certainly hitting Gram like a ton of bricks, but Emily was upset. She bit her lip, immediately feeling remorseful.

"Excuse me?" Gram had closed the book and set it on the arm of the chair. She didn't look surprised or angry. She looked completely perplexed.

She'd started now. She might as well keep going. "Did you love him?"

"How do you know his name?" Gram looked up as if the answer were there. "I haven't heard that name in a very long time…"

"Did you cheat on Papa?"

Gram's eyes grew round with the question as they landed back on her, but then she straightened out her expression. "Of course not."

"Who was he?"

"He was my husband."

"What?" Had she just heard Gram correctly?

Gram leaned forward, a gentle look on her face. "When I was a child, probably eight or so, I used to play with your Papa and his friends. We grew up together, did everything together. Then, when we were teenagers—too young to marry but old enough to experience those big feelin's—we would meet each other on Wiley's pier. Remember Tom Wiley? He built the pier so we called it that, but it was the public pier where we used to take you girls for picnics."

"I remember."

"We met on that pier every day after school and every mornin' in the summer. We'd sit there, side by side, our bare feet danglin' above the water, and talk for hours. I could always talk to your Papa." She smiled, giving significance to the lines around her eyes. "So, when Winston McBride, Papa's best friend, began to court me—askin' me to fancy parties and buyin' me flowers—I thought that if Papa wanted to intervene, he would. He didn't. So, I carried on. I stopped goin' to the pier, feelin' guilty for havin' feelings for another man while I was seein' Winston. I was in love with Papa, but he hadn't given me any indication that I should be.

"I didn't see Papa anymore and eventually, Winston and I married. The problem was that, even though Winston was a wonderful man, he wasn't the man I wanted, and I ached for your Papa. I wanted *him*. I cried myself to sleep every night, but what I didn't know was that Winston could hear. He was torn apart by it—he thought he was doin' somethin' wrong. Finally, he asked me about my cryin'. I told him how I wondered where Papa was, I wondered what he was doin', I wondered if he cried like I did. I held Winston's hands and I told him how very wonderful he was and how terrible I had been—although it was naivety. I thought I could love him. He was such a good man."

Emily was so still she had to remind herself to breathe. With every word Gram said, she felt so much better, like she was finally whole. Gram loved Papa—just as she thought. When all the sadness was gone, that would remain. She had faith in love again, faith in life.

"To my surprise, Winston understood," Gram continued. "He cried too and said he loved Papa and me. He said he couldn't live with himself if he didn't let me go. It was almost unheard of back then, but we divorced. I didn't know if Papa would want me after I'd been divorced, if he'd want someone else's wife. But because I loved him so much, I had to leave Winston whether Papa wanted me or not. It wasn't fair to him to stay." She looked down at the gold band she still wore, spinning it around her thin finger.

"So what happened?"

"I left. I sobbed all mornin', and I needed to clear my head. I went down to Wiley's pier." Gram's eyes became glassy with the memory, and Emily couldn't wait to hear the rest of the story. "I walked to the pier and sat at the end of it," she said, the tears falling down her weathered cheeks, "and, in the bright sun of that afternoon with water as far as I could see—enormous and rough, mirrorin' my emotions—Papa sat down next to me. He'd come to that pier every day— he'd never stopped. He'd thought I was in love with Winston so he didn't want to come between us. I held his hand that day on the pier and neither of us had to say a word. We were together from then on."

Emily wiped her own tears as they fell—this time they were tears of happiness. "But Gram, I don't understand why, with a story like that, losing Papa didn't break you into pieces?"

Gram smiled, her own tears still present for the man she'd loved her whole life—just like she'd always said. "Because, dear, for some reason, Papa went on to the next life before I did, and just like he had before, I know he's waitin' for me. And that makes me the happiest woman in the world because I know that the next time I meet him on that pier, it will be forever."

That night, when she went to bed, Emily wished that Papa had said something to Gram before she'd married Winston. It seemed silly now, knowing how he'd felt and how happy their lives were once they were together. People should tell each other when they feel something, she thought. As she lay there, she couldn't help but think about Charlie.

Chapter Twenty-Two

The movers were there to finish boxing up the house. There were things everywhere—mirrors leaning against the wall, boxes of dishes open in the middle of the kitchen floor, rugs rolled and taped for easy packing. As Emily looked at the chaos, she was glad that Jeff had offered to use his truck to take the things she'd marked to her storage unit. With everything in shambles, she wanted to get Papa's boat and the furniture she was keeping into storage where things wouldn't get bumped around or nicked. She'd helped him load them on and then she gave him the second key to the unit. He'd headed down the drive, taking all her favorite things with him.

The team of movers walked through the house, their boots scuffing the hardwoods as they toted boxes to their giant truck outside. Emily's first inclination was to ask them politely to watch the floors, but then she remembered that pretty soon these floors would all be gone.

She was dusty—her hands felt gritty from moving things all morning—her nose was sniffly from the dust, and the heat from the open doors had made her sweaty.

"Gram," she called into the living room where the single chair sat in an empty room. Gram was reading a book. "I'm going out to the beach one last time," she said.

Gram nodded and smiled, although she could've sworn she saw fear in her eyes. There was an airy smack when one of the movers shut the door, and the reality of what was happening had definitely set in. Emily felt that if she didn't get out of that house right now, she was going to suffocate, so she hurried across the yard and nearly ran down to the beach where she gulped in the fresh air. She sat on the swing that hung in the sand, the other one empty beside her. She didn't want to look back at the house because she didn't want to remember it that way—all a mess, boxes everywhere, empty rooms, piles of dust.

She sat there for a while, thinking about the rush of success as she'd brought the pub in Richmond into the limelight, turning it from a drab, insignificant location into an upscale, sought-after hot spot. She was doing it now with the inn, working slowly to add in changes that would eventually pay off and put it on the map. Emily was great at doing that—taking something run down and making it new again. She decided that her life was a little like that right now. One thing she'd learned over the years was how to build herself back up whenever she was knocked down, and this was no different.

She had one more thing to do, one more knock to take. She didn't want to face him because it was going to be too hard, but she knew that she'd better go see Eli one last time before he left the only home he'd ever known. She'd agreed to rent a little piece of land by Shelly's house. It was a wiry spot of grass along the main road, separated only by a small fence, cars whizzing by at all times of the day, but it was the best she could do with such short notice. She hoped to find somewhere better. Would he get spooked? Would he spend his final days wondering why Emily had broken her promise?

She made the long journey to the barn, her chest heavier with every step. When she got there, Eli was standing in the field, looking so strong and content. She let herself in and walked over to him, the lump in her throat rising with the tears in her eyes.

"Hey there, old boy." She could barely get the words out through her tears. She rubbed his side. He didn't nicker this time and she worried that he knew somehow. "I just wanted to come see you to say I'm sorry. I'm sorry I couldn't keep my promise." She wiped away a tear. To her surprise, Eli turned his enormous head and put it near her hands. She rubbed his face, feeling like she'd failed him.

"I tried to show Charlie how great it was here. I tried to let him see who we are," she said. "I tried." She tipped her head back to feel the sun, hoping it would calm her, but it didn't. "I promise I'll come see you," she said, feeling her face finally crumple with sadness. She wanted to spend more time with him. Perhaps she'd eventually assume responsibility for Eli herself, but only once she was settled and she could give her horse the attention he deserved.

Eli began heading toward the barn, so Emily walked alongside him. When she entered, she saw Papa's chair in the spot where she'd last returned it. Seeing it sitting empty and abandoned was a reminder of his absence. She said a final goodbye to Eli and went over to pick it up. It was big and awkward in her tired arms, but she carried it out of the barn, across the field, through the fence, down the long path and through the yard. In the middle of the grass, outside the house, she finally plopped it down where she liked it to be, leaning on it for support. In the daylight, there was something so beautiful about the age of the chair, as if it could tell its story just by looking at it.

Flash, who'd been in and out all day, came running up to her, unaware of what was happening. He was about to lose his freedom, and she felt guilty about that too. She rubbed his head behind his ears as he panted in the heat of the day. She sat down in Papa's chair and he lowered himself in the grass beside her. Emily took in this one last moment.

She felt like her heart was being ripped right out of her chest. In a perfect world, she would've loved to have taken Papa's hard work and put her spin on it. She'd have done something more with the pier, perhaps, maybe even planted some flowers in a garden outside.

She took in the salty air, let the sun's rays hit her face, and reminded herself that in time, she would be all right. The bay that had always given her calm was working its magic.

"You okay?" she heard a familiar voice from beside her. Rachel sat down in the grass and hugged her knees. Flash lifted his head to greet her and then put it back down on his paws.

"No. But I will be."

Rachel gave her a look to let her know she understood. "Did Jeff get all the things to storage that you're saving?"

"I think so. I want this too." She patted the arm of the chair. "What will happen to Papa's tractor?"

"I'll get Jeff to drive it to our house for now, but you can't keep it, Emily. Where would you put it?"

"I know I can't keep it." She remembered Papa's words: *It feels like I'm gone, but remember I'm right here.* She tried to tell herself that. "Did you know Gram mentioned she might want to stay in Clearwater?"

"Yeah, she said she might."

"She could stay at my new place if it gets too crowded at yours."

"It's fine if she stays with us. She and Clara will have a ball together."

"Gram said I could have some of the furniture that we've put in storage—the pieces you haven't marked that she's leaving behind."

"I'm glad you're keeping some too."

"They're beautiful pieces," Rachel said. "Gram had mentioned that you plan to call some antique shops in town for the rest. I don't mind doing that for you."

"Thank you."

They sat there in silence while Flash made his way up to the house to bark at the movers as they exited.

"Looks like they're done for the day. They're taking the last of it on Monday, I believe. I should probably get Gram to my house now. Her room's all ready," Rachel said. "Want to come over?"

"No, thank you. I'm going to move my things into the condo today. It's available whenever I'm ready, so there's no time like the present, I suppose."

"Want me to bring Jeff's truck over? He can drive your car while you're moving."

"That would be great."

"Need any help? I could organize things for you next week while you're at work."

"Thank you. I'd rather do it alone though, but I'll give you a key in case I change my mind."

Rachel nodded. It was clear that she knew Emily had a lot on her mind, and she'd had enough practice with that to know that it was better to just leave Emily alone when she asked. "I can't wait until you have everything moved in. You'll have to have us over."

Emily smiled. "Absolutely." She stood up. "Now, Let me help you with Gram."

Flash hopped out of the car and followed Emily up to the door of her condo. It was a short walk to the public beach access, but she had a nice view of it from where she was. She slipped the key into the lock and twisted the knob.

The first thing she noticed when she opened the door was the newness of the place. Everything was so nice—the stainless steel appliances in the kitchen, the carpets, the fresh paint on the walls. Having been a rental for vacationers, it was furnished and the pieces used were in an island colonial theme. Large glass windows covered the back wall to allow a view of the bay, gauzy white curtains hanging from embellished wrought-iron curtain rods flanking their sides. As beautiful as it was, it still didn't have the character that Oyster Bay had.

Flash was in the kitchen, sniffing his way around.

"Do you like this place, boy?" Emily asked, patting his head.

He looked up at her and snorted before resuming his sniffing. She was glad that no one had claimed him because it was nice having another being with her to keep her company.

She dropped the keys on the kitchen counter and walked back out to Jeff's truck, leaving the door open so Flash could come and go—he always stayed near her when she was around. She'd left most of her things in storage, but she'd brought a few pieces to make the home her own. She didn't want to bring too much since it was only temporary. Once she got settled, she'd be looking for somewhere to live after the summer was finished and perhaps even before then if Gram made up her mind to stay. She pulled the old floor lamp from the back of the truck. The stained glass top, in its reds and blues, would be perfect in the living room.

She brought it in and set it behind a leather recliner. The blue in the lamp matched the blue on the wall. She let her eyes roam the thick white trim framing the walls, and thought how lovely it was.

The cheeriness of the place and the bay breeze were giving her hope in new beginnings.

Emily had learned about grief as a child—Gram had taught her. Every time, Gram said, there was a moment when she'd learn to fly again. Like she had when she'd laughed with her sister and Jeff in the yard those nights, like when she'd thrown her hat into the air at college graduation, like when she'd worked at the pub, she'd fly again.

Emily went back out and got Papa's hat rack and a suitcase and brought them inside. Flash came out from behind the white curtains in the living room to greet her, and then followed her upstairs to the bedroom. It had vaulted ceilings and a paddle fan in the center. She set the hat rack on the large bed.

Double glass doors with more sheer linen curtains covered the wall. She pulled them back to reveal sliding doors. With a click of the lock and a hefty tug, she pulled it open, the curtains blowing out into the room with the rush of tidal wind. There was a small deck only big enough for one chair but the view was fantastic. She sat down on the chair and looked out at the enormous expanse of blue before her. The Chesapeake Bay was so large that in places she couldn't even see the other side. There was a sailboat out there today, and with the way the wind was blowing her hair, she knew it was a perfect day for sailing.

It made her think about the regatta she was planning for the inn. Emily wondered, would Charlie come back for it? But then she stopped herself. She needed to move on and feel what it was like not to have anyone to lean on. She hadn't heard from him again since that one text, and his silence made her think things were finally finished between them. Maybe she hadn't replied, but he hadn't said anything to fix the break between them either. She felt sorry for him, actually.

His upbringing hadn't taught him much about the importance of home and family. If he couldn't see the value in those things, if he couldn't see the reasons for compromise, or at least have a discussion regarding it, then maybe he wasn't the person for her anyway.

By the time Emily had unpacked the necessities and showered, Flash was a little stir crazy. He kept scratching at the door, and she worried about him putting claw marks in the paint. So she thought she'd take him down to the beach to play catch. She had to put him on a leash, and at first he didn't like it one bit, but as they walked, he must have realized that she had a firm grip on him and he slowed down, pacing beside her. She decided that if she was going to keep Flash, she'd better look for a rental with a yard.

Being a weekend, the public beach was crowded with people, but there was a marina nearby with a large strip of grass on the other side, so she took Flash there to play. He was so excited to be off the leash that he almost knocked her over. His relentless happiness made her cheerful. She threw the ball as far as it would go. Flash tore after it, and she could see the muscles working in his sides and legs. Keeping an active routine for him would be of the utmost importance this summer. She'd probably have to get him a crate for the days she worked because he might ruin the house trying to get out if she didn't, so he'd need a lot of exercise in the evenings.

Flash brought the red ball back and dropped it at her feet. She threw it again with all her might and he went chasing after it. Only then did she notice the beautiful surroundings. So many gorgeous sailboats lined the pier, their sails rolled and roped down, the boats rocking in the gentle tide of the bay. The sun was bright, like a white ball, casting rays onto the water and giving it its familiar sparkle.

As she played Fetch with Flash, she tried to pinpoint the things she liked about her new location: She liked the marina already—she even saw a restaurant with an open-air bar attached; she liked the view from her new bedroom; she liked how new everything was. She tried to focus on those things.

Chapter Twenty-Three

It had been a whole week since Emily had seen Charlie that day on the front porch. Seven days. Flash was settling in at the condo. They went to the marina every day after work to play Fetch and then she took him for long walks on the beach. Like it always had, the bay relaxed her. But she missed Charlie.

Today, she'd driven Flash to Wiley's pier, and they'd walked for miles in both directions on the sand before finally going out on the pier. It was a big day because today was Closing Day. Gram had signed over the papers for Papa's house this morning, and it was officially gone.

She sat on the pier like Gram had done all those years ago, hoping to feel the calm that Papa could always bring, Flash lowering himself down beside her. She handed him his bone. The weather was mild for a summer day. It was in the eighties with a nice breeze and not a cloud in the sky. As she looked out at the bay, she could almost feel Papa sitting next to her. She wanted to let him know that she was okay. That, even though she didn't have anything but his note and a few photos of him, she knew he was close by.

Something about her life, though, just didn't feel right, and it wasn't losing Oyster Bay. She hadn't imagined this for herself. Sometimes, when she was out walking Flash, she thought about what others around her must see—her upscale work clothes, her well-behaved dog, her new condo. She looked like a person she'd never wanted to be. She was supposed to be that woman who had a loving husband who would play out in the yard with their children; she was supposed to be that woman who took her kids to the pier, telling them stories about their great-grandfather and how he'd built one for her a long time ago; she was supposed to be the woman who spent all day on the beach, running with her dog in the woods, catching lightning bugs at night; she was supposed to be the woman who heard her children call out "Mommy" when she'd tucked them all into bed, put away their bedtime stories, and turned on their nightlights.

But she wasn't.

She wanted to call Charlie, to hear his voice, but she knew it wouldn't do any good. Maybe they'd just have to go on with life and see what happened. What worried her was that she wouldn't get to see what happened with him.

With a deep breath, her lungs full of fresh air, she stood up and patted her leg for Flash to do the same. He followed her lead, his bone in his mouth, his tail swooshing back and forth.

"Time to go home," she said. She was having her family over for dinner now that she was finally settled, and it was nearing time to get ready.

"Hey there," Jeff said, offering a side hug as he and Clara met Emily at the door of her condo. She let them in. "Nice place!"

Clara went running inside.

"Thank you."

Rachel helped Gram out of the car and Flash had already exited the house and made it over to them to say hello.

"Aunt Emily," Clara said, returning and tugging on her shirt at the back. "Are those cookies in there for us?"

"Yes! But I'll bet your mom will say you have to have your dinner first."

Flash had gone back inside ahead of Rachel and Gram. He nudged Clara in the doorway, asking her to pet him. She giggled and put her little hands on his face awkwardly covering his eyes, but he didn't seem to mind.

"This is lovely," Gram said as she reached the door.

"Oh! You've hung Papa's hat rack!" Rachel said, coming into the small entryway, helping Gram inside. "It looks great there."

Gram peered over at it for a little while before turning and heading toward the kitchen.

Jeff took Flash and Clara outside. Emily brought over a plate of casual hors d'oeuvres and set it down on the coffee table in front of Rachel and Gram as they sat down on the sofa.

"Wow. You didn't have to go to all this trouble," Rachel said, smiling up at her sister as she took a small puff pastry off the plate.

"I enjoyed it!" Emily liked entertaining, and this was the first time she'd been able to since she'd been back home. She'd found an unfussy dinner recipe that had been given to her by a friend in Richmond for salmon with lemon and dill over rice. "Eat up," she said with a grin, "before Flash comes back in and helps himself."

Gram picked up a pastry. "How do you like living here?" she asked.

"It's different." she said. "It's good! But I like having you all over and being together like we always have."

"Too bad Charlie couldn't be here. He was a lot of fun. Have you spoken to him?" Gram asked.

"No."

"Did you see this?" Rachel said, pulling a rolled magazine from her handbag. She opened it, and slid it toward Emily. "Rodger Simpson did a story on your guy… I thought you might want a copy."

"He's not *my* guy," she said, peering down at the professional shot of Charlie in his suit, leaning against a table in the Concord Suite, the beautiful room behind him and sailboats on the glistening water out the window, and then another of him at the pier—she remembered he'd mentioned that.

Emily had to work to pull her eyes from his face. She missed him. She felt bad for blowing up at him. A wave of mortification washed over her as she thought of how she'd acted sometimes around him, her emotions getting the better of her. But at the end of the day, she still regretted losing Oyster Bay.

"Thanks," she said, shutting the magazine and setting it on the coffee table.

"If it's meant to be, it will be," Rachel said. She looked down at the magazine before meeting Emily's eyes and smiling.

"Think so?"

"I believe so," Gram said. "Just look at me and Papa."

Emily wasn't convinced—she thought her grandparents were just lucky—but she hoped Gram was right.

"Has anything happened on the property yet?" Rachel asked. "Anyone know when they're starting to build?"

"I'd given Charlie the go-ahead as soon as we were out," Gram said. "There's no reason to hold things up just because of paperwork. But I don't know what's been done at the moment. I haven't been by to see it."

"I don't want to see it," Emily said. She thought about the tree swings being cut down, the yard overrun with machinery, the house falling to pieces. She didn't want that mental picture among her collection of memories. Emily stood up. "I'm going to have a drink. Would anyone else like one?"

"Would you please get us all one," Gram said. "I'd like to propose a toast."

She obliged and got them all a glass of local white wine. Then she took a seat in the living room, glad to have everyone together again tonight.

Gram held up her glass. "To family," she said. "And to life. It is a glorious ride no matter where we are! Cheers."

They clinked their glasses.

"Speaking of family, have you thought any more about staying in Clearwater?" Emily asked. "I was thinking that we could look for a place together."

Gram smiled and set her glass down, fiddling with the stem. "That's really nice of you. But I still need to think about what's best. I don't want to be a burden to anyone."

"You wouldn't be."

She nodded and then said, "Well…," like she did, letting Emily know she wouldn't have any answers right now. "No matter what, it'll all be okay."

"You're very positive in your old age," Rachel said. "I hope I can be as upbeat as you are."

"I fully believe both of you will be," Gram said.

"Why do you think so?" Emily asked.

"Because once you're sittin' on my side of this lifetime, you'll look back on all your struggles and know that they were just blips between the better things—the wonderful things—that happen. Yes, I lost my son but I got to raise his two daughters at an older age. I embraced it, and it was wonderful. Every time I brushed your hair and braided it for school, I stored that memory away so that it could warm me on those cold nights. Yes, Papa left us. But I got all those decades with him, all that time... I have more to be thankful for than I can even recollect in one sittin'. My heart is full."

Emily took Gram's words to heart. Her failed relationship with Brad, losing Papa's house, and Charlie... They were just blips. She wanted to believe that. She focused on the positive: She had Gram and the rest of her family right here at this moment. It was time to celebrate that. "Let me find Jeff and Clara so we can eat."

Chapter Twenty-Four

Emily knew better. She knew better than to take the long way to work and drive past Oyster Bay. Like her other losses in life, she'd finally made it over the coping stage, and now she could breathe again. While she missed the house terribly, she knew that she could handle living without it.

It was probably for the best, but the house was still mostly hidden from the road, and she couldn't pull into the drive because construction cones had blocked it off. As she drove slowly by, she couldn't see the entire state of the farmhouse through the trees—the bulldozers were lined up in front of it—but she caught a glimpse of an empty spot where she swore the roof had been, the spot where she remembered Papa patching it when there had been a leak.

She rolled her window down, the low hum of machinery coming from behind the trees, and her heart sank. Pretty soon the walls would be crumbling beneath the impact of a wrecking ball, the handprints on the pavement breaking apart as the jackhammers plowed into it. She hit the gas, speeding away from the scene.

At least with Charlie gone, she didn't have to try to avoid him. Long past his flight, he hadn't contacted her anymore, and she knew he was back in New York. Perhaps, by not getting in touch again, he was trying to make things easy on her. She needed to make a clean break and get him out of her mind. The only problem was that she'd fallen hard, and she couldn't deny the heartbreak that she felt without him.

Emily pulled into the parking lot and tried to clear her head. She saw Libby with a big smile on her face, standing at the entrance with two cups of coffee. She'd been there, waiting for her every day for the last week. As Emily walked up, she handed one to her.

"Can you see the construction at all yet?" Emily asked after thanking Libby for the coffee. She took a sip and let the warmth spread through her. It was a balmy, sunny day, but she felt cold on the inside after seeing the house.

Libby shook her head. "They haven't knocked down trees yet on this side. I know they've started, though. I already have invoices for materials from the architects."

Emily took a deep breath and let it out.

"Try to get your mind off of it." Libby said.

"It'll be okay," Emily told her friend.

"It's a go for the regatta by the way," Libby said, her eyebrows raised in excitement.

"Oh, that's fantastic! Now I can immerse myself in the planning of that." Before she knew it, the summer would be over. She'd be waist deep in paperwork and planning, Rachel would probably be back to work, and Gram would be in sunny Florida. How things move along...

Emily still wanted everyone together, happy, sitting on a back patio somewhere like they had when the summer began. At night, she thought a lot about Papa. Last night, she'd dreamed of him. He'd sat down next to her on Wiley's pier, the water completely obscured by fog. He didn't talk; he just held her hand while she tried to see the bay. The more she tried to see it, the more he squeezed until they were hugging out of nowhere. She was her younger self again and she could feel the cotton of his cardigan against her cheek. She took in the familiar smell of him, the strength in his protective arms, and her fear melted away.

Emily's phone rang in her handbag, pulling her from her thoughts. Libby offered a quiet wave, allowing her to answer the call. It was Rachel.

"Hello?" Emily said, waving goodbye to Libby as she passed by the front desk and headed to her office.

"I have some great news!" Rachel said.

"You got the job?"

"Yes! Oh, I'm scared and excited at the same time!"

"I'm so happy for you!" She closed her office door, sat down, and turned on her computer.

Then the line went silent, and she realized that her sister's delight was for show. She thought she heard a sniffle. "Jeff doesn't know if he wants to be with me anymore. He stayed with Jason last night."

"What? That's ridiculous," Emily said, frustrated. She knew how perfect Jeff and Rachel were for each other, and she just couldn't face them splitting up. "How can he give up on all those good years that you've had? Just because you want to live your own life and do something that makes you happy? It makes no sense at all."

"Ridiculous or not, it happened. And the worst part was this morning when Clara asked for her daddy. I didn't know what to tell her."

"What did you do?"

"I told her he went to work early. I can't lie to her indefinitely."

"Rach, you have to do what is right for you, and Jeff needs to support that. I can't believe that he isn't. He's always supported everything you've done. And I know that this might change the way in which you go through life, but it shouldn't change whether or not you go through life together!"

"It's simply not what he wants for his family." She got quiet and Emily allowed the silence. "I just always thought he was perfect for me. I guess I was wrong."

"I'm coming over," she said. Emily had already gotten up from her desk and was fishing in her bag for her keys. Rachel needed her.

"No, no. Stay at work."

"Absolutely not."

"It won't solve anything if you come. It'll just disrupt your day."

"Then disrupt it. Who cares? It's just work. You and Jeff are family and we need to figure this out."

"Well, we won't figure it out right now. Go back to work and I'll call you if anything changes."

Emily was frustrated, but she knew that it was something Rachel and Jeff would have to work through. "Life doesn't end up the way we expect it to, does it?"

"Not at all."

"When do you start?"

"In two weeks."

"That's awesome. You'll be great! I'll be here if you need me."

"Thank you. Well, I should be going. I just wanted to tell you the news. Have a good day at work."

Emily said her goodbyes, settled in at her desk, and then scrolled through her emails. There was nothing new—no requests for tours, no inquiries regarding facility rentals. She checked her phone. Nothing there. She even searched online for property listings for her and Gram briefly, and there were a few hopefuls she made a note to call. It was a slow day, and she didn't want a slow day. She wanted to be over-whelmed with work so she didn't have to think about everything. She picked up her office phone and decided to begin planning the regatta.

She set out scribbling down initial plans. With every idea, she felt more energized, more focused than she'd been in a long time. She was in her element. This was what she was meant to do. She searched for possible vendors and advertising options, she scouted locations in Clearwater where she could begin the race. As she planned, she imagined all those beautiful sailboats gliding past the inn. How stun-ning it would be.

By the time she left work, Emily had made a sizeable list of things she'd need to work out for the regatta, and she was feeling accom-plished.

But she wanted to share her good mood with someone. She want-ed to talk about nothing and everything, and she knew just the per-son she wanted to speak to. Emily took out her phone but then put it back in her bag. She wouldn't let herself call him. It was clear by his silence that he'd made his choice.

Chapter Twenty-Five

"They're starting to clear the land from this side," Libby said as she looked out the great window in the entrance to the inn. "I can see them lining up just out of sight of the guests." They'd been watching all week.

Emily shuffled up beside her, her heart pounding a hundred miles an hour. There was a considerable amount of acreage between the clearing of the farmhouse and the inn, so, even with those trees gone, it would probably take a few weeks before she could see the fate of her old house.

She was glad to be leaving work to take Gram to the doctor. She didn't want to have to think about Oyster Bay—it brought her back to all that sadness. If she thought about it, just like when she'd lost loved ones, it would pull her back into that grief. She wrapped up the last few items she had on her list for that morning, said goodbye to Libby, and headed out into the sunshine.

As she got into her car, Emily checked her phone. To her complete surprise, she saw a text from Charlie: *I still miss you.*

She stared at it, the thrill of knowing he missed her swallowing her up. She couldn't move; she was frozen with the phone in her hand. She missed him so much she couldn't stand it, but he'd gotten everything he wanted and it was at her expense. He hadn't shown her anything to prove that he would ever consider her feelings.

She decided to wait to text him back, unsure of how she wanted to respond. She dropped her phone into her bag and started the car.

"Your tests all look good, you have a normal EKG. But you'll need to continue the medication I prescribed," the doctor said to Gram as Emily stood with her in the small exam room.

"That's fine," Gram said with an uncomfortable smile. Was she just as worried about being far away from them as Emily was?

"I'd take it easy for the next few months," the doctor said as he read something in her chart. Then, he flipped the papers over and slipped them into a folder. "Do you have any questions for me, Ms. Tate?"

"None at the moment," Gram said.

"Well give me a call if you feel anything unusual—shortness of breath, or any side effects from the medication. Otherwise, you're shipshape."

"Thank you, Doctor."

As quickly as he'd entered, he exited, leaving Emily and Gram to collect their things and head back out to the reception area.

"I found a couple places we could check out if you decide to stay," Emily said as they walked through the double doors leading to the front of the building.

"Well…" Gram walked through the door, leaning heavily on her cane, as Emily held it open for her. "I'm not sure about living in Clearwater if I'm not at Oyster Bay. I just don't feel like I belong anywhere else. But I don't want to leave you girls."

They entered the lobby, the sunlight streaming in through the windows. Emily was sad that Gram couldn't imagine living here without Oyster Bay, but at the same time, she liked that Gram felt sentimental about it.

They walked outside, the blue sky above them full of pillow-like clouds. One slid in front of the sun, giving relief from the intense rays. "I wish you'd stay. I couldn't believe it when you said you were moving to Florida. It was such a surprise."

"Life is full of surprises. Enjoy them."

"It's hard to sometimes."

"Hello?" Emily said into her phone as she walked the aisle of the supermarket, browsing for something to make for dinner that night.

"Hey," Rachel said.

Emily was so glad to hear her sister's voice. She worried about her. The last time Emily had called to ask about Jeff, Rachel had said he still hadn't been home, and Clara was crying more at school, making Rachel worry about her choices. But today, it was clear by her voice, her sister didn't want to talk about her problems.

"Have you been by the farm?" her sister asked, something nervous in her voice.

"No, why?" Emily had stopped driving past the farmhouse because she wanted to move on with things, but Rachel's question made her wish she had. She should've taken in every single minute of the view of the woods because soon it would probably be a parking lot.

"You need to go see it right now," she said urgently.

"I don't want to." She wasn't far from it at the moment; she was only a few minutes' drive from there.

"When I saw it, I couldn't believe it. I know it's hard to go back, but you have to see what they've done."

"It's not the same, is it?"

There was a long silence. Emily hung on the sound of it, not wanting to hear an answer for fear it would be the wrong one. Then, her fears were confirmed.

"No."

"Why won't you just tell me?"

"Because I think you need to see it for yourself."

Emily could hear the sniffle in her sister's words and she could tell that she was crying. What had Charlie done? "Okay, I'll go," she said, feeling her chest tighten with anxiety. She didn't want to go, but Rachel's insistence had made her curious, and she'd see it eventually anyway.

She got off the phone, left the groceries in the cart, and ran outside to get back into her car. As she drove, the wind in her hair and the radio on low, the announcer chirping away, completely unaware of the heaviness that surrounded her, she tried not to picture what Oyster Bay had become. Flashes of pavement, new construction, barren land with only cookie-cutter landscaping, the natural trees all gone, the shoreline immaculately shaped. She cranked up the radio and took in a deep breath, her hands shaking.

The drive seemed to take forever, the roads stretching out before her, seemingly endless. She'd taken a different route to work every day, coming in from the other side, but even the longer route hadn't seemed as long as this. The closer she got, however, the slower she drove. She wanted to savor the last few moments before the image of new construction on her papa's land was burned into her consciousness forever.

When she finally arrived, Emily pulled her car up alongside the main road that ran in front of Gram's old property, and she had to close her gaping mouth. At the end of the drive, still covered in trees, right at the street, was a very familiar blue BMW and Charlie was leaning against the back of it, his legs crossed at the ankle, his hands propping him up. He was grinning from ear to ear.

"What are you doing here?" she asked, after getting out of the car. She shut the door and walked up to him. "You're back from New York?"

"I never left. I've been overseeing the construction. Take a walk with me?"

The construction on the other side hadn't taken down the trees completely, so she had no idea what she was about to see. She didn't know what to expect, but she couldn't squash the feeling of hope that he'd saved Papa's house, even though she knew that would be ridiculous. It was just wishful thinking, her hopes already feeling crushed.

"Close your eyes," he said as they walked down the drive toward where the house had been. She took in the smell of pine, briny air, and seawater—this place had a scent all its own and it overwhelmed her as she walked blindly toward it.

"Are you going to show me that you've left Papa's house exactly the way it was and you aren't going to build on the land after all?" she guessed as she stumbled along the rocks in the drive. He caught her and steadied her.

"No," he said, causing her confusion.

"Have you started building then?"

"We're finished."

It all made no sense, and the walk was so long that the anticipation was killing her. She couldn't wait to open her eyes, but as they walked, hand in hand, his fingers caressing hers, she didn't want their little walk to end either.

"I'm glad to see you," he said.

She tried to answer him but she couldn't talk.

He chuckled.

"Okay. Open your eyes."

She stared at the structure in front of her. It was Oyster Bay, but it was some kind of heavenly version of it. The bright white siding shone in the sun, the porch—completely repaired and painted to its original form—now full of rocking chairs, deep green ferns hanging in the open spaces between the posts and pots of red geraniums lining the stairs like they had when she was a child.

"How did you know it used to look like this?" she asked, barely able to get the words out. Her skin prickled with the emotion of it all.

"I saw it in your photos."

The old walkway with her handprints was still there. The yard was full of grass again, sodded in thick green, making her want to walk in it to feel the cool under her feet that she'd felt as a girl.

"Would you like to see more?" Charlie asked, leading her around back.

Emily nodded, unable to speak for fear that she'd start to sob. Was this what Rachel had seen? Was this why she'd been crying? They walked along the side of the house where the old sea grass still was. When she got to the back of the house, the tears finally came.

Papa's shed was there, but it was completely repainted and re-stored to its original form, and beside it, his boat sat along the edge like some sort of nautical landscaping, the seat with the tackle box painting like a little bench while the rest of the boat was full of pots with yellow and white wild daisies. The entire back yard was bright green—more perfect grass—all the way to the beach where Charlie had kept the small hill and the wild grasses to prevent erosion. As she let her focus fall on the yard, the old tractor path through the woods was now gravel, lined with sandy-soil shade-loving plants to make a natural border.

Charlie was watching her, his happiness undeniable, and she could hardly stand to look at him. She wanted to throw her arms around him and thank him for this, but she still wasn't sure what was going on—she'd seen the clearing of the trees beginning from the inn's side—and the emotion of seeing it all was overwhelming.

"Let's take a look at the patio," he said, putting his hands on her shoulders and turning her gently toward the area where the patio and the screened porch were.

She gasped as she walked up the steps. The entire back of the house had been transformed. The porch had been restored, the paddle fans whirring, and there were more ferns and rocking chairs. The newly whitewashed staircase fanned out at the bottom level, which contained more potted plants, wrought iron furniture, and a bright red patio umbrella.

"I hope you don't mind. I made some repairs to the roofline on this side and lifted the patio up a few feet," he said as they stood together facing the house. "Because"—he turned her around—"now you can see the entire bay." She clapped her hand over her mouth, her chest heaving up and down. She wiped the tears that were falling freely now. Just past the fire pit, her little spot on the bay was still there. The beach, that powdery sand, still there.

But better than all that was the lone chair—Papa's chair—in its same exact form, sitting empty, facing the bay just as Papa had placed it. How did he get all of this?

Her eyes couldn't stay still long enough to focus, but she could almost make out, against the pier, a little, wooden fishing boat like her Papa's tied to the post, bobbing in the water.

"I got you a new boat. This one is yours. There are brand new fishing supplies in the shed. Would you like to see the inside of the house?" Charlie asked, her emotion clearly affecting him. He cleared his throat.

"Yes," she said in nearly a whisper.

They walked the few steps to the back door and Charlie let her enter first. The old counters and the sink that lined the back wall had all been renovated—everything was like new. The kitchen table was there, the floors still rustic planks of hardwood, now perfectly even. She opened a cabinet, marveling at the beauty of the knobs now that they were shined—the cabinet was full of hand-painted wine and margarita glasses. She looked over at Charlie.

"I went to Francine's."

She laughed, closing the cabinet door.

"I hope it's okay, but I called Rachel this morning and asked if she knew of any way to let me into your storage unit. I was thrilled she had a key! I had to let her see the house first to make sure I'd put everything in the same spots. Follow me."

He took her hand and they walked into the hallway. It, too, was completely restored to its original form. A bright, shaggy runner ran the length of it, making it feel warm and cozy. Papa's hat rack hung as if it were on display, his hat dangling from one of the pegs.

She looked at him again for an explanation.

"Rachel took it from your condo this morning. She said you'd want it to be back where it had been."

Charlie dropped her hand and walked to the end of the runner where he bent down and picked up a corner, lifting it to reveal the hardwoods. The flooring was still the original boards, and, as she looked down at it, a smile broke out on her face. Under that runner the roller-skating scratches were still there, protected under the gloss that now covered the wood.

"We hand-sanded around them." He walked back over to her.

This was the best thing that had ever happened to her. No one had ever done something so grand, so fantastic. It made her admit to herself how much she cared for him. She didn't have to push her feelings away anymore. Finally, she threw her arms around his neck, burrowing her face in his shirt. "Thank you," she said.

"Because of you, I fell in love with it. I've never loved anywhere before, but," he said, "I only love it with you in it."

Suddenly, looking at him, Emily wondered if he'd visit often. She wished there was some way to make him stay, but she knew that she'd already had too many wishes come true with all this to have the right to yearn for more.

"What are you thinking about?"

She felt the heat in her cheeks from being caught in her thought. "I just hope you vacation here a lot."

"You do?" he said with an excited chuckle.

She nodded.

"I have to go home for a few weeks to get things settled, but then I can come back."

"How long will you stay?"

"As long as you'll have me."

"What about work?"

"It's only about an hour and a half flight from Richmond. I can fly in for a few days and then do the rest of my work remotely, but only if you want me to stay." He took her hand again.

"I want you to stay every single day."

He smiled, affection for her in his eyes. "I'd love to." He leaned down, took her face in his hands, and kissed her—just one quick kiss. The feeling of it was more like coming home for Emily than seeing the house. She was flying.

They went upstairs, and all the rooms were just as they had always been, but brighter, cleaner—perfect.

"I made just a little change to Gram's room. Let me show you." He took her into her Gram's old room. It had been repainted; the walls were highly glossed white panels with thick crown molding and baseboards.

There was a small button on the wall and she walked over to it. "What is this?"

"Press it."

She pushed the button and heard a hum. Then, the panel opened revealing a small elevator that had been hidden in the wall.

"It will take your grandmother to the hallway downstairs."

"Oh, Charlie, that's wonderful," she said.

Emily turned, startled as Gram came out of the bathroom. She'd been hiding out in there.

"Gram! What are you doing here?"

"Charlie called when he'd finally finished this place and I asked if I could be here to see your reaction. I'm glad I did," she said, her whole face lighting up. "I just love his changes. They'll make it so much easier for me to get around every day."

"So you're not going to Florida?"

"Not if you want me to stay."

"Absolutely, I want you to stay! It's *your* house!" She walked over to Gram and gave her a big hug. "Will you?"

"Of course." She leaned on her cane for support, but she stood a little straighter today. "Now that I'm not hidin' in the bathroom, I'd like to give this elevator a whirl and head downstairs so I can read on that beautiful patio." She was obviously allowing Charlie and Emily more time to themselves.

As Gram got into the elevator, Charlie led Emily out into the hallway. "Let me show you your room."

He took Emily's hand and they walked together. The wooden floors gleamed, the walls all painted in a bright island pink the light coming in through the windows. They entered her room and she couldn't believe her eyes.

There was a new addition. It was a real life doghouse in the corner. It was white with black shutters just like the farmhouse and it had the name "Flash" painted on a plank of wood above the rounded doorway. Inside it was a big fluffy cushion. The whole thing sat on a rug that protected the hardwoods beneath it.

"I love it," she said.

Charlie turned her around to face him. "You'd said I should show you how I felt about you..." he said, his eyes so familiar now, that smile playing at his lips.

Emily wrapped her arms around his neck for the second time. She pushed herself up on her toes to reach his lips, but he didn't kiss her. Instead, he ran his fingertips down her neck, causing a slight shiver through her arms, and then slid his hands up until his fingers were in her hair, his face serious. Slowly, he leaned down toward her, his lips excruciatingly close to hers, his breath deliciously near, and pressed his lips to hers. It was an intoxicating feeling, sending her head whirring as his lips moved on hers, his hands sliding through her hair and back down her back.

She now knew, without a shadow of a doubt, what it was like to feel that kind of indescribable spark that Gram had always talked about with Papa. She had no idea what would happen between them in the days or weeks or even years to come, but she knew one thing: She wanted to find out.

When she'd finally floated back to earth, Emily pulled back and asked, "But what about the clearing? They're clearing the land by the inn."

"Yes. I altered the plans to expand on part of the land, leaving a considerable amount of property, including trees, between it and the house. You won't even know it's there. I promise. I sat in a meeting with the architects and we thought long and hard about what would be the best way to use the land so that we could still expand but provide the privacy you're used to here. The expansion will be on a smaller scale than I'd planned, but it will pull in enough revenue to make it attractive to buyers and still provide income for Clearwater."

"So Rocky let you split the rezoning request into two different zones?"

"When I told him why, he rushed it through for you."

She smiled. "That was nice of him."

"Yes it was."

"Charlie, this is unbelievable."

"I'm so happy that you like it." He leaned in for another kiss. "I have one more surprise. But we have to go outside."

She followed him down the newly painted steps—not a creak beneath her feet; they were strong now and sturdy. They walked outside and through the yard together, headed down a new path. She heard Eli's whinny and tears sprung to her eyes. They didn't fall, though, until she saw the barn. It was classic red with white trim, all new hay feeders along the side of the brand new fencing. Eli was standing by the feeders. But then, she spotted something and her lip began to quiver. Nuzzling Eli was a pony—white like an angel.

"We brought her in a few days ago. Eli took to her immediately. I thought I'd let you name her."

Without even thinking, she blurted, "Hope." Because that was what she had today. She had so much hope for the future that she couldn't imagine anything better than this.

"Hope, it is then. Now, let's go get Flash at the condo and bring him over. We're having a family party tonight. Rachel is bringing Clara to the house in a little while and your Gram's here. I'm sorry we couldn't have Jeff come. Rachel said it wasn't a good idea."

"I'm sorry too. Maybe one day…"

He smiled. "Well, we should get going. I have a caterer for later tonight. He'll prepare all local seafood, and I've stocked the bar in the kitchen. What do you say we break in Francine's glasses tonight?"

"That sounds perfect."

Chapter Twenty-Six

"Watch this," Charlie said, hitting a switch inside the closet in the hallway. "I added one improvement for *you*." Immediately, music poured through outdoor speakers and into the house.

Emily leaned toward the open window to hear it.

"I have it set to the channel that you had on the little radio last time."

"You've thought of everything," she said.

"I wanted it to be perfect."

"It is."

When they went outside, Gram was in a rocker on the patio. "You know," she said, "I always loved this view, but I never knew how absolutely magnificent it was until I could see it from this height. Charlie, you have really outdone yourself."

"Thank you," he said, clearly proud. "I've never had a renovation project of this size that I've done myself, and, while I had a huge team working for me, I made sure to oversee it all to get every detail just right or it wouldn't have the impact that I wanted it to have."

"It is a grand gesture, Charlie." Gram was smiling, her happy self. She, too, was flying and Emily loved to see it.

"I was actually nervous," he admitted, and he looked over at Emily. "I've never done anything like this for someone, and the pressure to make you happy, Emily, was unbelievable. It was more stressful than any business deal. Making you happy was my number one priority."

Emily nearly stopped breathing. "What did you just say?" She made eye contact with Gram, and tears surfaced in her grandmother's eyes. Emily's gaze slid back over to Charlie, and she didn't even notice that Rachel had arrived. "Did you just say that my happiness was your number one priority?"

"That's what he said," Rachel said from the doorway, clapping her hand over her gaping mouth as she looked at him. Clara pushed past her and ran to Gram, climbing onto her lap.

"What?" Charlie asked, his eyes darting from one person to the other. "What did I say?"

Emily swallowed to keep herself from crying too with happiness. "You just said the most perfect thing." Suddenly, she wondered if Papa was there with them, for those all-too-familiar words of Papa's that Charlie had just uttered made her feel like her grandfather somehow had a hand in all this.

"Oh," Charlie said with a smile. "You had me worried there for a second." He took her hand and kissed the back of it.

Rachel shut the door behind her and settled on the patio, Flash running out from the woods to greet her. He hadn't stopped running since they'd gotten home.

Before long, the chef had arrived to cook their meal and Charlie went inside to get him acquainted with the kitchen.

"Any word from Jeff?" Emily asked. Clara was swinging down by the beach and Emily used the moment to check on her sister. It just didn't feel right without him there. She wanted Rachel and Jeff—the couple. She missed their laughter together and their love for one another.

"No. I haven't seen him. I texted him to let him know about the house and that we'd be here, but I got no response. He's avoiding me, I think. I missed him so much last night that I couldn't sleep. I even thought of giving up the job, but I know that wouldn't be the right thing to do." She fluttered her hands in the air the way she did when she didn't want to burden anyone with her troubles. "Don't worry about me!" she said. "I think Charlie has something else to show you."

"You're welcome to talk some more if you'd like," Charlie said as he returned from the kitchen, concern on his face.

"It's fine, Charlie. My problems will still be here when you get back."

"Get back?" Emily asked, eyeing Charlie.

"Yes. We have to take the boat for this. It's my last surprise."

They walked down to the pier, Flash following behind, then Charlie pulled the new wooden boat over by its rope. Emily stepped in, taking his hand to steady herself.

"Whoa!" Emily laughed as the boat shook. She tried to keep it from wobbling as Flash and Charlie got in, the three of them snug in the small vessel. Charlie rowed it out past the pier. "You're going to take us all the way out to the island at this speed," she said, watching in awe as he rowed.

"I want to show you something and I'm excited."

It didn't take her long to realize where he was headed—the pier through the woods that Papa had built all those years ago. She stretched to try to see what other surprises he had in store for her, and as they neared it, she was blown away yet again.

"How did you—?"

The entire pier was there, covered in candles in tall, narrow glass vases to keep them from going out, their flames dancing in the soft breeze. "I didn't touch this pier," he said. "I did nothing to it. I wanted to leave it in its raw state. This was the place where you finally stopped crying all those years ago, isn't that right?"

She nodded as Charlie hopped out of the boat, Flash following. He pulled it up onto the sand and held out his hand so she could get out.

He held onto her hands and looked down at her. "Right here, right now," he said. "I want you to know that, just like that day, you can stop being sad. Because whether you feel the same for me or not, I have fallen in love with you, and I will do my very best to make you happy." He pulled her close.

Emily felt as if her life could begin right from this moment. Everything that had happened, everything she'd prepared for, had led her to this. "I've never felt I could talk to someone like I can with you," she said, pulling back and looking into his eyes. "When I thought you were gone, I missed you so much. I'm blown away by what you've done here for me, and I don't quite know how to ever repay you."

"You've taught me what it's like to really care about someone. You are the first person I want to see in the morning and every time I have to leave you... Well, I don't want to. As soon as I realized that, I knew I couldn't go back to New York."

"You'll have to return at some point to work," she said, voicing her concern as she wrapped her arms around his torso, clasping her fingers at his back.

"Yes. But I will have a whole lot waiting for me here. That will certainly encourage me to finish quickly." He kissed her nose.

Emily looked out at the pier again, its entire surface glowing with those beautiful flames. "Thank you," she said at a loss for words. How could someone thank a person for a gesture like this?

"No, thank *you*. In a way, you saved me. You saved me from a life of never knowing what this feels like."

She held on to him. Just like Papa had held Gram's hand that day on the pier and then never left her side, Emily made a silent promise to do the same as long as Charlie wanted her to. And she would show him every day how thankful she was, not only for what he'd done, but also for him.

"Shall we leave the boat for now and take the tractor up to the house?" he asked with a grin, and it was only then that she saw it parked where she'd always left it when she drove to this pier. "I need to get back to check on the chef."

"That sounds perfect," she said, unable to control her smile.

"Oh," he said turning toward her. "I got oysters…"

She offered a devious look. "Well I hope you have wine for later, too," she said with a wink.

When they returned, Rachel and Gram were touring the house together while Clara played with her dolls on the living-room coffee table. More candles were lit on the old farm table in the dining room, the wax bubbling in jagged drips down each candlestick, and the whole table was set with plates, silverware, and some of Francine's painted glasses. The chef had set several covered silver dishes on the serving table along the side of the room.

"Take a seat," Charlie said, pulling out her chair. "I'll round everyone up."

As they all trickled in, Clara climbing up on a booster seat at the end, Gram and Rachel on either side, and Charlie sitting next to Emily, she looked around at her family and prayed that she wasn't dreaming. But she knew she wasn't when the chef came in and collected the extra plate on the other side of Rachel. If it had been a dream, Jeff would've been there, too.

"This is a feast of a supper, Charlie," Gram said, looking small against the large furniture. Emily was so glad she'd decided to stay. She couldn't imagine this house without her.

"Well, I wanted to celebrate." He turned to Emily. "And, not talking to you for so long was killing me, but I would've struggled to keep this a secret. I wanted enough food tonight to keep us here for a while. I want us to talk so long that we run out of things to say." He winked at her.

The doorbell rang—it sounded like wind chimes, the old broken buzzer gone. "I'll get it," Charlie said, putting his napkin on the table. He stood up and left the room. When he returned, to Emily's surprise and excitement, Jeff and Jason were with him.

"Daddy!" Clara nearly fell out of her chair trying to get down. Jeff steadied her and held her in his arms, his attention on Rachel.

Rachel tore her eyes from her husband to greet Jason. "Hey there!" she said. "Long time no see! We're about to eat. Come join us for dinner."

"Oh, no. You all are having a family meal," Jason said. "I was just dropping Jeff off."

"Stay," Gram said. "There's plenty. And you're lookin' right skinny these days. They got food in Nashville?"

"Ah, I was only there a little while."

"Why don't you sit down and eat," Gram said. "And then, if you would, you could play some of your new songs for us. I know you've got that guitar out in your truck."

Jason laughed. "I do." He took a seat at the other end of the table. Jeff set Clara back down and then pulled out the chair next to Rachel. The chef returned the plate and silverware, and also added a place setting for Jason.

"Rachel," he said. "I came to tell you something, and I don't mind saying this in front of our family and friends." He set his hand on top of hers on the table. "I'm so sorry. I needed to be away from you to realize that you are more important than any plan I have for how my life should play out. I love you as much as I did the day I married you, and I was miserable without you."

Rachel twisted her hand under Jeff's and intertwined her fingers with his, tears brimming in her eyes.

"I'll support you in whatever makes you happy," Jeff said.

"He was a complete sap," Jason said from the end of the table. "He blabbered on about you so much that I wrote a song about it. It could be a hit actually," he said with a laugh.

"You must play it for us later," Gram said with a little giggle.

"Definitely."

The wine was poured, the dishes filled, and a family was finally sitting around a table again in that old house. Emily looked around the room, and for the first time, she could see her future right there in front of her.

Epilogue

Charlie took Emily's hand, and she looked lovingly at their two children, John and Alice, as they both puffed up their cheeks and blew out their birthday candles at Gram's old table. Charlie had refinished it but it still sat in its same spot in the kitchen at Oyster Bay.

Four years ago today, Emily had nervously wakened in the wee hours of the morning and shaken Charlie, rousing him from sleep. She was scared, grabbing her belly as the pains came one after another.

"Get me a bag with some clothes," she'd said as she hurried around the room, looking for things.

But Charlie slid on his jeans and gently took her hand just like he had now. "The car is already packed," he said, no fear at all in his eyes.

"What about things for the babies?"

"In the car." He smiled at her, leading her toward the door.

"Flash…"

"I've put his food out for Gram, and Rachel will be by as soon as I text her."

And now, here they were, celebrating four whole years with their twins. John looked exactly like Charlie except he had a dimple on his right cheek, and Alice was a good mix of the two of them—she had Emily's eyes and Charlie's smile.

"Let's have cake and ice cream and then we can ride the horses!" Emily said. She turned to Charlie. "Are Hope and Junior saddled up?"

He nodded, complete happiness in his eyes.

They'd worried about introducing a new colt to Hope—she'd only ever known Eli. But after Eli had passed, Emily didn't want her to be alone, and they'd gotten another horse right away. Just as Eli had welcomed Hope, Hope had done the same for Junior. The new colt had been a similar coloring to Eli, the same build, and after a few years with him, they realized he even had a comparable temperament. So, when they'd decided to name him Eli Junior, Junior for short, they'd made a good choice. Emily and the twins took the horses out for daily rides and they let them swim in the warm months. Shelly still came over to take care of them. She even entered them into competitions. Junior, it seemed, was a natural, and his ribbons were hanging in the barn.

"Gram, would you like cake?" Emily asked, her fingers now full of icing as she tipped a large wedge of vanilla cake onto a paper plate.

Gram, still as sharp as a tack, but resting a lot more these days, was sitting in the corner, her hands on her lap and a smile on her face. "I'd love a piece, dear," she said. "But let the children have some first."

Emily handed the first piece to Simon who would also be four in a matter of days. She couldn't believe it when Rachel had told her she was pregnant. Their due dates were only a week apart. True to form, her sister was still doing it all—working full time and raising her two children. Jeff had been with her every step of the way.

"I'll help Simon," Clara said. She was tall and lanky like Jeff, her brown hair now laced with golden streaks from days in the sun with her friends. She took the plate from Emily and sat down next to her brother.

Charlie had moved over to chat with Jeff while Rachel poured the juice into little paper cups that said "Happy Birthday," placing them in front of each child.

As Emily looked on, she couldn't help but think how that house had seen almost her entire life. Those walls had been witness to her childhood, her teenage years, her wedding to Charlie, the stairwell done up in magnolias and white roses just like Papa's pier, where, in a flowing dress and bare feet, with her family and friends looking on, she'd promised to love Charlie for the rest of her life. And now those walls were there to witness her raise her own children. She hoped with everything she had, that one day, she'd be sitting in that chair where Gram was, celebrating the life of her great-grandchildren.

She wondered about Papa from time to time, and this was one of those times. But she remembered his words: "It feels like I'm gone, but remember I'm right here. I'm just a thought away, wherever you go." And he was right. He was always just a thought away, evidence of his life and hard work all around her. It was true: Papa had built her a great house. But he'd built an even better family.

Letter from Jenny

Thank you so much for reading *Summer at Oyster Bay*. I really hope you found it to be a heart-warming summer treat!

If you'd like me to drop you an email when my next book is out, you can **sign up here**:

www.itsjennyhale.com/email/jenny-hale-sign-up

I won't share your email with anyone else, and I'll only email you when a new book is released.

If you did enjoy *Summer at Oyster Bay*, I'd love it if you'd write a review. Getting feedback from readers is amazing, and it also helps to persuade other readers to pick up one of my books for the first time.

Until next time!

Jenny

P.S. If you enjoyed this story, and would like a little more summer fun, do check out my other summer novels—*Summer by the Sea* and *Love Me for Me*.

Lightning Source UK Ltd.
Milton Keynes UK
UKOW05f0737191016

285639UK00012B/205/P